BB

Fear in the Cotswolds

a&b

Fear in the Cotswolds

REBECCA TOPE

First published in Great Britain in 2009 by
Allison & Busby Limited
13 Charlotte Mews
London W1T 4EJ
www.allisonandbusby.com

A CIP catalogue record for this book is available from
the British Library.

10 9 8 7 6 5 4 3 2 1

13-ISBN 978-0-7490-0747-8

Typeset in 13/16 pt Adobe Garamond Pro by
Allison & Busby Ltd.

Paper used in this publication is from sustainably managed sources.
All of the wood used is procured from legal sources and is
fully traceable. The producing mill uses schemes such as
ISO 14001 to monitor environmental impact.

Printed and bound in the UK by
CPI Mackays, Chatham ME5 8TD

REBECCA TOPE is the author of fourteen previous crime novels. She lives on a smallholding in Herefordshire, with a full complement of livestock, but manages to travel the world and enjoy civilisation from time to time as well. Most of her varied experiences and activities find their way into her books, sooner or later. For example, bee-keeping, milk recording, spinning, arguing, undertaking and gardening. She is also currently the membership secretary of the Crime Writers' Association.

www.rebeccatope.com

Dedicated to lifelong friends far and wide:

Bobby in Bulgaria
Flo in Chicago
Sue in Canada
Hilary in Australia
Judy in New Zealand
Cheryl in South Africa

Author's Note

Hampnett is a very small place – even smaller than I have made it appear in this story. I have stretched distances slightly for dramatic effect. As before, all the characters are products of my imagination, as are the farms and houses in which the action takes place. The church, however, is very much as described.

Chapter One

Chapter One

It was much smaller than a village – a hamlet, then. Hampnett was a hamlet. Thea played with the words as she drove along the A429 watching for the sign that would take her to her latest house-sitting commission. The bare trees that dotted the landscape, along with the short colourless grass, created a whole different world from the Cotswolds in their summer lushness. Now the palette was all greys and browns, as the low January cloud sapped light and clarity from the scene. It fitted her mood alarmingly well. After a dutiful Christmas and New Year spent with her recently widowed mother, and an assortment of other relatives, she felt as drained as the surrounding countryside. The past months had been gruelling in a number of ways – the death of her father, the ending of her relationship with Phil Hollis, and a very difficult time with her older sister, Emily. She was ambivalent about the forthcoming house-sitting commission, which involved a month in this isolated little place, in the depths of winter.

The tops of the round hills were indistinct, misty with the damp vapour settled on them. Shapes with fuzzy edges came and went along the roadside, as the small car climbed the gentle incline towards its destination. As always, the sheer unpredictability of what lay ahead of her was both enticing and unsettling. But this time there was a new element: an unwelcome feeling of apprehension. If it hadn't been so foreign to her nature, she might almost call it fear. An insistent tightening of her insides, a faster-than-usual heart rate, a dryness in her mouth – her body was telling her that it was uneasy, however strenuously she tried to ignore it, and however irrational it might be.

Hampnett had two approaches: one from the A40, which ran roughly east–west; the other from the A429, which crossed at an angle, south-west to north-east. The hamlet sat in one niche made by the intersection, to the west of it. At least, that was how it looked on the map. In reality, all awareness of the main roads disappeared within seconds, once you'd left them behind. Thea had experienced before the sense of passing through an invisible curtain into a different universe, as she approached a hidden Cotswold settlement. Temple Guiting, Cold Aston, Duntisbourne Abbots, and dozens of others, were all tucked away behind folds of land, invisible from any thoroughfares and almost forgotten even by tour leaders and walking groups. But Hampnett was closer to the bustle and security of the twenty-first century than most. It would be a ten-minute walk from the church to the A40, twenty minutes to the other road. The town of Northleach was almost within shouting distance. Yet another road ran Roman-straight to the west, only a few fields away.

So why, she asked herself, with a questioning glance at the spaniel beside her, did it feel so very remote?

Lucy Sinclair had been shameless in her explanation of why a house-sitter was required. 'I've got to an age where English winters are intolerable,' she said. 'So I'm going off to the Canaries for a month.' Her cat, donkey and five lion-headed rabbits all needed somebody on the premises, it seemed.

'Lion-headed rabbits?' Thea queried, trying to imagine such freaks.

It turned out that they were fairly ordinary rabbits with a lot of fur in the head area and quite short ears. They were four does and a buck, of assorted colours and sizes – and surprisingly appealing. Lucy plucked one from its palatial quarters and thrust it into Thea's arms. 'This is Jemima. She's very friendly. They all are, except Poppy. She scratches rather.' The buck, named Snoopy, had his own cage, and sat looking somewhat sulky. Thea stroked Jemima, who was a blue-grey colour, with a frosting of a lighter grey.

'She's lovely,' she said. 'And quite heavy.'

'You should feel Snoopy. He's a monster.'

Thea liked Lucy. In her late fifties, she was divorced and self-employed. 'I fix people's computers,' she said, briefly, with a sideways look at Thea. 'The last bastion of male supremacy, for some reason.'

More relevantly, Lucy's mother had died a year ago, leaving a substantial property for her daughter to inherit and sell for an astonishing figure. 'Quite against the trend,' she laughed. 'Plus I get the state pension in another couple of years. I've never felt so rich, even when my ex was raking it in, in the Eighties.'

The rabbits seemed an anomaly, even more than the donkey did. 'It's a long story,' Lucy had laughed. 'To do with my daughter and an allergic boyfriend.' She rolled her eyes and sighed. 'I knew it would happen, right from the start. Kitty got Snoopy first, before all the does, and I fell for him the minute I saw him. He's getting on a bit now – you will take good care of him, won't you?'

But it hadn't been the rabbits or the cat or the donkey that Lucy was primarily concerned about. There was an even greater reason for spending fifteen hundred pounds on a house-sitter. Leading Thea through the house to a conservatory at the back, she grimaced ruefully before opening the door. 'It breaks my heart to leave him,' she said. 'After the life he must have had, it's the last thing he needs.'

A skeletally thin grey dog was curled on a bed in a corner of the room. Tufts of hair barely covered the skin. A ratty tail flickered as he lifted his head to gaze questioningly at Lucy. 'Hello, Jimmy,' she crooned. 'This is Thea. She's going to look after you when I go away next month.' Thea reached down her hand for the animal to sniff. Politely, he touched it with his cool nose.

'Jimmy?' she repeated. 'He's called Jimmy?'

'That's what I named him. I don't know what he was before. I found him at the side of the road, two years ago. He's not as old as he looks. He's a lurcher, so he's meant to be thin. But his wits have gone. He's not going to get any better now.'

Oh God, Thea groaned inwardly. Just when it had been looking reasonably easy, this scrawny glitch had to gum up the works. 'Will he be all right with my spaniel?' she asked.

'He'll ignore her. He doesn't have any problem with other dogs. It's people who've betrayed him.' Lucy stared angrily at the dog. 'Has it occurred to you that the whole thing between humans and dogs is about betrayal?'

Thea had heard a news report, only that morning, in which the soaring numbers of abandoned dogs had been presented as a sign of harsh economic times. Unable to meet their mortgage payments unless they made serious savings, people were giving up the dog – dumping it in rescue centres, for the most part. What must the poor creatures think – ousted from their beloved family, through no fault of their own, with no warning? 'Yes,' she said. 'That had occurred to me.'

'It makes me sick.'

'And yet I've met people who'd go without food themselves in order to make sure the dog or cat's all right. The very idea of abandoning the animal is unthinkable.'

'Right. Those are always the people one knows, aren't they? It's always some faceless moron from the city who doesn't know how to make a commitment, who quits when things get a bit rough.' If possible, Lucy's expression grew even angrier. 'But that's rubbish. *Everybody* would do it. The difference is in the justifications they give. That's not important to the dog, is it?'

'Devoted old ladies break their hips, or die,' said Thea mildly. 'They're forced to give up their dog then.'

'I know that. But it still feels like betrayal when you're on the receiving end. Don't you see?'

It was too much for Thea. She held up her hands in surrender. 'So what's the answer?' she said. 'Nobody should ever have a dog or cat, by that reckoning.'

'Right,' said Lucy again. 'Exactly right.'

'And then there wouldn't *be* any dogs or cats.'

The smile finally came, as Thea had trusted it would. 'So take good care of Jimmy for me, will you? Make sure there's always something that smells of me in his bed. Don't let him run away.'

Recalling a previous experience, Thea shuddered. 'No, I won't let him run away,' she promised.

* * *

The house was isolated, down a lengthy track that ran alongside a small copse, half a mile before the centre of the hamlet. Hampnett consisted essentially of a remarkable church and a farm, with a handful of other stone buildings scattered over the rolling ground to the north and west. Lucy Sinclair was the proud owner of a converted barn with three acres of land. The conservatory was a carefully designed addition, with no embellishments that might be deemed out of keeping with the local style. 'I bought it twelve years ago, and oversaw the conversion myself. It would never suit anybody but me.' Where most people had created huge airy spaces inside their mutated homes, Lucy had chosen to divide it into five or six modestly sized rooms. 'Easier to heat,' she said. 'And who wants to feel as if they're living in a barn?' A lot of people, Thea could have replied.

Now, on 6th January, Thea arrived nearly two hours before Lucy had said she would have to leave for Birmingham airport. Being in charge for almost a month was by far the biggest commitment she had made since she began the work. It hadn't seemed nearly so demanding to watch over a homestead for a week or two – although she had experienced too many difficulties and alarms during most of her commissions to be complacent.

Jimmy seemed even more decrepit than before, still huddled in his conservatory and showing very little interest in whatever might be going on around him. 'He doesn't like the cold,' Lucy explained. 'But he's not happy in any other room than this. I think he must have spent his life outdoors. He gets agitated in the house. I built this specifically for him, but it's not very easy to heat.' Thea stared at her, open-mouthed. She built the addition for the dog? Was that possible?

'He looks comfortable enough, and besides, winters aren't as bad as they used to be,' said Thea optimistically. 'His bedding looks very warm.'

'It's felt,' Lucy explained. 'They use it in Mongolia, so it's probably going to do a good job. I gather they've had massive snowfalls in New York this week, though. It often seems to get here a fortnight later.'

'Lucky the main road's so close, then,' said Thea.

'First get up my track. Even a quarter of a mile's a lot of digging,' Lucy laughed. 'But I've filled the freezer with bread and milk and plenty of basics, so you should be OK.'

It felt like a joke at the time. Thea shared the laughter at the idea of being snowed in. That never happened in Gloucestershire, did it?

Chapter Two

The two hours they had together passed slowly, Thea wishing Lucy would hurry up and leave. She had already been shown the animals and the house, a list of important phone numbers taped to the door of a kitchen cupboard; it seemed a waste to have them both hanging around with nothing to do. Outside there was a sharp east wind, the sky a dense blanket of grey cloud. 'My father always used to hate January,' said Thea. 'I think he got it from my grandad. He was a farmer and had to be outside in all weathers. I remember wondering how he could bear it, year after year.'

'We've got soft,' said Lucy. 'I find myself feeling sorry for the poor sheep and other things outside all year round. And then I remind myself how daft that is. After all, in olden times, everything had to survive on what they could find. There haven't always been people to bring them hay and mangolds.' The last word sounded odd and Thea repeated it.

'Mangels?'

'You know – mang'l'worzels, like in Worzel Gummidge.'

'No. What are they?'

'Vegetables. Like sugar beet. Sheep love them. The farmer down the track gives them to the sheep, even now. I walk that way sometimes to watch them at feeding time. She scatters them in an old muck spreader.'

Thea watched the woman's animated face, wondering at the childlike pleasure she was displaying at the thought of a farmer feeding her sheep.

'How nice,' she said uncertainly. 'Can people eat them?'

'Probably. Might be a bit indigestible. But we eat swedes and parsnips, much to the horror of the French. They'd be much better than nothing in a famine, I'm sure.' Again there was a faint air of relish in Lucy's voice, as if the idea of a famine was secretly rather appealing.

At last it was time for her to go. 'Look,' she said, waving a cheque under Thea's nose. 'I thought I ought to give you half the money now, and half when I come home. Is that all right?'

'Oh! I don't usually – I mean, people generally pay me at the end.'

'Well, I'm not "people". I can't leave you destitute for a whole month, can I? You'll need to buy some food, and fuel for your car, and presumably pay your own bills at home. Here, take it. Otherwise I might spend it all on cocktails and gambling in the sunshine.'

Thea heard this as 'gambolling in the sunshine', and giggled at the image. 'Well, thanks,' she said, trying not to show the small thrill she felt as she read the figure on the cheque. Seven hundred and fifty pounds – and that was only half the full sum. Lucy Sinclair had made no demur about paying her the fifty pounds a day that Thea had tentatively suggested was the going rate for a sitter who took up residence. It still felt like being paid for having a holiday and doing almost nothing, despite the many pitfalls she had encountered since she started the work.

Lucy leant down and kissed Jimmy, then stood up with tears in her eyes. 'Selfish cow that I am,' she sniffed. 'You will take good care of him, won't you?'

Thea drove her temporary employer to the station at Moreton-in-Marsh and waved her on her way. Driving back down the A429, she recognised much of the road from previous sojourns in the area. She passed Lower Slaughter just a short way off the road to her right, and then Cold Aston, a few miles further west. But she knew hardly anyone in either village well enough to count them as friends. There was a woman in Cold Aston, who she had first met a year ago, and again the previous summer – their relationship had taken some knocks on both occasions, and Thea was in no hurry to risk a third bruising encounter. And there was a man in Lower Slaughter; a man who had got under her skin more than she had liked to acknowledge to herself at the time. Knowing he was going to be so close by for the next month created a small flame of interest at the back of her mind. She had persuaded herself that there could be nothing between them, that the whole idea was folly – and yet, he had taken root in her consciousness, and intruded uncomfortably often into her dreams.

She cruised unhurriedly down the hill to the crossroads, with Hampnett ahead and slightly to the right, Northleach to the left. On a whim, she turned right onto the A40, and then left into the small road leading through the hamlet, past the church and its neighbouring farm.

Old man's beard straggled over the hedges, adding to the general greyness of the landscape. The January light was poor, with a faint damp mist covering everything. She met no other cars, and saw no living creature until she had passed the minimal village centre and was approaching the turn for Lucy's Barn. A few yards before the junction there was a man walking along the road, facing the oncoming traffic, so that Thea had to pull out to avoid him. He gave no sign of awareness that there was a car alongside him, although she was close enough to get a good look at his face.

He was tall and thin, and somehow the same shade of grey as the surrounding winter hedges. There were deep lines on his face, which sported a straggly grey beard, and his narrow shoulders were slumped. Something about his loose gait suggested bony knees and fragile ankles. His longish hair flopped around his face, and his beard disappeared into a grubby-looking scarf.

'I wonder who that is,' she said to the dog beside her. Hepzie appeared as impervious to the encounter as the man himself had been.

Preparations for the winter month in the middle of nowhere had been made carefully. For Christmas, Thea had requested DVDs, computer games and books. She had compiled a list of long lost friends and relations to whom she would write rambling letters. She would take things slowly, reading a daily newspaper and listening to the radio. And she would teach herself lacemaking – a secret ambition she had nursed for twenty-five years. Her sister Jocelyn had given her a lace cushion, two dozen bobbins decorated with beads, a book of instructions and several reels of cotton. It was magically tantalising, in its own cotton bag with large red flowers printed on it, and she was itching to get started.

She visited the donkey when she got back to the house, stroking its long ears, burying her hand in the soft hair and mumbling daft nothings to it. The donkey was, Lucy had assured her, the easiest of all the animals. 'He'll patrol the paddock twice a day, whatever the weather,' she said. 'But apart from that he'll mostly stay in the shed. I think he dreams a lot. Watch his face and you can see he's remembering happy times.'

The donkey was about thirty years old, and had no

cause for complaint about his lot. He had belonged to a family not far away, living with his jenny mother until she died. Then the family opted to move to Spain, initially deciding to take the donkey along. At the last minute, the expense and bother of this had changed their minds, and he had come to live with Lucy quite cheerfully. 'He never had a name,' Lucy said. 'Just Donk, mostly.'

He was a big brown individual, not like the furry grey donkeys of seaside tradition. His face was on a level with Thea's, as she talked to him. Hepzie sat tolerantly at a distance, not tempted to join in the exchange. The paddock was about an acre in size, sloping downwards away from the barn, and fenced with a new-looking wire-and-post arrangement. A metal gate led into another field at the bottom of the slope, which Lucy had explained as recently installed. 'It's the only way a large vehicle can get in and out of the paddock,' she had said. 'Although that field doesn't belong to me. There are beef cattle in there for most of the winter.'

The lower field was an odd shape, and Thea eventually worked out that it had at one time included Lucy's paddock. One corner had been carved out of it, leaving a narrow strip to the north, and a much larger rectangle to the west.

The cat was a slinky black female, barely a year old. 'She's called Spirit,' Lucy had told her. 'She's very self-sufficient. The worst thing is the creatures she catches and brings into the house. There was a slow worm not long ago. I suggest you keep all the bedroom doors closed. Otherwise things die under the beds and make a dreadful smell.'

The bedrooms numbered two, and were suspended over the ground floor rooms on a platform which ended about two thirds of the way along the length of the former barn. A gallery overlooked the living room, with a balustrade to prevent accidental falls. The stairs were open-tread, rising from the hallway, and leading to a corner of the gallery. It was, according to Thea's inexpert judgement, very cleverly designed to make best use of the limited light. The bedrooms each had a small square window, while downstairs most of the lighting came from one large area of glass at the far end of the building, by the odd device of having the partitions between the rooms only eight feet high. Above them there was empty space. The idea of walls without ceilings was peculiar, and Thea was momentarily reminded of lavatory cubicles. The room furthest from the big window was a study, full of computer-related hardware, with only the scantiest of natural illumination.

She had, of course, been in barn conversions before, but had never properly considered the process of transformation. Lucy had been very ingenious in the way she'd conformed to the regulations restricting what was allowed. 'Though why on earth it should matter that the thing continues to look more like a barn than a house escapes me,' she had sighed. 'And the real irony is that when I needed to put up two new sheds outside for the animals, there was nothing to control what they looked like. I could have erected steel bunkers, or glass-and-concrete monstrosities, just as long as they weren't too enormous.'

Lucy's voice echoed in her head as she explored the house in which she was to spend the coming month. Every small remark was magnified into significance, a clue as to how that month would be. The only mention of neighbours came with a brief comment about the continuing track past the Barn. 'That leads down to the next farm. They're busy at this time of year – you probably won't see anything of them.'

Thea had experienced neighbouring farmers before, and knew how reclusive they could be. On the other hand, it made sense to know something of her closest neighbours. 'Is it a family?' she asked.

'Not really. Old Kate and her aged parent, that's all. He's not well, so she's got her work cut out.' She shuddered gently. 'It tends to make her irascible, so try not to annoy her. That woman's temper is legendary.'

'Old Kate?' Thea raised an eyebrow at the less-than-respectful epithet, but nothing more was forthcoming. Lucy had been in overdrive, rushing her surrogate from one part of the property to another, throwing out random pieces of information as she went.

The heating was on, the modern insulation of the conversion efficiently keeping it where it should be. 'Underfloor,' Lucy had informed her. 'It cost a fortune, but is pure luxury.' *Not luxury enough,* thought Thea, *if*

you have to bolt for the Canaries when January arrives.
The mournful presence of Jimmy in the conservatory nagged at her through everything she did. Hepzie, too, was intrigued by the other dog, and whined at the door every few minutes. 'Come on, then,' said Thea. 'Let's go and talk to him.'

As predicted, the lurcher ignored the spaniel when they entered the room, but he raised his head to gaze enquiringly into Thea's face. She knelt down beside him, and cupped his head in her hands. 'You poor thing,' she crooned. 'It's not much of a life, is it? What are we going to do with you?'

Jimmy sighed and laid his head back on the felt of his warm bedding. Hepzie approached cautiously and nosed him gently. He turned to look at her, and to Thea's amazement began to lick the spaniel's head, right between the eyes. Hepzie melted, lying down full stretch against the sparse grey hair of her new friend's side. Thea almost cried. 'Hey!' she murmured, 'well done you.' And then she remembered that they'd be leaving again in a month, and perhaps two doggie hearts would be broken by the separation.

Outside it was already getting gloomy at half past three, and Thea was unsure what to do next. The rabbits would want to be fed, as would the donkey, but it seemed far too early to settle them down for the night. She could phone or email her daughter, to say she'd arrived and was already in harness. At the back of her mind was the thought that whatever she did today would become the routine for the next month, which meant she should give it some serious thought.

As she moved to leave the room, both dogs watched her. 'Come on, then,' she invited. 'Why don't you both come outside for a bit?'

Hepzie was at her side instantly, but Jimmy didn't move. He was, however, quite alert to his new friend's behaviour, and when she looked back at him, he slowly got to his feet. 'Good dog!' Thea applauded. 'Come and have a bit of exercise.'

She tried in vain not to think of the sadistic treatment he might have endured at the hands of people she could not begin to envisage. The expression in his eyes spoke of hesitation, wary anticipation of pain or abuse. 'It's OK, Jimmy,' she crooned. 'I'm not going to hurt you. But you do have to go outside sometime, and it might as well be now.'

He made no move to follow her, so she took down the lead that was hanging from a hook on the wall, and fastened it to his collar. He cooperated when she pulled him gently, but was plainly far from enthusiastic.

Outside, on the patch of grass that Lucy had identified as his toilet, he relieved himself, and then stood passively waiting for whatever might happen next. 'Jimmy, you're going to break my heart,' Thea told him. She could feel tears at the back of her nose, and an accompanying annoyance with herself for being so sentimental. But hadn't Lucy used almost the same words? Was not this the legacy of the dog's ill-treatment – that softer souls would grieve for his hurt, for years after the event?

The day closed down, leaving hours of winter evening to be filled. Briskly, Thea got herself organised, stacking her DVDs on top of the television and plugging in her laptop where it sat on a small round table in a corner. 'Move anything that's in your way,' Lucy had said. 'It won't bother me at all.' And there had been things to be moved. Lucy Sinclair was not unduly tidy, with old computer magazines and other clutter on most surfaces. 'This is nothing – you should see my workroom,' she had laughed. When Thea went for a look, she was genuinely shocked. All four walls were shelved, the shelves groaning with an eccentric mix of discs, boxes, cables, potted plants, books, mysterious pieces of computer hardware, large and small. Everything was dusty. It felt like a cave.

'Wow!' she gasped.

'I know. I was determined not to let it get like this, but it's an occupational hazard. If you go to any computer geek's house, it'll be the same. If you don't mind, I'll just close it up and suggest you stay out. If anybody phones, wanting my services – which they will, I promise you – just tell them I'm away until the seventh of Feb. Don't let them leave anything here. I don't want to come home to a stack of broken PCs.'

Thea's experience of computers was not great. Her husband, Carl, had used a standard machine for his work, and Thea had borrowed it for emails and letter-writing, until she'd got a laptop the year before he died. So far, nothing had gone wrong with it. But she knew there were people who were crippled without their computer; immobilised by panic as if their right arm had dropped off. 'Is there anybody else I could refer them to?' she asked.

'Not really. Don't worry about it. There are plenty of us in the Yellow Pages. Don't let them dump their problems onto you. The women are the worst – they get hysterical if the screen freezes for two minutes.'

Until then, Thea had not considered the need for computer doctors as being almost as urgent as that for the more traditional kind. She had a vision of a tower console being belted into a passenger seat and rushed to Lucy for emergency attention. 'I bet you're popular,' she said.

'I am sometimes, yes. But if I have to declare the thing dead on arrival, it can get scary. I've had my face slapped for it, though only once.'

The phone rang at seven-thirty on that first Saturday evening, and when she answered it, Thea was regaled with a confused story about a virus message which had begun replicating itself endlessly all over the monitor screen. 'Sounds nasty,' she said, 'but I'm afraid Lucy isn't here to help you. You'll have to find somebody else. Sorry.' She put the phone down on the anguished female yowl that met this information.

Not only, it seemed, was Lucy's work desperately needed – it knew no civilised restrictions concerning evenings and weekends. The prospect of more such calls was irritating, but it was a more difficult emotion that Thea found herself assailed by in the strange building with its peculiar spaces and absolute silence. She found herself to be nervous, jumping as the cat came noiselessly into the room, checking that the doors were all locked against the dark and chilly outside world.

The second bedroom was sparsely furnished, as if kept strictly for guests. There were paperback novels in a small free-standing bookcase, a lamp on a table beside the bed, and a wardrobe with a drawer beneath the hanging space, which Lucy had invited her to use. The bed was a generous single, with ample space for Thea and her dog – but not for a second human being. What if Detective Superintendent Phil Hollis had joined her again, as he had done in Cold Aston and Temple Guiting? What if she met a likely man and wanted to bring him back with her? Improvisation, she concluded. The lack of a double bed had never stopped a couple from copulating, she was sure. But the thought of squashing into this particular one with anybody, however appealing he might be, was not tempting. 'Just us, then,' she said to the spaniel. Hepzie wagged her long tail reassuringly.

The situation with Phil remained unresolved. There had been no final ending to the relationship, nothing spoken that rendered it irreversibly terminal. As far as she knew he had no other female friend competing for his attentions. They had discovered aspects of each other that they weren't sure they liked, and Phil had been the one to voice his feelings first. Thea had not behaved very well in Temple Guiting. And in Lower Slaughter she had recognised more and more of the flaws and failings in the relationship. She couldn't see quite what a committed relationship with Hollis would bring her in terms of happiness and fulfilment, while at the same time she felt upset and apprehensive at the prospect of losing him completely.

'But what is it you *want*?' he had demanded of her, a few months earlier.

Good question – *very* good. Much easier to list the things she did *not* want: the constraints of constantly having to account for her movements; the endless discussions about food and mealtimes; the daily compromises; the sheer claustrophobia of couplehood. She had tried to say some of this, and Phil, to his credit, had listened carefully.

'I agree with you,' he had concluded, thereby almost changing her mind completely. 'I don't want those things, either.' She heard an added *with you, anyway*, that he never spoke aloud, and she felt irrationally rejected, despite everything. She had not liked it when he confronted her with the truth of her own feelings. She had both wanted him and not wanted him, and the craziness of this alarmed her.

She was nearly forty-four. Her birthday would be on 3rd February, while still here at Hampnett. Like any woman of the same age, she was perpetually aware that there was still time for another baby – or even two. She knew women who had given birth at forty-six. Her only child had been born when she was twenty-two, and she had not wanted any more, for reasons she could hardly now explain. The triangle created with Carl and Jessica had suited her perfectly. He had his little girl, who thrilled him beyond expression. There was a comfort and complacency to this small nuclear family which Thea used as a sort of cocoon. She passed her twenties and thirties in a haze of coffee mornings and outings, friends and conversations that had felt entirely sufficient at the time. She never had a proper job, having taken a degree in history, marrying Carl two weeks after graduation, and delivering Jessica thirteen months later. The degree had mainly been a matter of writing essays constructed from facts gleaned in the library. It had been completely unreal, and left scarcely a mark on her consciousness.

And then Carl had died. Killed in a car crash that nobody could ever have predicted. The indescribable pain of the loss and shock had lasted a year or more, a time of stunned bewilderment that she could hardly remember now. Everything she had taken for granted had dissolved into futility, and since then she had struggled to maintain any kind of purpose. Drifting from one Cotswold village to another, taking a superficial interest in the events that swirled around her, living for the day – it had been enough to keep her alive. More than enough, when Phil appeared and she felt herself being drawn to him as if wound in by a nylon fishing line. Sleeping with a man who wasn't Carl had been a richly emotional exercise. With no sense of guilt, she had allowed herself to become lost in the sensations of novelty and recovery. But the novelty had worn off much too quickly, leaving them both wondering what it had all been about.

There had never been the slightest hint of marriage or another baby or a shared home. They had been joined together by a series of police investigations, in which Thea had found herself involved more or less directly, with not a great deal else to talk or think about. Phil was in his late forties, divorced, with a son. His daughter had died of an accidental drug overdose, effectively putting a stop to any furtherance of his police career beyond the level he'd reached. He was bruised, as Thea was, weary from life's blows and recently physically damaged by a slipped disc. A decent man, sometimes insightful, mostly kind... but... but...shouldn't there be something more than that?

Her family had done their best to be warily understanding about Phil. As a shattered young widow, Thea had been the object of appalled sympathy from her siblings and parents, who could find little to say. They had gathered round and offered varying kinds of support, until the advent of Phil Hollis had brought about a collective sigh of relief. She could be treated normally again, now she had another man. When it became evident that this was not to be a rapid courtship and second marriage, they held off and waited patiently for what might happen next.

And so it was that this well-paid exile in a wintry hamlet was also in part intended to be a time of reassessment. She had another forty years of life, in the normal nature of things, and she had no intention of wasting it. Already she had rediscovered some of the pleasures of history, laid out for her on a plate during some of her house-sitting commissions. Walking the deserted uplands, where medieval villages had been abandoned, and megalithic bodies had been buried, she had sometimes felt a strong connection with bygone times. The notion of further organised study held some appeal – a year or two at a university doing a master's degree, perhaps. But the prospect of such an intense commitment gave her pause. She doubted whether she had the application for it, having found how much she liked the flying-Dutchman existence of a house-sitter. A few weeks in one place, getting to know new people, many of them under the stress of a sudden violent incident, brought out something she hadn't known was within her. A clear-sightedness; an ability to make connections and see through prevarications and evasions, had manifested itself, and she liked this new talent.

Sunday was again cloudy, with a spiteful east wind cutting across the wolds. The animals were accorded over an hour's attention, first the rabbits, then the donkey and finally the unhappy Jimmy. Except the dog seemed less miserable than before, thanks to Hepzibah. The spaniel had gone straight to the conservatory after coming back from the donkey shed, and reintroduced herself to the lurcher. Again he licked her forehead, and she sat amicably beside him until Thea broke it up and took him out to his toilet. He drank a bowl of milk and settled down again on his warm bed.

Later in the morning, she decided it was time for a good walk. She had yet to locate the many public footpaths, or to visit the famous church. Not that a Sunday morning was the best time for that, she realised, unless she joined in the service. Church services were not part of her normal experience, and she inwardly cringed at the thought of trying to join in with a handful of aged parishioners, intoning hymns she didn't know and repeating words from a prayer book which had no meaning for her. Except, of course, there was little chance that such a small settlement continued to enjoy weekly services. Places of this size were lucky to get sufficient share of a vicar for more than once-a-month attentions. The whole business was slowly dying away, and few people of Thea's age and below cared enough even to notice.

So she bundled herself into a thick coat, with scarf and woolly hat, and set out to see what Hampnett might have to offer.

Chapter Three

As chance would have it, there was a service taking place in the church, and as Thea and her dog approached, the strains of organ music wafted down the grassy bank to greet her. Three cars were aligned along the edge of the grass, and as Thea strolled past, people began to emerge from the church door. Ahead of the small group came a young woman, head tucked between her shoulders as the wind nipped at her. She wore a thin coat, and looked pinched with cold.

Curious as always, Thea paused to watch this unlikely churchgoer, and as the girl reached the gate leading out of the churchyard, their eyes met. Thea smiled, and it was as if she had held out a hand to someone dangling over the edge of a deep abyss. 'Hello,' she said, unable to repress a slight question in her tone at the naked hope and relief on the face in front of her.

Hepzie, as so often happened, provided the necessary lubricant by jumping up at the new acquaintance, who responded with a small cry of delight. She grabbed the long soft ears and bent down to gaze into the dog's eyes. 'Who are you?' she murmured. 'Good little dog.'

The accent was marked, but not instantly identifiable. She looked up at Thea. 'I am Janina, from Bulgaria,' she said simply.

Thea mentally transposed the Y of *Yanina* into a J, remembering a student friend of the same name. 'Oh. Pleased to meet you,' she said. Bulgaria was well beyond her scope, she realised as she quickly scanned her memory for anything at all. Nothing. Did it have mountains? Was it east or west of places like Poland or Hungary? Or did it neighbour Yugoslavia – were the people Muslim? The girl had dark hair and eyes, but her skin was the same hue as Thea's. 'Do you live in Hampnett?'

'I am nanny, over there.' She waved a hand to a point vaguely northwards where there was a handful of farms and old stone houses. 'I am free for half a morning, so I go to church.'

'I see.'

'I am not interested in church, you understand. It is the only place to escape, where I can sit in quiet. People look at me, but I close my eyes and forget them.' The English was carefully good, the sentences constructed slightly in advance of their utterance. Thea wanted to retreat from this premature confession, this exposure of an unhappiness that she would far rather not have to face.

'How long have you been here?'

'Six weeks,' came the answer in a flash. Janina shivered. 'Six long weeks.'

Why did they come? Thea wondered. What sort of life did they expect here – and was it really so much better than what they had at home? Could mere money ever compensate for the loneliness and low status and general unpleasantness?

They had begun walking away from the church, taking the small road in the direction that Janina had indicated. A car passed them slowly, the elderly female driver ducking her head to stare at them shamelessly. This, more than anything, forged a bond between Thea and the young woman. Instinctively she closed the gap between them.

'How many children are there?'

'Two. Benjamin is six and Nicholas is almost four. He is to have a birthday party next Saturday.' The gloomy resignation in her voice made Thea snort with a brief laugh. 'Yes, it is funny, I know. A party should be happy, with games and a lot of food. Perhaps that will be how it is, but only if I make it so.'

Thea murmured an encouraging syllable. 'His mother hates me,' Janina announced. 'Because she is stupid and I am not. Because she has made big, big mistakes and is now in a trap. She can see that I know her to be a fool, and that makes her hate. I understand it all, but what can I do? Every time I look in her face she can see what I know.' This emerged as a prepared speech, and Thea wondered whether the hour in church had been spent in thinking it through. 'She is a terrible mother, with no love for the boys. She pays me to love them for her.'

'Where's their father?'

'Hah! The father is Simon, who works in a hotel near Stow-on-the-Wold. He is always working, but at home I never saw a more lazy man. He drinks beer. He watches football on the TV. He says he is tired from the guests who bother him every moment of the day.'

Probably true, thought Thea. She had always considered hotel work to be amongst the most demanding and exhausting imaginable. 'What does their mother do?' she asked.

'Oh...she works in advertising. She abandons her boys for such *worthless* work. Worthless,' she repeated. 'It brings no good to anybody. It is about lies and deceit and nothing more. Stupid woman.'

'What's her name?'

'Her real name is Beatrice, but we call her Bunny. *Call me Bunny*, she says as if that were a sort of gift. A grown woman, forty years old, named Bunny. That is stupid.'

Thea began to feel a flicker of sympathy for the maligned employer. This high-minded nanny must be rather a strain to live with, if indeed her scorn was as visible as she believed it to be. There was an uncomfortably obsessive element in this outpouring of bile to a total stranger.

'My name's Thea Osborne and this is Hepzibah,' she said. 'We're here for a month.'

Janina paused, as if arrested by a firm hand laid on her arm. 'Ah, I am sorry,' she breathed. 'I have talked too much. How rude. Thea,' she repeated. 'And Hep—?'

'She answers to Hepzie. It was a silly choice of name. I've regretted it ever since.'

'So change it,' said the Bulgarian, as if the obviousness of this was almost beyond any need to state it. 'A dog cares nothing for a name.'

'Too late,' said Thea lightly.

Janina shrugged. *Not my problem*, was writ large on her face.

'Did you qualify as a nanny in Bulgaria? Your English is excellent.' She stopped. Any more questions and it might sound like an interrogation.

The girl pouted contemptuously. '*Qualify!* What need for study to care for young children? It is crazy. I have four young brothers – that is my *qualifying*. I mean *qualification*,' she said the word emphatically, even boastfully. 'My mother took a new husband when I was twelve and...' she made a hissing zipping sound, flicking one hand in a horizontal sweep '...then there were four small brothers, all in four years, like a magic trick.'

'Gosh,' said Thea faintly.

'Fortunately, I like small boys. They are funny and warm and brave and wild. I was happy to come here to take care of Nicholas and Benjamin, for money. It is good money, I think. And the food is not bad. But the woman is...' she looked around as if afraid of eavesdroppers '...she is a monster. I am sorry to say it, but it is true.'

'Well...' said Thea helplessly. 'I'd better go back now. I suppose I'm rather like you. I have to take care of a woman's animals, and her house, while she's away. And my money's pretty good, too. We're the new domestic servants, you and me. It's like it was two centuries ago, when rich women paid other women to do the dirty work.' Even as she spoke she felt a pang of remorse at this small betrayal of Lucy, who clearly didn't object to dirty hands at all.

'I too have more duties,' said Janina with a sigh.

'I'm sure I'll see you again. This is a very small village.'

'It is not a village, not at all.' The raised voice contained a genuine fury and frustration. 'Here nobody cares for each other, no sharing, no place to gather. This church, today, I expected all the people to come. Instead there were six very old ladies, a man who seemed to be in some deep trouble inside himself, and another man, also very old, who talked aloud to himself. It was like a hospital – a place of dying. They are all there because they are afraid and hope for rescue. But they know it will not come.' She shook her head in despair at the follies of the English that she had somehow fallen amongst. 'I will not go there again,' she added. 'It was worse than my room in Bunny's stupid house. Except for the decorations, of course. The decoration is a glory. It reminds me of Rila Monastery at home.'

'Oh?'

'You have not seen it?'

Thea glanced towards the church, where a knot of people still hovered in the porch. 'I've heard of it. I'll come back another day for a proper look.'

'Any day but Sunday,' Janina said with a shiver. 'No more Sundays for me.'

'Cold in there, I expect.'

Again Janina shrugged. 'Not so cold as Bulgaria in winter. I come from Plovdiv, close to the mountains. There is snow.' She stared wistfully at the grey sky.

'Well...' Thea tried again.

'Yes, you must go. I too. No free time for me now until next Sunday.'

'Surely that can't be right,' Thea objected. 'What about the evenings?'

'They go out, to see their friends, two, three evenings each week, so I must babysit. And why should I object? I have nowhere to go, nothing to do. The children like me.' Her face became pinched. 'Too much they like me. When I leave, they have to begin all over again, to like a new person. It is cruel. They are boys – they should learn about trust and security, if they are to make good husbands and fathers when they grow up. All these two learn is how to bear it when women walk away from them. It will be what they learn to expect – they will push everyone away from them. It makes me very sad.'

Thea's eyes widened. 'You've really thought about it, haven't you?' she said.

'It was my degree subject – psychology. I did my postgraduate course on how children learn to form relationships. I understand too much,' she added darkly. 'Too much for comfort.'

It was, Thea gathered, all rather a shock for the poor overeducated clever girl, finding herself in the role of servant to a stupid woman. Could it be possible that she earned more in Gloucestershire as a nanny than she would as an academic in her own country? Why did she submit to such a miserable fate, otherwise?

'Well, I'm glad I met you,' she said, and then had a thought. 'Maybe you could bring the children down to the Barn. There's a donkey and some rabbits they could play with.'

'Barn?'

Thea explained, and a vague promise was made. They parted with wistful smiles.

A rhythm established itself over the next three days, which left Thea quite contented. She did her routine shopping in the little town of Northleach, where life appeared to have stopped around 1955. The market square was bordered by shops selling basic requirements – bread, groceries and pharmaceuticals, with a post office added for good measure. The excessively large church, built with wool money, stood protectively to the north, but Thea did not visit it. The people she met were almost all over sixty, and she found herself imagining her widowed mother living there, readily establishing new friendships. But then she noticed a card in the post office window on which a woman in her sixties pleaded for companionship, and wondered about the drawbacks. Northleach was no Blockley, with its legions of clubs and outings and talks and exhibitions. It was calm and quiet and forgotten, entirely beautiful, and probably perfect for a week's holiday. Further than that, she couldn't say. But she enjoyed her visits, which she made by car, despite it being scarcely half a mile from Lucy's Barn to the market square. One day, she promised herself, she'd make the trip on foot, discovering the hidden nooks along the way.

She set up the lacemaking cushion, but found it much more complicated than expected. Putting it back in the bag, she regretfully decided to abandon it until she could find someone to teach her.

Almost she could accuse herself of complacency. None of the dramas that had taken place during previous commissions were going to happen here. How could they, in this tiny place, with the low grey skies and almost total lack of activity?

But there was one small unexpected drama on the Wednesday; the kind of drama nobody could object to.

She had gone out to feed the rabbits as usual that afternoon. They were in no hurry to partake of the food Thea gave them, and only three emerged from the bedroom area in the cage containing the four does. Carefully, Thea unlatched the door into that section, and peered in. A pretty blue-grey ball of fluff was crouched in the corner, nose twitching, eyes wide and bulging. Thea identified Jemima, the one she had cuddled under Lucy's scrutiny. In another corner was a nest, apparently made of hay, but with some wisps of hair protruding from it. 'Uh-oh,' said Thea, capturing a distant memory of rabbits owned by her younger sister, twenty-five years previously. 'What have we here, then?'

With the gentlest probing fingers, she investigated, and found a toasty warm huddle of babies buried under layers of fur and hay. 'And how did this happen, hmm?' she demanded of the wild-eyed mother. 'Oh well, you seem to know what to do. I'd better give you some extra rations.'

It was a greatly consoling thing to find. New life, the hairless helpless scraps so perfectly protected in the midst of a grey January – it suggested a whole range of happy hopeful feelings. But it also added to Thea's responsibilities. The other rabbits probably ought to be removed, especially if one of them was an undiagnosed male. Males were unreliable around babies, and should not be permitted to cause trouble.

But where to put them? The second cage, containing Snoopy, was quite large. Perhaps the three exiles could go in there, and the buck be found some smaller temporary shelter. Meanwhile, everything appeared peaceful in the new family, and she was reluctant to interfere for the time being. Jemima was big enough to defend her offspring against the other three, if it came to it. She would see how things stood in the morning.

Chapter Four

Thursday 11th January arrived, and Thea woke early with a sense of something having changed. Curtains were closed across the small window, and everything was silent. It was half past seven – a time when it was still almost dark in January. Instead, there was a flat eerie light coming through the curtains, which Thea took some minutes to understand.

'Snow!' she exclaimed, when she finally went to look out. 'Masses of it.' Her initial reaction was a childish excitement, combined with awe at the absolute beauty of the scene. The yard between the house and outbuildings was a pristine expanse of glittering white, the sheds rising starkly to present vertical planes of muted colour, before more white obliterated their roofs. There was no flicker of life – no bird or fox or stoat seemed to have left any footprints in the snow.

'Gosh!' Thea muttered to Hepzie, a few minutes later. 'This could give us some trouble.' Quickly, she did a mental scan of food stocks, and the basic needs of the animals in her care. Water – the outside pipe would be frozen, so the donkey would have to be supplied from the house. Would the rabbits be warm enough? How would she get Jimmy out for his lavatory trips?

'Oh well,' she went on. 'Snow never lasts for long in this country. It'll all be gone by tomorrow.'

The donkey was not impressed by the change that had come over his world. He laid his ears back and shook his head firmly, standing in the open doorway of his shed. So much for Lucy's assertion that he patrolled his patch whatever the weather. Thea fetched hay and water and left him to it. Walking across the virgin snow in her wellingtons, she was alarmed to discover that it was a good nine inches deep. Progress was exhausting, even over the fifty yards to the donkey shed and back.

The rabbits showed no sign of having noticed anything different in the weather and the nest of new babies seemed undisturbed. Jemima's companions lolloped appealingly around their large two-storey cage, snatching eagerly at the cabbage leaves and carrots proffered by Thea. 'Make the most of it,' she told them. 'It might be short rations from here on.' There seemed little reason to start moving them, the new mother appearing relaxed to the point of complacency.

Jimmy was even less disconcerted by the snow. He picked his way to his usual toilet corner, and performed exactly as if nothing at all had happened. His pee left a yellow streak in the snow. Hepzie, in contrast, thought the whole thing was laid on especially for her. She reverted to puppyhood and cavorted ecstatically, forging a gully for herself through the cold white stuff, getting more and more clogged with chunks of it sticking to her long hair. Thea wished there was a child with her, to justify building a snowman and throwing handfuls of snow around. As it was, she had to make do with the dog, who was already showing signs of having had enough of the novelty. 'You can't come in the house like that,' Thea told her. 'You'll make a flood when all that ice on you melts.'

She compromised by putting the two dogs together in the conservatory, where the stone floor wouldn't mind some wet. Then she tuned the radio to a local station, feeling a sudden need for human voices and relevant information.

The snow, it seemed, had brought civilisation to a standstill. Schools were closed, trains and buses cancelled, roads barely passable. 'And there's a lot more to come,' added the newsreader, barely concealing his glee. 'Another six or seven inches of snow is forecast for this afternoon and evening. Brace yourselves, folks – this lot could last a week or more.' Thea felt the thrill of a crisis, a surge of adrenalin at being forced to cope alone in an isolated snowbound house. 'We can always eat the rabbits,' she told Hepzie and Jimmy. The glass roof of the conservatory was grey with the weight of snow, and made occasional creaks that Thea tried to ignore. She had a feeling you were supposed to clear it off this sort of roof, which was not designed to take anything heavy.

At least the power was still on, so the freezer and lights would work. Presumably the underfloor heating needed some kind of electrical input, as well. If that died on her, she'd have to assemble the livestock and huddle under blankets until the thaw came. She focused fiercely on the practicalities, the essentials for survival, trying to ignore the clenching spasms in her lower belly which gripped her every time she recalled the pessimistic forecast. She was, after all, trapped. The snow had obliterated the track, in both directions, and walking even a quarter of a mile in deep snow would take more fortitude than she believed she possessed. So she had to stop thinking about it, and keep to the feeding routines.

The worst part was seeing to the donkey. She went out again at three, following in the same footsteps she'd made that morning, hoping some sort of track might form, which would make the walking easier. The hay was fortunately in an enclosed corner of the same shed, but water had to be carried in a black rubber bucket that was awkwardly large. Despite the expanses of white in all directions, the overall impression was of a pale grey, as the short day began to close and the sky sagged heavily just above her head. The silence too had a greyness to it, with no traffic or birds or animals audible. All sensory experience was muted, she realised. There were no smells, either, and nothing to taste or touch but endless cold white nothingness.

For supper she took out a prepared frozen curry and microwaved it, boiling rice to go with it, and tracking down an almost-full jar of mango chutney at the back of Lucy's store cupboard. The hot spicy food brought a welcome explosion in her mouth, warming her both physically and emotionally. If only a real log fire could have been blazing in the non-existent hearth, she could have felt quite cosy.

She found herself constantly wrestling with anxiety. Of course she was in no danger whatsoever. She could surely walk out to the main road if really necessary, where there was sure to be traffic passing. She had her phone, and Lucy's radio and her computer. Treat it as an adventure, she adjured herself. Enjoy it. Think what a good story it'll make later on. But what if it lasted a week or more, nagged the worried little voice. How will you get food? What if the pipes burst, or the donkey falls ill, or...or...?

But so far, nothing troubling had happened. There was food and water enough – the pipes must be made of some kind of frostproof material, in such a new building. And it wouldn't last a week, *of course* it wouldn't. Outside there was already a flurry of fresh snowflakes falling, just as the man on the radio had said.

She went to bed early, Hepzie following her and curling up at her feet, as usual. For a while she read an absorbing novel about Australia, where it was always too hot. Then she slept soundly, dreaming about driving along a straight white road, where a windmill waited for her, some miles away in the distance.

The next morning was a rerun of the first. She went to the window, and tried to assess whether or not more snow had fallen. At first it wasn't easy to be sure, until she focused on a low stone wall between the house and the yard, where she remembered sweeping all the snow off, just to gauge the depth of it. Now the area she'd swept was covered again, and the rest of its length had a higher step. Another three or four inches must have silently fallen during the night.

Doggedly, she stamped her feet into the boots, the double pair of socks making it a tight fit. A woolly hat, which she had found in the drawer of Lucy's Victorian coat stand, was pulled down over her ears. But when she went outside, her first sensation was not of cold, but of a renewed wonder at the transformation of the mundane world of fields and trees into a hummocky featureless expanse where even the hedges had been swallowed up. It took her a while to realise that this meant it would be difficult to locate the track up to the road into the village. She could easily find herself floundering in a ditch, or setting off across a field because she had forgotten the precise bends and turns of the lane.

But she could still see the donkey's shed, and the trail of footsteps leading to it. She had even taken the first few steps before it hit her. There ought not to be any footsteps still visible. Everywhere else, all signs of yesterday's activity had been erased.

Somebody else had walked across the paddock that morning. The ice that swept through her had nothing to do with the weather. She was abruptly frozen with fear – her arms and legs crackled with it, her stomach clenched. Without conscious thought, she turned and struggled back to the house, the puzzled spaniel slowly following her, when she called. Not until she had slammed and locked the door did she stop to ask herself why she was so frightened.

She ought to phone somebody, she told herself, to ensure that she was linked to the outside world. Somebody who could assure her she was all right, and talk her through her panic. In fact – why hadn't Jessica or her mother called already, as soon as the first snow had arrived? Didn't anyone *care*?

They wouldn't have understood how isolated Lucy's Barn was, of course. They'd think she had neighbours and a shop close by, and all the usual services of civilisation.

So she phoned her daughter, praying that there would be a response.

'Hi, Mum,' came the breathless voice of the young police constable. 'I bet you've got some amazing snow there, haven't you?'

'You could say that.'

'What's the matter? Can't you get the car out?'

'I haven't tried – but no, there's no way in the world that I could move it. I can't even see where the track goes.'

Jessica paused, as if absorbing the fact that her mother was not excited at the adventure, as she ought to be. 'But you're all right, aren't you?'

'Yes, I suppose so. But there are footprints outside, Jess. Somebody's been here in the night.'

Stupid, of course, to expect the girl to understand the geography, to grasp immediately that there should not be people walking across the donkey's paddock in any weather, at any time of day – and certainly not during a snowy night. She did her best to explain.

'Somebody got lost, perhaps?' Jessica suggested. 'Did you notice which way they were pointing?'

'Of course I didn't.'

'Well, if they were leading towards the house, you've got more to worry about than if they were the other way – haven't you?'

Slowly the sense of what Jessica was saying sank in. 'If they were coming this way, the person would be here,' she said. 'In one of the sheds, at least.'

'So just go out and have a proper look. It's not like you to be so timid – what's got you so jumpy?' Jessica was genuinely curious to know, and yet there was no hint of concern in her voice. That alone made Thea feel better.

'I think it's the idea that someone was prowling round here while I was asleep. It was such a shock, seeing those footprints. At first I thought they were mine, but then I realised the new snow had covered mine up.'

'Well, whoever it was obviously didn't mind if you saw the tracks. Come on, Ma – listen to yourself. Get a grip.'

'It's fine for you to talk,' Thea protested. 'I've got rabbits, a donkey, a cat and a daft old dog to look after. It's not easy in all this white-out, you know. I can't find the paths, and keep thinking I'm going to fall into a ditch.'

Jessica laughed. 'But it's an *adventure*. Stop sounding so middle-aged about it. Throw a few snowballs, why don't you? You're lucky. We didn't have anything here except a bit of sleet.'

'Mmm. So I have to get out there and feed that donkey – is that what you're saying?'

'Precisely. Call me again any time and update me, OK?'

'Aren't you on duty?'

'Technically, yes, but it's Friday, and there's not much doing, for a change.'

'Well, you'll probably get plenty of snow over the next few days, and then there'll be people skidding into each other, and pipes bursting.'

'Not my department,' said Jessica complacently.

So Thea took some deep breaths, reminding herself it was broad daylight, and that a few footprints really were nothing to fear, and ventured outside again.

Carrying the donkey's water bucket, she followed the line of the prints, peering at them to see if she could distinguish toe from heel. It wasn't easy, but she eventually concluded that they did indeed lead away from the house. When she reached the donkey's shed, she saw that the person had veered to the left, rather than dive into the warmth of the shelter, where she might have found him sitting on the donkey's hay. Puzzled, her gaze followed the wavering line of prints which went away to the left, and the neighbouring field.

The donkey seemed to have grown resigned to the weather, and had even made a little track of his own, where he had emerged for a short walk at some point. Not his usual circuit of the paddock, but at least a brief bit of exercise, down the slope towards the big new gate. The snow was scuffed, as if the animal had been frisking as he went – and he must have retraced his own tracks, creating quite a definite pathway. 'You've been walkabout, I see,' Thea said. He nuzzled her amiably, and ate the hay she gave him with slow crunching movements. Quite how animals made soft hay crunch was a mystery she had stopped trying to solve some time ago.

Outside again, she took another look at the footprints that had so alarmed her. Where had the person gone? What kind of a struggle must it have been to walk across open fields, negotiating fences and hidden hummocks? And *why*? Was it a recognised short cut?

Belatedly, she recalled Lucy's reference to 'Old Kate'. Was there an even more isolated and struggling woman than Thea herself, further down the track? Had she made the footprints, walking home late at night, for some reason? In an instant, the walker was transformed from a sinister threatening stranger, male and aggressive, to a floundering elderly woman, stoically traversing the snowy expanses in an effort to get home.

Hepzie had obviously exhausted her playfulness, and had not followed Thea to the donkey shed. Instead she remained in the yard, idly sniffing at the rabbits in their own quarters. Were they all right, Thea wondered? Did rabbits freeze to death in weather like this? They had seemed fine the day before. The niggling worry was swamped by the much larger concern about the maker of the footprints. Instead of rushing indoors in such a cowardly fashion, she should have thought about the poor person out in the cold, who obviously had no harmful intent.

Doggedly she accepted that she ought to investigate. She ought to go to Old Kate's and make sure she was all right. After all, it would be good to share the difficulties, and talk to another person, even one with a formidable temper, according to Lucy. And so she set out cautiously to follow the footprints and see where they led.

It took ten minutes to traverse the paddock beyond the donkey shed. When she reached the wire mesh fence, she found no way through. The unknown walker must have climbed over, which a close examination of the prints confirmed. 'Must have longer legs than mine,' she muttered, before throwing one leg over the wire and finding herself uncomfortably straddling the fence, with no alternative but to pitch herself over, landing on her hands. Thankful for the woolly gloves, she picked herself up and pressed on.

The field tilted downhill, the tracks following the fence down to a shallow bowl, typical of the Cotswolds where the ground undulated crazily like a rumpled duvet on an untidy bed. In the same field, but at some distance, she could see a small group of Hereford cattle, their red coats shaggy against the white snow. They were standing up to their knees in snow, and Thea paused a moment to worry about how they could find anything to eat. They had trodden down the snow for a wide area from the fence almost to a patch of trees at the other side of the field.

But they had not followed the human track closely enough to obscure it. Thea spied it snaking away to the right and down a sudden slope. As she began on the same course, she could see something dark in the snow, huddled in the hollow, close to the point where the new fence turned at a right angle to form the northern boundary of the donkey paddock.

Rapid movement was impossible, every step a heave and a plunge, the snow almost reaching the top of her boots at times. As she got closer, the dark patch resembled a heap of abandoned clothes, with a smaller item close by. A scatter of snow formed odd patches on the heap, which remained stubbornly shapeless and impossible to identify.

But Thea had little doubt as to what she was going to find, from a distance of thirty yards. She approached steadily, her head thumping, her teeth clenched tightly together. As she came closer, she focused on the incongruity of a glass bottle standing upright in the snow, only the neck and shoulders visible. She barely glanced at it, only taking the time to recognise it as having held alcohol of some kind. Infinitely more significant was the person who had drunk its contents, and then removed his coat and waited for the painless oblivion of death by hypothermia. He was lying on his side, his back to her, his bare head half buried in the snow.

Chapter Five

It took an impossibly long time to flounder back to the house, call 999, and try to explain that it would be a major operation to get any sort of vehicle to the spot in question. 'Even a tractor would have difficulty,' she said. 'I don't know what you're going to do.' As if to add emphasis, snow had begun to fall again – fat, fluffy flakes that settled comfortably on top of their fellows. The gentle soundless stuff made everything seem less urgent, as if rush and trouble were examples of human folly and nothing more.

The girl at the end of the phone was clearly unfamiliar with rural realities. 'I'm sure they'll cope,' she said dismissively. 'What's the postcode?'

Thea opened her mouth to reply with her own home address, before remembering where she was. 'I have no idea,' she said. 'It's called Lucy's Barn, to the south-west of Hampnett. It's not very easy to find.'

'Could you stand somewhere they can see you, then, and wave when they arrive?'

'Not really. It's at least a quarter of a mile from here to the road, in snow a foot deep. I can't even see where the track runs. I don't think you're quite getting the picture. Even if I did struggle up there, it isn't possible for anything to drive back to the Barn – and even less feasible to get to where the body is.'

'Oh.' The thread of panic in the girl's voice found an answer in Thea's insides. She was trapped here until the snow cleared. Nobody could get in or out, without an industrial-scale snowplough. There was a dead man two fields away and nothing anybody could do about it.

'You *are* sure he's dead, aren't you?' the girl asked, having exchanged some muttering with another person.

'I think so,' said Thea, suddenly not sure at all. 'He was very cold and stiff. I tried to shake him, but he didn't respond at all. Oh yes, he must be dead. It looks as if he committed suicide.'

'Helicopter,' said the girl. 'Is there somewhere we could land an air ambulance?'

'I doubt it. Can they manage snow? The field isn't very level.'

A defeated silence rebounded between the two women. It appeared that there was no script for such a situation, as all the modern means of transport were found wanting. Thea found herself wanting to say, 'A horse could manage it,' but bit it back. You'd need two horses and a cart, at least. Or a team of huskies and a nice big sledge. Or a couple of woolly yaks, accustomed to slogging up and down snowy slopes dragging dead meat and heaps of felt and wood which would transform into a cosy ger.

'I'll pass you to my superior,' said the girl wearily. 'I'm sure she'll think of something.'

In the end, a group of well-clad police personnel arrived on foot, an hour and a half after the phone call. Four of them came clumping down the track, in single file, one of them with a phone clamped to his ear, with which Thea had directed them to the Barn. They introduced themselves as a sergeant, a constable, the police doctor and a photographer. The last two carried bags containing their equipment, the photographer looking breathless and rumpled. The snow had stopped and the sky had cleared, the sun shining coldly on the sparkling snow, having no thawing effect on it at all. In fact the temperature had fallen, if anything.

'Can you lead us to it?' the sergeant asked her, scanning the surrounding landscape apprehensively.

'I suppose so,' Thea sighed, with considerable reluctance. She had become increasingly agitated as she waited for them to arrive, checking her phone repeatedly, and then clearing pathways around the yard, from rabbit shed to barn and linking the garage to the house. She stayed at the back of the house deliberately, trying to close her mind to the wretched scene she had witnessed. At one point she heard the donkey braying, and Hepzie yapping in response, but she remained where she was, persuading herself that the clearance work took priority.

It was hard work, the shovel cutting sheer cliffs in the snow. She checked her car to see whether it might be possible to move it, but was daunted by the prospect of having to dig tracks for it for a substantial distance. She was already exhausted by her exertions when the rescue party finally arrived. The fresh snowfall continued relentlessly, threatening to obliterate the work she'd accomplished.

'You took your time,' she accused, when the men finally arrived, just as the sky cleared. 'Where did you have to come from?'

'Cirencester,' said the sergeant. 'But that's not the reason we were delayed. Never mind, we're here now. Could you just show us what you found, do you think?'

Wearily she escorted the police across the donkey's paddock as far as the shed and then pointed out that she had climbed over the fence away to the left, when they might prefer to go through the gate at the bottom, and walk along the fence to the spot where the body lay. The donkey tracks could be seen going down to the gate, and coming back again, the snow sufficiently broken up to comprise a relatively inviting pathway. The men agreed to the suggestion with no hesitation, their heads hunched into hoods and their knees getting wet from melting snow, which had clung to their legs as they sank into the deeper parts, and was then turned to liquid by the heat from their bodies. The doctor looked especially damp, and the photographer sniffed. Looking at him more closely, Thea noted that his nose was red, and his eyes bleary. 'Have you got a cold?' she asked him.

'Probably,' he said thickly.

It all took an unreasonable length of time. A biting wind had sprung up. Every step took effort, and Thea's legs were aching. Few words were exchanged, everyone silenced by the unusual conditions. For most English people, snow recalled carefree childhood memories, with the schools closed and dads extracting half-forgotten toboggans from the back of the garage. It represented a sudden holiday, something to relish for its beauty and strangeness.

'How much further is it?' asked the young constable.

'Just at the end of this fence, in a dip down there,' Thea told him. 'And then you're going to have to carry him all the way back to the road – aren't you?'

'Eventually,' said the sergeant, who was the nominal leader of the group. 'First the doctor has to certify life extinct, and a close examination of the scene undergone.'

'Yes,' said Thea, fully aware of the procedures. 'And he has to be identified. And I don't have any idea who he is.' As she spoke, she suddenly remembered the tall grey man she'd glimpsed on the first day.

'Plenty of time for that,' said the sergeant. 'Once we've seen what sort of a state he's in.'

Finally the corner of the fence was visible. 'There,' Thea pointed, knowing the men would be able to see it before she did, walking ahead of her as they were. The photographer was in the lead, raising his camera to look at the display screen, swinging it round as if making an amateur video.

'Where?' said the sergeant, his head following in a slower arc to that of the photographer.

Thea surged ahead, impatiently. 'That last lot of snow must have covered him up,' she panted.

She was in the corner, with fences stretching in two directions, her arms outstretched in a gesture of bafflement. 'He's gone,' she said unnecessarily.

Opinion instantly divided as to whether Thea was mad, bad or simply incompetent. 'Must be the wrong field,' said the constable.

'If this is a hoax...' began the doctor, who was middle-aged and overweight and had grown increasingly breathless during the walk.

'Are you absolutely sure he was ever here?' said the sergeant.

'Look,' Thea ordered them. 'You can see there was something here.' The snow was indeed compressed and disturbed in the place they were all staring at. 'He must have got up.' She pointed towards a clump of trees less than a hundred yards away, and a muddled track of prints leading to it. 'Something's been over there,' she added.

'Those cows, look,' said the photographer. Sure enough the Herefords had moved to the lee of the trees, and were standing in a ragged group, heads down.

'If it was your dead man, he'll be home by this time,' said the sergeant.

The photographer snorted as if at a joke.

'We ought to follow that track and see,' Thea urged. 'He might have managed to crawl that far, and *then* died. But he *was* dead. I know he was. He was cold. The snow was settling on him. And there was a bottle,' she remembered. 'He wouldn't have bothered to take the bottle.'

All four men looked at her. The doctor was the only one to manifest anger. The photographer examined her with his head tilted as if assessing her potential as a model. The two police officers simply looked tired, as if this sort of thing happened just that bit too often.

'I don't think so,' said the constable. 'The cows made those tracks, if you ask me. They don't look human.'

'And before long they'll all be covered up anyway,' said the photographer. It seemed to Thea that this only added urgency to their quest for the dead or dying man, but none of the others appeared to share this view.

She had never felt so stupid. Had she mistaken a sleeping drunk for a dead man, and caused all this bother for nothing? She remembered the apparently empty bottle as a much more significant detail than she had previously acknowledged. She stammered out a confused theory, which the four men heard in silence, whereby an alcohol-induced stupor had been mistaken for death. 'But he was so *cold*,' she repeated, 'and *stiff*.

He really did seem dead. The snow hadn't melted on him.'

The enormity of the situation seemed to engulf them all. The snow stretched obstructively on all sides, making any decisions about a search utterly daunting. Gradually Thea regained her self-possession. 'He *was* here,' she insisted. 'You have to believe me. Even if he did get up and stagger away, he'll be ill and freezing somewhere. We ought to search for him. It's barely two hours ago, after all.' She looked at her watch. 'Well, nearly three now,' she amended. 'You took such a long time to come.'

'We do believe you,' said the sergeant, slowly. 'Why would you invent such a story? The question is, where would we begin to look for him? We could have a look in those woods, I suppose – but I'm inclined to agree with Paul that those tracks were never made by a human being.' He walked a little way towards the trees, peering closely at the ground. The photographer plodded after him, holding his camera.

'Come back,' pleaded the doctor. 'This is getting beyond a joke. I'm not here to search for missing bodies.'

'Aren't you?' muttered the constable, giving Thea a wink. The sergeant and photographer paused indecisively.

The snow was disorientating: an endless white blanket covering mysterious humps and bumps, which could be anything. Thea knew there was little prospect of further investigation. 'Why would the cows come over here?' she wondered aloud.

'Curiosity,' said the photographer. 'If there really was somebody lying here, they'd come over for a look.'

'So the fact that they then went up to the woods means they *followed* him,' she said earnestly. 'And so should we.'

'No!' Again it was the irascible doctor. His nose had turned blue, and his teeth were chattering. It made Thea feel a lot colder, just to look at him.

The sergeant was rubbing his chin vigorously. 'We can't see any human footprints on this side of the fence except for ours,' he repeated. 'Nor any wheel marks, so there hasn't been a tractor over here this morning. Even if we wanted to, we wouldn't know where to start searching. Best get back,' he decided. 'Nothing we can do here for the time being.' He gave Thea a look that was almost kind, when compared to the doctor's baleful glances. 'No harm done,' he added.

'But—' Thea felt a surge of alarm at the implications. The afternoon was already half over, the long hours of darkness not far off. 'You can't just *go,*' she pleaded. 'I'm absolutely sure he was dead. Somebody must have moved him.' She shuddered. 'And why would they do that?' She wasn't sure which explanation was more alarming – that a dead man had been spirited away, or a live one had dragged himself off somewhere and was in the process of dying that very moment. She tried to spell this out for the sergeant. 'What if he's over there in those trees?' she demanded.

'If he could get that far, he could get to a house,' said the sergeant, with a shake of his head. 'It'd be a wild goose chase to go off trying to find him. We'd be better waiting to see if there's a missing person reported.'

The four men were arranged in a semicircle around her, all embarrassed to a greater or lesser degree. 'It isn't very likely anybody took him, is it?' The doctor spoke for them all. 'Let's face it – it would be quite a job to lug a dead body anywhere in all this. Look how worried *we* were at the idea of having to do it.'

'Besides, it would leave marks,' said the photographer, repeating the obvious, much to Thea's irritation. He had been scrutinising the ground assiduously for the past five minutes, with an air of frustration. 'There's no sign that anything was dragged away from this spot. Is there?' he challenged to nobody in particular.

Thea's fertile imagination conjured images of a half-dead man crawling doggedly over the fields to Lucy's Barn, and then either dying on the doorstep, or forcing entry to the house and accusing Thea of interfering with some complicated plan. These were quickly followed by even more alarming visions of a hugely strong man, carrying the frozen body out of the field and away to some unspecified point where nobody could find him. There he would lurk, dangerous and unpredictable, until the snows melted.

'Come *on*,' whined the doctor. 'Why are we standing around like this?'

'Good question,' muttered the constable, and by mutual accord they began the return journey.

Hepzie and Jimmy were curled together in the grey light of the conservatory, the snow on the glass roof obscuring much of the daylight. Spirit, the black cat, was on the back of the sofa, staring out at the snow through half-closed eyes. The donkey had been standing with his head and shoulders out of the shed, observing the unfamiliar world with a very Eeyore-like expression. Thea had been left to the company of the animals by the bemused police people, with a half-hearted instruction to call them again if anything more happened. She almost felt sorry for them, watching them struggle with the impossible facts. Tempting as it might be, they couldn't go so far as to disbelieve her whole story. There *were* marks in the snow, compatible with a human body lying there. Easiest to assume he had only been asleep, not dead, and had simply got up and stumbled home. During the return to the Barn, this was what they had concluded, slowly exchanging remarks that fortified the theory, until Thea herself was close to believing it.

She knew she should apologise, abasing herself for the outrageous waste of police time. But that would be to admit the credibility of the theory that the man had not been dead, and this she could not do. He *had* been dead. The snow wasn't melting on him, there was no sign of breathing, he was stiff to the touch. The convenient explanation was understandably the one the men adopted – but she knew it was wrong.

Chapter Six

Darkness closed in shortly after four, the sky having clouded over again. Tuning to the local radio station again, Thea heard with dismay that there was no foreseeable prospect of a thaw. Aged countrymen were rounded up to recall the five-week freeze of 1947, or the barely less unthinkable Big Snow of 1963. With irritating relish, the presenters had already decided that this was another memorable winter which would go down in history for the length of the white-out.

The police had expressed a fleeting concern for Thea's plight, unable to get the car out, and with no guarantee that the electricity supply would survive. Heavy branches, weighed down with snow, could bring cables down. Snow could do unpredictable things, as everybody knew. 'So could you ask the council to send the snowplough down here?' she suggested, trying to keep her nerve.

The sergeant pursed his lips. 'Not our department, I'm afraid.' Every time he spoke, she heard a ghostly unspoken *madam* at the end of each sentence. Didn't they say that any more? Had it gone the same way as *love* and *pet*? How were they supposed to address female members of the public these days?

When they first arrived she had waited to see whether they knew who she was – the former girlfriend of Detective Superintendent Phil Hollis, and active participant in investigations into a number of violent deaths in the Cotswold area over the past year or two. By the time they'd reached the second field she had concluded that her anonymity was safe. There was no hint of any familiarity with her name, or role as house-sitter. She was just a slightly unreliable woman in her forties who had brought them out on a wild goose chase, possibly because of a hormonal problem, or the trauma of the snowfall.

'OK,' she said to the dogs, having taken a deep and bracing breath. 'You two have to go out, like it or not. The rabbits need fresh bedding, and I ought to find the cat. Then tomorrow, we're going to walk out to the road and see what's going on in the bustling community of Hampnett. We will not give dead bodies another thought. Right?'

Hepzie looked at her, with a slow tail wag, but Jimmy merely sighed gently and laid his long nose on his narrow paws.

* * *

The evening was an ordeal, by any standards. The enveloping blanket of snow created an unnatural silence that led to the impression that the world had disappeared, leaving nobody but Thea and the animals in her care. And perhaps a superhuman figure who could bring himself back to life at will. Repeatedly, the memory of the tall ghostly man from Saturday intruded into her mind, embellished by subsequent events, until she was convinced he had been the same as the 'dead' man in the field. The mental quote marks around the word annoyed her, even while they refused to go away. She argued obsessively with herself about the logic of believing him to have been a genuine ghost. Logical, because it fitted at least some of the facts; impossibly foolish because she had *touched* him and found him to be all too convincingly solid. Ghosts were insubstantial, fading away at the very idea of touching them. No, she reproached herself – they weren't even that. They were nothing, they did not exist.

Although, persisted a small inner voice, if they were ever going to exist, this was absolutely the right setting for it. How many ghost stories began with snowy nights, and a lone woman in an isolated house, awaiting the attentions of a supernatural visitor?

She turned the television up loud, watching a costume drama which made no less than fifteen blatant historical mistakes in ten minutes, with such a hopelessly anachronistic tone to the whole thing that she could hardly bear to stay with it. But all the other channels were even worse, and she couldn't summon interest in any of the available DVDs, so she left it on. At least it helped her to forget the various threatening aspects of the world outside.

At last it was ten-thirty and she could decently go to bed. Jimmy was escorted outside, to a point only five yards from the house, where he cooperatively relieved himself in the beam of light shining from the open front door. The snow was becoming a fixture, the strange light and the absence of sound already half familiar. But Thea barely looked at it, her attention fixed on the welcoming light from the house, and the shivering dog at her heels.

Saturday morning dawned with a fleeting hope that by some miracle all the snow would have vanished in the night, only for it to be dashed immediately. There was no mistaking the flat light and muffled silence outside the window. 'Here we go again,' she sighed as she rolled out of bed and went to the window.

Automatically she was sweeping the visible scene for fresh footprints, for a renewed reason to fear that inexplicable things were going on out there during the night. There were plenty of footprints, but she was satisfied that they had all been made the day before, and their visibility meant that no further snow had fallen. Her resolve to walk up to the road was firmly in place, and she dressed in layers of warm clothes, with this intention in mind.

The rabbits were subdued, but their shed felt bearable, temperature-wise. The nest of babies was just as before, and a quick check reassured her that they were still very much alive. 'Better muck you out today,' Thea told them. 'You're a bit whiffy.' Lucy had shown her a bale of wood shavings behind the hutch, used for their bedding. She would do the living area, letting Jemima's sanctuary remain as it was for a few more days.

Jimmy was much as usual but the donkey's temper wasn't good. He tossed his head irritably when Thea tried to stroke his ears, and she saw that he had been lying in a pile of his own excrement. 'You're meant to do that outside,' she reproached him, realising she was in for a second session of mucking out at some stage that day.

As she returned to the barn, she heard the phone ringing. 'Another broken computer, I suppose,' she muttered to Hepzie.

But she was wrong. It was Lucy Sinclair, speaking from the Canary Islands. 'I've just heard about your snow,' she began, her voice warm with lazy sunny days. 'I can't even imagine it. Are you all right?'

'Oh yes,' said Thea, without even pausing to think. 'It's all rather an adventure.'

'Have you seen Kate? Has she come past?'

'No, I don't think she can get along the lane. The snow's quite deep.'

'Oh, she will. She'll use the tractor if necessary. I'd have expected her to have done it on the first morning. She's very resourceful, and she likes to be useful.'

'I ought to check that she's all right, then – do you think?'

'You don't have to worry about her. She can get out the other way. It's *you* I'm concerned about. She's your best hope of clearing a path. Try phoning her.' Lucy gave the number from memory, and Thea jotted it down. 'Although she's one of those annoying people who lets a phone ring if she's not in the mood to talk. She hasn't even got 1571, so you can't leave a message.'

'I might walk down later on, if there's no reply. How far is it?'

'Over half a mile. If the snow's as bad as you say, you'd better not. It's quite a winding track, with a lot of stones and potholes. But you can see the house from the first bend – you could have a look to see if there's smoke coming from the chimney, or any other sign of life. How's Jimmy?' The question burst out as if it couldn't wait another second.

'He's absolutely fine. Hepzie has won him over and they're good friends. He licks her.'

'Mmm.' Lucy did not sound enthusiastic about this news. 'I hope he won't miss her when she goes.'

'I know – I wondered about that. But I couldn't really stop them.' She could, of course. She could keep her dog out of the conservatory fairly easily. The truth was she didn't want to – it was sweet seeing them snuggled together.

'I expect he'll just forget her. I don't think his memory works much any more.'

'Probably,' said Thea vaguely, wondering which piece of news she ought to disclose next. 'So you're having a good time, are you?'

'Wonderful,' breathed Lucy. 'Total bliss. I'm sorry you've got the hassle of snow, but if I'm honest I have to say it convinces me I did the right thing. I could never see the attraction of snow, and you sound as if you rather enjoy it.'

Stifling the flash of resentment this caused, Thea merely laughed. 'I expect the novelty will soon wear off,' she said.

'Oh, it'll all be gone in a day or two. Like we said last week – snow never lasts for long in England.'

Stop tempting fate, Thea wanted to shout at her, but all she did was laugh again, before drawing breath to say, *A man died and the rabbit had babies.*

'Oh, gosh, I'll have to go,' Lucy hissed suddenly. 'There's a man I'm trying to avoid, and he's just come round the corner. Thanks a million, Thea. I'll call again soon.'

All Thea could do was bid Lucy goodbye.

She did not really regret her failure to tell Lucy about the man in the snowy field. It was ingrained habit to shield her employers from bad or disturbing news, for as long as she could. Terrible things happened, sometimes

even to the creatures left in her care, but she had come
to the conclusion that bad news could generally wait,
and it was kinder to leave it until the people came back,
and had to take up the reins again. It had not been her
fault that Lucy rang off before there was a chance to
get everything said.

But she did feel a mild sorrow at the missed
opportunity to share the experience of the baby rabbits.
That was the sort of news liable to bring amusement and
pleasure, surely. So much more difficult to talk about
death, with the response entirely unpredictable. What
if Lucy had said, 'Oh yes, that must have been Kevin.
He's always doing that – drinking himself into a stupor,
so everybody thinks he's dead. Why…there was even a
woman a year or two ago who called 999, thinking she'd
found a body.' How reassuring that would have been –
and how unlikely!

Outside again, muffled in hat, scarf, gloves and one of
Lucy's thick coats, she was aware of a dilemma as to
which direction to take. To the left was Old Kate's farm,
where all was still and silent, as far as Thea could tell.
To the right was the road, and people, and the prospect
of rescue from the growing feeling of being trapped.

There was no real contest. With impeccable logic,
she persuaded herself that even if Old Kate was in
difficulties, there would need to be a way forged out
to the road, and Thea needed to work out for herself
what was feasible. She followed the trail made by the

four men the day before, noting with amusement a
place where they had obviously followed each other
onto the side of the track, where a low stone wall
was completely covered with snow, to the point of
invisibility. Somebody had apparently fallen over it,
sweeping the snow away and exposing some of the
mossy stones. Footprints mingled and circled close by,
and then led back to the middle of the lane.

She had Hepzie with her, the lead in her pocket for
when they reached the road, which just might have
traffic passing. Although she suspected that anybody
wanting to drive in and out of Hampnett would use the
other approach, which was much closer to a main road.
Even so, she expected to see tyre marks and slush and
other signs of near normality.

Emerging from the lane with aching legs and a very
cold nose, the first thing she saw was three figures
walking towards her from the direction of the village.
One much taller than the others. A woman and two
children. She fastened the lead to Hepzie's collar and
went to meet them.

'Hello, again,' she said to Janina-from-Bulgaria.
'These must be Nicholas and…' She had forgotten the
other boy's name.

'Benjamin,' said the older boy with a scowl. 'I'm
Benjamin.' It was instantly obvious how much more
prepossessing the younger boy was. Dark hair and
long eyelashes above deep soulful eyes made him the
sort of child that everyone wanted to hug. His brother

was very different – a long face, with mud-coloured eyes set too close together, and a discontented expression.

How unfair, thought Thea. 'Well, I'm pleased to meet you,' she said. 'I suppose you're having a bit of a holiday, with the schools being closed.'

Three unsmiling faces stared at her as if she was mad.

'Mummy's gone,' said Nicholas, with a wide-eyed look. Thea found herself wondering for a crazy moment whether the body she knew she had seen had been the apparently stupid Bunny, and not some disreputable man, as she'd assumed. She looked at Janina for an explanation.

'She has not *gone*, Nicky,' she said, shaking his hand gently as it clung to hers. 'She can't come home because of the snow. She's sent you a text, remember?'

'Which he can't read,' muttered Benjamin.

'Where is she?' asked Thea.

'Bristol, she says. The roads are too slippery, she says. She will not risk it.' Janina's words were redolent with scorn.

'She's going to miss my party,' the younger boy said, fury suddenly seizing him.

Thea began to give more credence to Janina's assessment of her employer. 'It's today, isn't it?'

'How do *you* know that?' demanded Benjamin.

'I met Janina last week, and she told me. It sounded like a big event.' She waved an arm at the wilderness of white still masking fields on all sides. 'But will your friends manage to come?'

Janina groaned quietly. 'The phone has been ringing all day, yesterday, with people saying they will try. I think most of them will make it.'

'And you have to organise it all,' Thea sympathised. 'Where's Dad?' She cocked an enquiring head at the boys.

'He's…he's,' Nicky stammered.

'He's going to clear all the snow away from the front drive when he gets home from work,' supplied Benjamin coolly. The air of weary cynicism in a six-year-old was uncomfortable to witness and difficult to respond to.

'That'll be useful,' said Thea feebly.

'This country is pathetic,' Janina said, with much the same tone as her older charge. 'In Bulgaria we can deal with snow. Here, life comes to a stop.' She spread her hands in a helpless gesture.

'I know,' said Thea. 'I can't get my car out. Has a snowplough been through the village?'

Janina shook her head uncertainly. 'A tractor from the farm by the church pushed it aside, up to the top road. We wanted to see how it was this way, didn't we, boys?' The children nodded without enthusiasm. All four let their gaze settle on the inadequately cleared road. A single track ran down the middle, two black lines of dirty crushed snow, with grey ridges on either side, and the road verges still virgin white.

'I like your dog,' said Ben, who had clearly been eager

to embrace the spaniel from the first few moments. His fearlessness endeared him to both Thea and the dog. Janina laughed quietly. 'His mother says he should not be so friendly with dogs, but he has a special feeling for them.'

'It's OK,' Thea assured her. 'She won't hurt him.'

'I know that. In Bulgaria sometimes they have rabies, but here the dogs are harmless.'

'This one is, anyway,' said Thea, thinking of bull terriers trained to attack by their inadequate masters, and then to the depressing conversation she had had with Lucy about the endless betrayals of dogs.

They seemed to have reached a hiatus, and Thea found herself hoping the others wouldn't abandon her for a few more minutes. 'I can't get my car out,' she told them again. 'It'll have to wait until the snow melts, I suppose.'

'Have you got food?' Janina asked with belated concern. 'You could walk to Northleach, perhaps.' She grimaced doubtfully at the prospect.

'Oh, I'll be fine. There's plenty of food.'

She was increasingly desperate to tell the story of the dead man in the snow, the disappearing body and her consequent embarrassment – but she couldn't broach such a subject in front of children. The prospect of returning to Lucy's Barn and its disconcerting mysteries was less and less attractive as the minutes passed.

'What time is it? The party, I mean.'

'Two o'clock,' Janina told her.

'There must be a lot to do. How many are coming?'

'Seven or eight. It's all done. We had a lot of extra time to prepare.' Janina rolled her eyes expressively, and Thea glimpsed the long snowy days spent trying to keep two young boys amused and reassured in the absence of their mother.

'You can come if you like,' said Nicky, and Thea almost hugged him.

'Oh! Are you sure? What about my dog?'

'Both of you,' said the child. His big brown eyes met hers and she wished she could read the thoughts behind them. At four, she wasn't sure a birthday fully registered, apart from the presents and the fuss. What did 'being born' mean to somebody his age, especially if there had been no more babies after him? This anniversary of his birth must seem arbitrary and inexplicable – but still this little boy was rising to the occasion, and asserting his claim to be special at least for a day.

'But I'm not dressed for a party,' she said, looking down at her old trousers.

Janina and Nicky both laughed at this. Benjamin looked less amused. 'The knees are dirty,' he observed.

'It's only wet, I think,' said Thea. 'I stumbled on the snow and landed on my knees. I could go back and change.' She cast an unenthusiastic glance at the snow-covered track back to Lucy's Barn. 'And catch up with you later.'

'No, no,' said Janina firmly. 'Come with us now. We can have a small lunch and you can be a big help with all the coats and boots and stuff like that.'

Thea dimly remembered children's parties, and the miraculous mountains of clothes and possessions that accompanied four-year-olds everywhere they went. They would bring presents for Nicky, and even possibly contributions of food, as well as the inevitable outdoor clothes. Hats, gloves and scarves would augment the coats and boots. 'Right,' she said.

Nicky looked up at the au pair. 'Will George come?' he asked in a hesitant voice. 'I want George.'

Janina squeezed his hand, through two gloves. 'No, I don't think so, darling. I haven't seen him since the snow started. He won't want to come out.'

It seemed that the party was to be significantly diminished by the absence of this George, but when Thea raised an enquiring eyebrow at Janina, there was no responding explanation.

Chapter Seven

The walk to the boys' house was over half a mile, and Thea found herself relieved that she had Hepzie with her for the return journey, which was likely to be in darkness. Even so, she shivered inwardly at the prospect. Would one of the party parents give her a lift, she wondered? Not down the final leg, obviously – and that was the part she was already starting to dread.

It was midday when they got there, and she wondered where the morning had gone. Everything took so long, trudging through the snow and stopping to gaze at the transformed landscape every few minutes. Janina's employers lived in a large detached house, constructed of the ubiquitous Cotswold stone sometime during the nineteenth century, or so she judged from the mellow colour and generous size. Even in the snow, it was obvious the house had had a couple of centuries to settle into place and took whatever the elements threw at it completely in its stride.

It lay to the west of the church, down a small road which had been comprehensively cleared of snow as far as the boys' house. Beyond their entrance, there was still a foot or so waiting to be shovelled away. Janina led the way around the back, where everybody ritualistically divested themselves of damp outerwear in a small room boasting a row of coat hooks and racks for boots. 'How very organised,' Thea remarked, thinking of a Victorian household with a routine for everything.

Trooping through the kitchen into a handsome room with a high ceiling and warm terracotta-hued carpet, they encountered a man holding a cloth with which he had apparently been cleaning a window. *How about that – a male cleaner*, Thea thought with amusement. Then he looked at her, following up quickly with a questioning glance at Janina, and she realised he must be the man of the house.

'This is—' Janina began, then put a hand to her mouth, with a girlish chuckle. 'I forgot your name,' she confessed.

'Thea. Thea Osborne. Pleased to meet you,' said Thea, proffering a hand.

The man took it in a dry, gentle grip and smiled into her eyes. 'How do you do?' he said with equal formality. 'I'm Simon Newby.' He was tall, with Nicky's dark eyes and Benjamin's long face. A certain languid air reminded Thea of Janina's criticisms of him – lazy, beer-drinking. But now she saw them together, it seemed to her that there was a relaxed atmosphere between Simon and the nanny that was at odds with the earlier description.

'Janina and the boys asked me to the party. I'll try to make myself useful.'

'Do we know you?' The question was as gentle as his handshake, but he obviously needed to hear the answer.

'No, you don't. I'm house-sitting for Lucy Sinclair. You probably know her.'

'You saw a dead body in a field yesterday,' he stated carelessly. 'I've heard all about you.'

Thea glanced worriedly at the two boys, but they were absorbed in a corner with what had to be Nicky's new birthday presents, the boxes still in evidence on the floor. Hepzie had joined them, politely watching their faces for any signal as to what was expected of her. 'Oh?' Thea said.

'The police photographer is my brother. He came over here last night to bring Nicky's present and he told me the whole story. Pretty pissed off he was, to be honest. Says he's sure he's caught a cold from so much standing around in the snow, and was crying off the party. That's a shame, because the boys are very fond of Uncle Tony. And vice versa – see all the photos to prove it.' He waved a hand at a wall on which hung eight or ten framed photographs, in sepia and black and white. They were all studies of the two boys, with Benjamin, somewhat to Thea's surprise, obviously the favoured one. The photographer had caught the less overtly attractive child in quirky, characterful poses: Benjamin eating an ice cream with his face besmirched; the two brothers hand in hand under a big tree; Ben looking back over his shoulder, someone perhaps having just called his name. The word that came to Thea's mind was *innocence*. Tony had managed to eradicate the slightest suggestion of unsuitable feelings associated with these images. How brave, she thought, in these paranoid times, to get so carried away with photographing children. Nicky's long eyelashes and round cheeks made him a natural subject for the cameraman – but Tony had chosen instead to focus on the longer face and smaller eyes of the older boy. Although Nicky had not been entirely ignored; the pictures of him verged on the saccharine almost to the point of parody. There was some sort of message here, she felt – one that perhaps she would rather not probe too deeply.

'Wow!' she exclaimed. 'They're brilliant. He seems to have a lot of talent.'

She realised that she had not taken a great deal of notice of the photographer in the snowy fields, except to register that he was in his thirties with wavy brown hair and narrow shoulders. Simon was superficially similar, she supposed, and a few years older.

'We think so,' smiled Simon. 'But he has difficulty making a living at it. Hence the police work. They pay rather well.'

'Because he has to be on constant call,' nodded Thea.

'Right. That's the bit he hadn't really bargained for. When the mobile went off yesterday, he says he was only half dressed, and in the middle of doing something tricky on the computer. But at least he only had a mile or two to go.'

'Oh?'

'Yes…he lives just the other side of the A40, at Turkdean.'

'Oh, I know Turkdean,' said Thea, remembering a brief visit there a year or so before. 'Well, he probably got there ahead of the others. They came out from Cirencester. What a waste of time it was for all of them, though. I felt really bad about it.' The impossible mystery of the vanished body washed over her again, leaving her paralysed for a moment. 'And very confused,' she added.

'It wasn't your fault,' said Simon, his attention on his older son, who was sitting on an old armchair, cuddled up with Hepzibah, as if the dog had been his for years. 'At least, I don't suppose it was. Tony said there was absolutely nothing there.' He frowned as if the puzzle were too hard for him, as well.

'I really did see a body,' she said defensively.

'I believe you. It's too bizarre to be a complete invention. Even Tony believed you, more or less.'

'It's not true that there was absolutely nothing, either. There were marks in the snow.'

'Mmm. That was all he had to take pictures of. He was rather looking forward to his first corpse, you see, in a professional way. There's a whole procedure laid down for getting the picture as accurate and helpful as possible.'

'Oh dear. Well, the body might yet turn up, I suppose, and then he'll be needed again.'

'You're still sure he was dead, then?'

The relief of finally being able to talk about it was enervating. She looked for somewhere to sit down for a moment. 'I certainly don't see how he could have recovered enough to just walk away,' she said from the small sofa she'd sunk into.

'Have you ever seen a body before?'

'Oh, yes. And I'm perfectly certain that the man I saw yesterday was just as dead as the others.'

This, on a raised note, attracted the attention of Benjamin, who turned round and stared at her with very much the same expression as when she had first met him. A look that said he had a distinct impression that she was mad.

'Sorry,' she muttered to Simon. 'He wasn't meant to hear that.'

'Lunch!' Simon clapped his hands in a parody of a children's television presenter. 'Come on, everybody, into the kitchen.' In a low mutter to Thea, he added, 'That'll distract him, you see.'

Benjamin wriggled slowly off the chair, sighing deeply. Not a happy child, Thea diagnosed. Must be missing his mother, she supposed.

Over lunch she asked Simon about his hotel job. 'Assistant manager,' he nodded. 'I get a lot of the unsocial hours. It's relentless. We do a lot of conferences – something I'm not at all sure is worth all the hassle.

The rooms are all full, but it's at a reduced tariff, and the catering's a nightmare.'

'How big is it, then?'

'Fifty-five rooms. Not massive, but we can fit seventy or so in, provided there are plenty of couples.'

'At conferences? Unlikely, surely?'

'You'd be surprised. I'm not saying they're all married to each other, obviously.' He grinned significantly, and she gave a smile in return that took an effort. When had she become such a prude, she wondered? What did it matter to her what businessmen got up to at their silly conferences?

The party ran its course, with Simon far more involved than Janina had led Thea to expect. He operated the music for musical chairs; blew up an endless supply of balloons to replace those that one small boy persistently burst; wiped up spilt juice and diplomatically intervened in an epic conflict between Benjamin and a screeching girl who had been delivered along with her younger brother who was apparently Nicky's best friend. Thea had been intrigued by the woman who brought them – at least fifty-five, with an intimidating fringe and sturdy leather boots. Grandmother, Thea concluded. Ages of the party guests ranged from two to six, with the noisy girl the undisputed senior. They all lived within two or three miles of Hampnett, it seemed.

Nobody mentioned the absent Bunny directly, but Thea quickly gained the impression that the party was going with a much greater swing without her than it would if she had been there. There was an air of mischievous liberation, especially in Simon, that suggested the lack of a repressive hand that would otherwise have held sway.

Janina too seemed quite relaxed. She swung in and out of the kitchen with trays of delicious food designed to delight any small child, treading lightly and smiling broadly. Nicky followed her adoringly, finding pretexts to gain her attention, often winning for himself a quick hug. Thea remembered the conversation outside the church, when Janina had bemoaned the cruelty of gaining a child's affection only to disappear from his life within a few months. She quailed to think of the pain of the inevitable separation.

Then she heard what the child was saying: 'Where's George? He said he would come to the party. I want him. He never gave me a present.'

Janina put her arms round him. 'Maybe he's busy with the snow. He might be working for people, digging it away from their doors. He likes to help.'

'Yes. But I want him to help *me*.'

'That is selfish, Nicholas.' She tempered the words with a smile.

'I want to go to his house and see him.'

'You can't. Tomorrow maybe. Now you have to be nice to your party guests.'

Thea's own role was very small. She enforced a few

game rules, selecting winners and consoling losers. She monitored food consumption, checking a chubby little boy after his fourth meltingly delectable home-made doughnut, and offering him a slice of fresh pineapple instead. She listened to garbled anecdotes about the snow from several youngsters who had been amazed at this unprecedented gift from Mother Nature. And before she knew it, it was four o'clock.

'Gosh, I'll have to go,' she cried, feeling like Cinderella. 'I've got animals to feed.'

Simon looked up from the party bags that were to be issued shortly. 'If you wait until everyone's gone, I'll drive you,' he offered.

'I can't. That'll be another half hour or more.' As yet, no parents had arrived to collect their child. If recollection served, it could be a very protracted process. 'I'll be all right walking. I've got the dog.'

The dog had to be enticed off the same armchair as before, where she and Benjamin had spent the major part of the afternoon. A flicker of worry about the withdrawn child went through Thea, and she began to say something to Simon about it, before he cut across her.

'Dorothy's dad might be going your way,' he suggested. 'They live in Northleach.'

'Dorothy?'

'The pugnacious one with the little brother.' He indicated the child who had been fighting with Benjamin.

'Ah yes. The ones that were brought here by their granny.'

'Uh?' Simon blinked. 'Oh, no...that was Barbara. She's their stepmother. But Bernard is meant to collect them, if I've got it right.'

'So where's their real mother?' she asked boldly, always curious about unusual family patterns.

'Philippa?' His attention wandered back to the roomful of children. 'She has them sometimes, but she lives in a flat and works full time. Barbara's more or less retired, so she minds them mainly. Dorothy was born the same week as Ben. Bunny and Pippa got friendly at the clinic, or somewhere.' He smiled tolerantly. 'She's a bit volatile, as anyone will tell you. Bernard is much better off with this one. She's his third, and you couldn't find three more different women.'

'Unusual,' said Thea. 'Normally they just go for a younger version of the same person.'

Simon drew in a hissing breath. 'Ooh...cynical!' he reproached.

'Not at all. Simple truth,' she defended.

'Anyway, he might be good for a lift.'

Thea was increasingly anxious to return to her responsibilities, and since there was still no sign of any parents, she decided to walk. 'I can do it in twenty minutes or so if I bustle.'

'Up to you,' he said, which made her blink. She realised she was accustomed to men who took charge and tried to manage her, which generally made her defiantly independent. Now this one was letting her go out into the freezing darkness alone, she felt a quiver of resentment.

'Right, then.' She retrieved the dog and went out to the boot room to collect her various garments. At least there was no new snow falling. And it wouldn't really be dark once she got outside. The fluttering in her stomach was entirely groundless.

Calling brief goodbyes to Janina and the boys, she wended her way around the house and back towards the church. Two cars were approaching from the north, and she heard them slow and turn down towards the house she had just left. *They won't be any use to me*, she thought, assuming they returned the way they'd come, up to the A40.

She was within sight of the turning down to Lucy's Barn before a car came towards her. It was proceeding slowly on the inadequately cleared road, with its headlights on full beam. It passed her, leaving a wide berth, and she could get no glimpse of the driver. So much for any prospect of a lift, she thought. Besides, no car would have ventured down the final quarter mile – and that was the part she had been increasingly dreading.

The track was dark, shadowed by overhanging trees, some of them evergreen. Without Hepzie, she wondered whether she would ever have had the courage to keep on. The spaniel, however, had a reassuringly clear idea of where they were going, and was in some hurry to get there. Perhaps it was Jimmy who called to her, or simply the prospect of a warm house and dry feet. They plunged down the middle of the track, which was tolerably passable thanks to the passage down and back by the four police people, as well as Thea's own upward trek. At least she could be fairly confident of avoiding any unexpected pitfalls, so long as she stuck to the tried-and-tested pathway.

The house was in complete darkness, and Thea reproached herself for leaving it for the best part of the day. She would have to feed the donkey and rabbits by torchlight, and give Jimmy a chance for some exercise in the yard.

Without warning, Hepzie made a lunge, squeaking with excitement. Holding tightly to the lead, Thea was dragged towards the front door of the barn, protesting, 'Hang on, damn it. We'll be there soon enough. What's the rush?'

And then something strange was happening. Hepzie was on her hind legs, scrabbling at something hidden in the shadows close against the barn wall. 'Hey, hey,' came a strong female voice. 'That's enough of that. God, woman, what kept you so long?'

Chapter Eight

In a confusion of unlocking the door, spluttering half-sentences of introduction, and Hepzie's excessive hospitality, the two women got themselves into the house and the lights switched on.

'I'm from the farm further down the track,' the visitor managed to explain, at last.

Old Kate! Thea had forgotten all about her. But this woman wasn't old. Mid fifties was Thea's instant guess. Despite the weathering on her cheeks, her hair retained its colour and her neck was smooth. 'Oh!' was all she could manage. 'I've got to do the donkey,' she added distractedly. 'He'll be waiting for his hay.'

'He can wait a bit longer. My need is greater than his, I promise you.'

'Oh, all right. Are you stranded by the snow?'

'Me? Of course not. I've been going in and out through the top road, same as I always do. I never thought of you until this afternoon, so I came to see if you were managing. When I found it all locked up and dark, I thought you must have deserted your post.'

'I did, I suppose,' Thea smiled ruefully. 'I was at a birthday party.'

'Oh...that must be young Nicky. You've met that family already, have you?'

'I bumped into Janina last weekend, and then again this morning. They very kindly invited me. Sorry to have been away, though. It gets dark so early – there never seems to be time to get things done in daylight.'

Kate shrugged. 'Well, you're here now. The point is, would you like me to bring up the tractor and clear your way up to the road?'

'Oh...well, if it isn't too much bother. I mean – maybe the snow'll melt in a day or two, anyway.' What would Lucy have done, she wondered? It was awkward not knowing the protocols, and whether the offer was to be regarded as normal neighbourly behaviour.

'No chance. There's more due later tonight; haven't you heard?'

'Oh, God, there isn't, is there?' Thea felt weak at the prospect.

'Never good to have snow in January – there's no strength in the sun, so it hangs around for weeks. You ought to hear my dad on the subject. He's like a pig in muck, with his weather stories.'

'Does he live with you?'

Kate huffed a brief laugh. 'Oh yes. That was never the plan, but he came for the New Year, two years ago, and hasn't got around to going home again yet. He's eighty-nine, and remembers back to the 1920s as if it was last week. Gets tedious, I can tell you. He's been poorly over Christmas. I knew from the start he'd never go back – after all, it was his farm all his life. We got him a nice little cottage to retire into, but it was never going to work.'

Thea's eyebrows lifted at the thought of a 'little cottage' standing empty for years. Little Cotswold cottages were worth very serious sums of money. 'What'll happen to the cottage?' she asked.

'It's got a tenant in for the time being. If you can call him that, when he doesn't pay us anything.' The woman's expression suggested that she was not inclined to discuss the details of the family properties, for which Thea could hardly blame her.

'You must be busy,' she said. 'There's no hurry for the tractor, if it's a nuisance. I walked out to the road today – I can get to Northleach on foot if I need some shopping.'

'Trust Lucy to go off like this. Fine thing, ducking out of it when things get tricky.'

'She was quite open about it, and she's paying me well. I knew what I was doing.' And only then did she remember the dead man in the field, who was already acquiring a dreamlike quality in her mind. Had it really happened at all? Should she say something about it to Kate? It seemed to follow, in some back-to-front way, from what she had just said. 'Although I hadn't bargained for a visit from the police yesterday.'

Kate's eyelids came down warily. 'Oh yes?'

'You haven't heard, then? I found a dead man yesterday in the field below the donkey's paddock. Or I thought I did. When I took the police back to the place, he'd gone.'

The woman avoided Thea's eye, and chewed a bottom lip. Her colour changed to a lighter hue. 'Mmm. I heard a commotion.'

'Did you? When?'

'I don't mean it was noisy. But I had to take hay to the Herefords, and could see there'd been people trampling about.'

'Didn't the police contact you? It is your field, after all.'

Kate shook her head vigorously. 'Why ever should they? Can't have been anything to worry about, if he'd got himself up and away.'

'I was certain he was dead. I think somebody moved him.' Short of a direct accusation, she could hardly say any more. It suddenly seemed inescapably obvious that Kate was the person in question.

'Well I hope you don't think it was *me*,' the woman said sharply, picking up the unspoken thought. 'I've got better things to do than mess about with dead bodies, let me tell you.'

'And you didn't see anybody there? What time did you take the cattle their hay?'

'Don't you go questioning me.' Kate's eyes narrowed.

'If I tell you I saw nothing, then that's the truth of it. It'll all get explained soon enough, without either you or me having to worry. Leave well alone, that's my advice.'

'But—' What was she missing here? How bizarre was this apparent lack of concern? 'I mean, he might be injured or ill, and still out there in the snow somewhere. Nobody seems to realise that.'

'I doubt that. What did he look like?'

'I couldn't really see. Grey hair, fairly long. A beard, I think. His face was almost buried in the snow, and I didn't move him.'

'Well, if you ask me, he can't have been really dead. Surely you'd have checked pulse and breathing? Anybody would.' The defensive fury seemed to have passed, Kate's tone back to something more normal.

'I was convinced he was dead. I touched his shoulder and it was stiff. The snow wasn't melting on him.' She felt as if she was doomed to repeat these lines for the rest of her life.

'So what? Snow doesn't melt on a coat when you're outside, does it? Even a living body isn't warm enough to melt it through three or four layers of clothes.'

'He was dead.' Thea spoke with greater certainty than she felt. 'Somebody moved him.'

Kate shook her head, still pale. 'The police obviously don't believe you. They know better than anyone that you can't just leave a dead man out for the birds and foxes to dispose of.'

'Right. I hope you're right. But I still think there should be a search party.'

'Maybe there would be if it wasn't for this weather. Everything's different in this snow. But you're right – there should have been a search for him.'

Somehow they'd reached a fragile understanding, for which Thea was grateful. The brief glimpse she'd had of Kate's steely temper had not been reassuring. Far better to stay on the right side of her, if possible. But what did the woman *really* think had happened? How much had she already known? There was an uneasy sense of being humoured, lurking somewhere.

A brief silence followed, and Thea took the opportunity to try to assess her temporary neighbour's credibility. She was tall, straight-backed and decisive. It was easy to visualise her driving a tractor or striding across the hillsides after a large flock of sheep. But beneath that there was a kind of camaraderie that Thea found appealing. She had met a number of well-intentioned women during her spells in the area, and this seemed to be another to add to the list. The temptation to take her at face value and make use of her as a friend and helper was almost overwhelming.

But there had been others, Thea reminded herself, who had not been what they seemed. There had been women capable of murder, habitual liars, their rage concealed beneath amiable exteriors. And Lucy had spoken of a violent temper. 'There was a bottle beside him,' she offered. 'That disappeared as well. I think it was empty.'

Kate merely nodded, as if enough had been said on the subject. In the silence of Lucy's big living room an antique clock ticked loudly. 'I really must feed that donkey,' Thea remembered. 'And the rabbits. And take the dog out. He's been in since the middle of the morning.'

'Jimmy,' Kate said. 'That poor creature. How are you coping with him?'

'He's easy enough,' Thea shrugged. 'It was noble of Lucy to take him in.'

'She's like that,' said Kate, flushing slightly. 'I wouldn't have the patience.'

It occurred to Thea that Kate could have done the job she was doing – popping up to the Barn twice a day to feed and exercise the animals. Was it possible that anybody could be too busy for such neighbourly tasks? But even as she thought about it she remembered that Lucy was away for a whole month, and that Kate was probably lambing – and it had snowed. And Jimmy would be left, hour after hour, in his lonely conservatory.

Which prompted her to waste no more time before attending to him, after which she had to slog across the paddock to the donkey's shed and throw him another slice of hay. Kate readily accepted that her visit was over, but on the doorstep she said, 'You never told me whether you want me to bring the tractor up.'

'Not much point if there's going to be more snow. Leave it until tomorrow, and we can decide then.'

It had not been the correct response. 'I wasn't proposing to come this evening,' came a snappy reply. 'I'm not sure how much free time I'll have tomorrow, after the way you kept me hanging about this afternoon.'

The injustice burnt in Thea's breast, but she resisted the urge to argue. 'Well, it's up to you,' she said with dignity.

'That's right.' She gave Thea a long assessing look. 'Seems to me you've taken on a lot, here. I wouldn't like you to get into any trouble. You know where I am – come down to the farm any time, if you need to.'

'Thanks,' mumbled Thea, feeling horribly small and young and feeble.

Chapter Nine

There was more snow during the night, but it made little impact on a world already uniformly white. Thea's footprints across the yard and paddock had filled in to roughly half their previous depth, but were still clearly visible. There were no fresh ones to alarm her, she noted with relief.

It was Sunday, she remembered. A week since she had walked up to the church and met Janina. A quarter of the way through her house-sitting commission. Apart from the little matter of a vanishing dead man and record-breaking snowfalls, things weren't going too badly. So why did she have such flutterings of anxiety in her midriff? Why was there such a strong sense of impending disaster hanging over her? Knowing there was a capable woman close by ought to be enough to remove the sense of isolation and burdensome responsibility. But it didn't. There had been something challenging about Kate, as if she expected Thea to fail and come crawling to her for rescue. The effect of her visit had been to bolster Thea's determination to manage by herself, and refrain from asking favours. She could walk to Northleach, as she'd said – although not on a Sunday. Tomorrow – she would find a big shopping bag and go out for milk and cake and a bottle of wine, and not request any helping tractor to get her there.

Sunday was also a day for contacting family and friends and catching up with the news. After her conversation with Jessica on Friday, she was unsure whether or not her daughter was eager to hear more about the mysterious footprints in the snow. She had been unusually cavalier about it at the time, when her normal stance was to express concern at her mother's repeated escapades during the house-sitting commissions. But might she not have heard about the much more mysterious body, and the fruitless visit from the police? Wouldn't that make a story good enough to reverberate around the various local stations?

But, she reminded herself, Jessica wasn't with the West Midlands force, but was finishing her probationary period in Manchester, well beyond the scope of any gossip concerning the Cotswolds. She should hear about it at first hand from her mother. She might even have a credible suggestion as to what might have happened.

And then, when it came to it, Jess's phone went unanswered, and her mobile was turned off, so Thea decided to leave it until later in the day. Instead, a little voice whispered, she could try Detective Superintendent Phil Hollis, who had until recently been her significant other, her lover and boyfriend and partner in detection of murderers. She and Phil had gone cool on each other, awkwardly giving permission for other relationships to develop, but promising to remain on friendly terms. Phil respected her judgment when it came to understanding malign motivations, or noticing revealing details concerning events in the Cotswold villages. He would believe her when she insisted the man in the field had been dead. And more and more, it seemed important that *somebody* should do that. It was forty-eight hours since the body had vanished, and the worry of it was increasingly debilitating. If the man had crawled away to shelter, wouldn't he have really died long since, out in the cold? Phil would know what the police were doing about it, if anything. He would tell her why there seemed such a complete absence of activity, when common sense suggested that a concentrated search ought to be under way.

She tried, over and over again, to see the whole business through official eyes. A woman, known to be rational and even helpful in past investigations, had reported the discovery of an apparently dead man. When sent to investigate, the police team found nothing but ambiguous tracks leading to a patch of woodland. Snow had fallen all day, making any effort at following tracks difficult. Nobody had been reported missing, and no questions had been asked in the local area, as far as she knew. Possibly the connection with the freelance photographer, who lived in the area, had reassured the authorities that nothing was amiss in Hampnett.

Still, she concluded, there should have been some effort made to check. Somebody ought to have at least gone as far as the woods, to make sure the man wasn't lying under the trees. Where was the caring spirit, the safety net of police concern that should have followed up her discovery and ensured there was nothing to worry about?

It had been that doctor, and his whining about the cold, that made them turn back. The sergeant and constable had not been senior enough, or committed enough, to pursue the matter. There had not been enough of them to effect a thorough search – and she wondered whether the presence of a small herd of Hereford cattle had been another deterrent. They would have gone back to the warm Cirencester station, filed their report stressing the absence of any meaningful evidence, and persuaded themselves that there was nothing more to worry about. Some other more urgent urban crisis would have arisen to distract them, and the whole thing would have been shelved – at least until the snow melted away, or somebody was reported missing. The police were only human, and nobody was going to relish slogging through deep snow on a hunt for a wild goose.

* * *

The day stretched ahead in the familiar Sundayish way that Thea hated. It ought to be that the high level of social interaction the previous day would carry her over, giving her plenty to think about – but the opposite seemed to be the case. She wanted to return to Janina's household, and chat more with her and Simon. They were nice people, and it would be interesting to find out whether Bunny had come home yet. Plus there were other absentees, apparently. The beloved George and the sneezing Tony had also disappointed young Nicky. From sheer idle curiosity, Thea would have liked to hear the next part of the story.

But a far more compelling story was hanging in limbo on her very doorstep. She remembered a convoluted dream where the body she had found was in the same corner again, frozen solid with ice on his eyelashes and lips. Then he was gone and she was searching desperately for him, with Hepzie digging insanely in a snowdrift, and five large Hereford cows watching thoughtfully. The sense of obligation remained with her now she was awake.

Could she face another trudge across the fields to the patch of woodland which had struck her as significant on Friday? She could go and look for herself, just in case the man had managed to get himself there. She needed, for her own peace of mind, to have a look. If the man had reached the woods unaided, he had probably eventually got himself home and warm and sober, forgetting the whole embarrassing episode. That would be absolutely fine with Thea, and she held the thought close, like a talisman. But there were insistent connections forming in her subconscious that made her afraid that the reality would be quite otherwise.

She waited until late morning, pleased to see a weak sun filtering through hazy clouds. No risk of further snow, then, and surely some scope for optimism that a thaw was on the way? Old Kate's aged father could be wrong. Everybody knew – didn't they? – that those times were over when snow could last for weeks, and great freezes take hold of the country. Now it was never more than a few days, and then the worries would all be of flooding caused by the rapidly melting snow.

She debated with herself as to whether to take Hepzie with her, and concluded that it was a bad idea. The dog would be a distraction, liable to get lost and probably useless in tracking someone from two days ago. Making sure the doors were firmly closed, she set off alone, wearing hat, scarf and gloves as well as Lucy's fleecy coat.

The novelty of the snow had long evaporated. It had a different feel under her boots – the surface crisp and crunchy, but beneath that it was much less dense, turning to crystals with spaces between them, collapsing at the impact of her feet. As if equally fed up with the alteration of his world, Donkey had emerged from his shed, and was walking with great deliberation round his perimeter fence. His route coincided with Thea's at the bottom gate, and it seemed to her that he was gazing rather wistfully towards the trees where she was headed. For a crazy moment she imagined riding him through the snow, giving him some work to do for once in his life. But there was no harness, and even though she was small and light, and he was bigger than many donkeys she had met, it seemed like an unfair exploitation.

The tracks were still visible, but the fresh snow of Friday afternoon had softened and blurred them. The Herefords were still milling around aimlessly. They had been given a quantity of hay, she noted, in a large circular metal cage some distance away. Their coats were shaggy, their breath steaming in front of their faces. Thea paused to admire them and the picture they made with their red coats vivid against the white snow.

It was relatively unusual to leave cattle outside all the year round – only the hardiest older breeds could withstand this sort of weather, and even they would need a lot of supplementary feeding. The workload for Kate had to be greatly increased by the snow, and yet she had not seemed unduly strained by it. It was a lifestyle that Thea could scarcely begin to imagine, despite her brief forays into the world of animal husbandry.

She brought her attention to the events of Friday: the timings especially. It had been about ten-thirty when she found the body, ten forty-five when she'd called the police. They had arrived at the barn not long before twelve-thirty, by which time the body must have gone. If the man had indeed been dead, then someone must have moved him during that time. Thea would not have seen anything, because she was at the back of the house, and besides, this hollow was invisible, even from upstairs in the barn. It all seemed entirely reasonable, as she stood in the snow and thought about it.

She puzzled determinedly as she headed for the fatal spot. Small tentative clues were offering themselves to her, along with theories: the cattle might have been deliberately driven over the place to obscure evidence with their footprints; someone might have been watching her from the woods, seeing her discovery and waiting for her to go away before they ran down and dragged the dead man away. Doing her best to behave like a detective, she examined the fence itself for shreds of fabric or hair or blood, only to find nothing at all. It was a well-made barrier, the wire forming squares, firmly fixed to quite new-looking posts every ten yards or so. But there lacked the usual strand of barbed wire along the top, much to Thea's relief. Even if it might have yielded evidence, the damage to her own skin and clothes as she climbed over it would not have been welcome.

The patch of woodland was the only viable cover, and even that was far enough away for the idea of hauling a dead body over the snow to it to seem doubtful. The ground sloped upwards in that direction, and somebody stumbling along dragging a corpse would leave a trail impossible to conceal. Even so, she was resolved to investigate. Doggedly she trudged across the field to the patch of trees.

The trees were bare, standing proud of the snow and making a clean stark picture that Thea paused to admire. She could imagine it as a striking photograph or oil painting. Even better as a woodcut, with William Morris-like overtones, tendrils and holly leaves poking through the enveloping snow. *I'm delirious*, she thought. They'll find *me* curled up dead in the cold, at this rate. She turned and looked back the way she'd come, able to see the roof of Lucy's Barn but nothing more, despite being on higher ground than the natural bowl where the body had been. It looked a dauntingly long way off.

There were two strands of wire between the field and the woodland, which looked old, but still effective in keeping out the cattle. Thea ducked between the strands, managing to avoid falling over. Only when she had straightened up and looked around did she wonder if this barrier was enough to cast mortal doubt on her hypothesis. How would anyone get a dead man over it, without again leaving telltale signs? Under the trees, the snow was only a few inches deep, but enough to be noticeably disturbed by the kind of activity she had in mind. There were brambles and dry stalks of bracken and other undergrowth to negotiate. There was no sign of a path.

And then she saw, in startling clarity, a trail. Deep grooves carved in the snow, about two feet apart, beginning seven or eight yards to her right and leading away from her in a northerly direction. Between the grooves was a line of footprints. She stood staring at it for two full minutes before she worked out that it could only have been somebody dragging a sledge. Somebody had loaded the dead man onto a vehicle with runners, and dragged it towards the village. She was rather pleased with herself for arriving at this deduction. How many times did such a thing happen in modern England? It conjured old Christmas cards, or rural life in the frozen north.

OK, she reasoned carefully, I was right all along. She went to the place where the track began, and found the wire sagging, and a jumble of animal footprints on the field side. Somebody had somehow carried the body across the field into these woods, and then put him on a sledge and towed it towards... She tried to work out where the tracks would lead if they continued in the same direction. The village centre, near enough, came the conclusion.

She easily followed the trail to the far side of the wood, and out into a field that was almost level for a change. The marks were less easy to see out in the open, where the most recent snowfall had almost filled them. But the weight must have been considerable, and the runners had made grooves of sufficient depth to show through as slight indentations. They ran alongside a hedge, heading more or less north. At this rate, Thea mused, she would emerge onto the road – and who would have risked dragging a sledge containing a dead body along the public highway?

The answer came at the far end of the hedge. The marks turned at a sharp right angle, along the lower side of another hedge, through a conveniently open gateway and on in the same direction, running roughly parallel with the road leading into Hampnett itself.

She had lost all sense of distance, despite frequent backward glances to monitor where she was in relation to Lucy's Barn, but knew she'd been walking for at least twenty minutes. It came as a surprise to see the tower of the church ahead of her, only a few hundred yards away.

Again the same question arose – wasn't it impossibly risky to take a dead man into the centre of the village? Perhaps, she thought doubtfully, she was merely following the tracks of an enterprising wood collector. Someone who had gone to the clump of trees to gather dead boughs and take them home for the open fire.

But she carried on with her quest, following the parallel lines in an almost hypnotic state of mind. Her nose was cold, and even through her gloves her fingers had gone numb. Her legs felt heavy, the muscles down the back of her calves complaining at the weight of her boots and the clogging resistance of the snow.

And then she was onto a paved road, with well-tended hedges on both sides, signs of a few walkers and animals under her weary feet. The snow was still very evident, but there were signs that a car had turned around on the spot where she stood. It was a cul-de-sac, with a scattering of houses on either side. But it was not until she saw the church tower directly ahead that she understood that she had emerged into the very heart of Hampnett.

She walked on a few yards, still following the marks of the sledge. Abruptly, she found herself beside a small opening to the left, a little gate standing open, revealing a virgin patch of garden in front of a very small cottage. There, miraculously, were the sledge tracks again, with the footprints between them, heading right up to the front door along a pathway between two areas of garden.

It must have been somebody scrumping firewood, then, she thought with a pang of disappointment. Nothing to do with the dead man, after all. She was no further forward, and had just wasted a lot of time getting cold and lost for no good cause.

But then she noticed the door was ajar, which seemed strange in this security-conscious time and place. And the sledge was nowhere to be seen. And she could hear voices that sounded for all the world like young children.

Cautiously, she approached the little house, listening intently. She pushed the door wider and went in, transfixed by the scene in front of her in the shadowy room.

Chapter Ten

There was a jumble of humanity on the floor which took a few moments to distinguish. A body was on its back, legs drawn up, hands clutched in front of its chest. Two smaller people knelt on either side of it, and Thea slowly recognised Benjamin and Nicholas. Then she saw a straggly beard, and narrow shoulders, and made two distinct deductions. This was the body she had seen in the field, and the body was of the man she had met in the road, over a week before.

'What happened?' she cried, in a state of appalled surprise.

The boys looked at her as if an angel had arrived to save and terrify them. 'It's George,' said Nicky. 'He's frozen dead.' The older boy simply stared at the lifeless face, his mouth open, his skin a greenish white.

Thea approached the tableau gently, aware of a host of conflicting imperatives. 'Where's Janina?' she asked, desperate at the idea that these young children had discovered a body all on their own.

To the boys this was entirely irrelevant. 'It's *George*,' Nicky repeated, with the exasperation of a child being wilfully misunderstood by a stupid adult.

It unquestionably was the same man. Thea had established that in the first glances. The beard, the narrow shoulders and long legs were all entirely familiar.

'You two have to go home, right away,' she said with gentle authority. 'I'm going to telephone the police and they'll take him away. Has your mum come home yet?'

Benjamin made no move from where he knelt. His mouth was working, but no words came out. In contrast, the younger boy was hyperactive, jumping up and trotting to the door, turning back and jigging on the threshold.

'Ben?' Thea coaxed. 'Get up now. I need to take you home.'

Not until she laid a hand on his shoulder did he move, and then it was more of a flinch than a genuine response.

'Where's Janina?' she asked again.

'Gone for a walk,' said Nicky.

'And Daddy?'

'He's on the phone.'

It seemed futile to enquire again after their mother. If she had indeed returned, then wouldn't she have been with her children, after so many days of absence?

'OK. Well, we have to go – now.'

'Is he…? Will he…?' Ben's cracked voice emerged in a whisper.

'He's dead, Ben,' said Thea. 'He'll have to be taken away. He won't get up again.'

'He won't ever talk, will he?'

'No. He's gone for ever.'

'Has *Mummy* gone for ever as well?' asked Nicky, still jiggling.

'No, of course not. Maybe that's who Daddy's talking to on the phone. Let's go and see, shall we?'

She held out a hand to each, and slowly Ben got to his feet, a deep frown marking his brow. 'You don't know,' he said. 'You don't know where Mummy is.'

'That's true. But I'm sure she'll be back any time now.'

'Yes,' said Nicky confidently. 'Yes, she will.'

Ben said nothing.

It turned out that the boys' house was literally next door to the cottage. Thea reproached herself for being so slow to work it out. Finally, she could see how the two approaches she had so far made to the village centre could in fact converge.

Out in the trampled snow, they turned left and there was the house that Thea had been in only the previous afternoon, twenty yards away. It was in no way startling that Nicky and Ben had been allowed to walk along to George's cottage, apart from some slight danger from traffic. Cars evidently did come past, but hardly enough to present much hazard.

Simon was in the kitchen, the room full of the smell of roasting pork and apple sauce. Lunchtime, Thea realised. She'd been out all morning, and it would be dark again in less than four hours. And she might have to walk back to the barn as before, her nervousness drastically increased by the bizarre knowledge that somebody had dragged a dead body across several fields in deep snow, two days earlier.

'Hey, boys, there you are!' The tone was forced, in a very poor piece of acting. Even before hearing the news, Simon was suffering from some profound worry or shock. He looked at Thea with a frown, as if trying to remember where he'd seen her before. 'Hello?' he queried warily.

'George is frozen dead,' said Nicky, loud and clear. 'In his house.'

Simon puffed a breath of amused disbelief. 'Surely not,' he protested. 'His house might be draughty, but it's not *that* cold.'

'It's true,' said Thea urgently. She was bursting to recount the full story about following the sledge tracks, and having seen the man earlier, walking along the road. But the children inhibited her. It was one thing for them to absorb the simple fact of death, quite another to introduce a sinister figure lurking out in the fields, behaving alarmingly. 'We'll have to call the police,' she added.

Simon closed his eyes and leant back against the kitchen worktop. 'What?' he muttered. 'What are you saying?'

'Where's Janina?' Thea demanded. She had the feeling she was going to need help in dealing with this.

'Here. I'm here,' came a voice from behind her. 'Hello again.' She was unwinding a long woollen scarf from her neck, and then pulled off a matching knitted hat. Her dark hair frizzed out untidily, and her cheeks glowed pink from the cold. 'Am I late for lunch?'

Only then did she scan the four faces in front of her, and understand that something had happened. 'Is it Bunny?' she asked, with an undisguised note of contempt. 'Is she still trapped by the snow?'

Simon made a soft bleat of protest, but Nicky drowned him out. 'It's George,' he said, importantly. 'He's frozen dead.'

Janina blinked, and inspected all the faces again. 'No,' she said. Then she met Thea's eyes and found confirmation of the story. 'Good God,' she gasped.

'The man in the snow,' said Simon slowly, also seeking Thea's gaze. 'Was that him, then?'

'Almost certainly,' she said. 'Although I didn't see his face properly. Look…we really do have to call the police.'

'Yes, yes. Well…you do it. You've seen him. You'll know what to say.'

Reluctantly, Thea nodded. Already she could imagine how the conversation would go: the bland failure to grasp the important background story on the part of the girl who took the initial call, the difficulty of describing the exact location, the endless bloody *snow* obstructing everything. 'I'll phone Phil,' she decided. 'He can find the man who came on Friday.' Foolishly, she had made no mental or physical note of his name, and was not about to face the complicated business of identifying him to the same uncooperative female she knew would be on the end of the phone. Then a memory popped up. 'Your brother!' she said. 'He'll know who it was. It might be simplest just to get hold of him.'

'Tony? No good. He's gone home to nurse his cold. He's not answering the phone.'

'You're joking!'

Simon shook his head ingenuously. 'No. He gets like that when he's ill. He wouldn't be any use to us, believe me.'

Thea shook her head impatiently. She was acutely aware of the two small boys listening to everything that was said, with Janina still holding her hat and scarf, her face a picture of bewilderment.

'Oh, for heaven's sake.' Thea grabbed at the phone and keyed the number of Phil Hollis's mobile, which was still clear in her memory, despite not having used it for some weeks.

He answered quickly. 'Hollis,' he barked.

'Phil, it's Thea. Um…I'm phoning from a house in Hampnett. I'm afraid there's a dead man next door.'

'Oh yes?' His calm was ominous. Undercurrents of irritation and worse were detectable. She could hear him thinking she only came to him when there was trouble, and that this was a kind of trespass on their former relationship.

'Listen,' she urged him. 'I found the body on Friday – there'll be a record of it. Two police officers came out, in all that snow, and when I showed them the place, the body was gone. Well, now I've found it again. It's a man called George and he's in his own house, here in Hampnett.' Despite herself, she felt rather smug at this impeccable summary. 'So can you find who it was who came out, and see if he's on duty today? It would be best if the same man came again. He was a sergeant.'

'Why? Why should it be the same man? What's his full name?'

'Hang on.' She held the phone away from her head, and asked Simon. 'Jewell,' he supplied. 'George Jewell.'

Thea relayed the information, aware that the police were always glad to have a name to hang everything on.

'Why are you calling *me*?' he wanted to know. 'It's a 999 matter, surely.'

She tried to explain to him that she'd just thought it would be so much preferable not to have to start all over again with a fresh face. That there was somehow something dreadfully *embarrassing* about being the person to summon the police. Something out of kilter and awkward. Phil stopped her.

'All right, I get the idea. I'm off duty, actually,' he said. 'And Thea…this has to go through the proper procedure. You'll have to call 999 to get it logged in the proper way.

I can't pretend the story makes a lot of sense, the way you've told it, but I'm sure it will all become clear. You're not suggesting anybody killed him, I take it?'

'Well, no. He seems to have died of exposure, out in the snow. But, Phil—'

'Sorry, but my food's getting cold. I was just sitting down when you rang.' And he dismissed her with no further ado. She felt choked with the pain of rejection, as she put the phone down.

'So?' demanded Simon. 'Are they coming?'

'Not yet. I've got to make another call.' She swallowed down the cold sensations of foolishness and abandonment and made the call, speaking briefly to the young man at the call centre, who showed admirable concern and understanding.

'There'll be somebody with you in twenty minutes at the most,' he said.

Same constable, same doctor, different sergeant. Pity about the doctor, Thea thought, seeing the identical irascible expression on the man's face as there'd been on Friday. She took them to the cottage, leaving Simon, Janina and the boys behind. Simon was fidgeting about his pork, turning the oven down to its lowest setting and bemoaning the spoilt and soggy sprouts.

'Is that his wife?' the constable asked Thea softly, as they walked.

'Au pair,' Thea told him. 'From Bulgaria. The wife's stranded by snow somewhere.'

'Oh? Like where?'

'I have no idea.'

'Most of the country's OK, you know. It's mainly confined to Gloucestershire and Wiltshire. If it was any other month of the year, we'd probably have floods. We might anyway, when this lot decides to melt.'

There was no time to pursue the topic before reaching George's front door. 'This is the bloke you saw in the field on Friday, then,' the new sergeant said, showing himself to be impressively well briefed.

'I'm sure it is, yes. I tracked him here, you see.'

'Pardon?'

She explained about the marks left by the large sledge. 'At least I suppose that's what it must have been. Something with runners.'

'How far was it?'

'I'm not sure. Half a mile or so, I would guess. I had no idea it would end up exactly where I was yesterday. It's a big coincidence.'

'Not really,' judged the sergeant. 'Not much of a village, is it? Nowhere else to go but this little bunch of houses.'

'No sign of violence, then?' The sergeant turned his attention to the doctor, who was kneeling beside the body, delicately removing instruments from his case.

'Not for me to say,' muttered the doctor.

'So can we remove him?' the police officer continued patiently.

'No photographer this time?' asked Thea.

'We could call one if we thought it necessary, but that's only for the scene of a crime, basically.'

'So you assumed on Friday that there'd been a crime?'

'Not as I understand it – though I've not seen the report. It was probably down to the snow, see. After you said how hard it'd be to reach, they brought the whole team just in case. Normally it'd just have been the two officers and a doctor.'

'Right,' nodded Thea. 'But isn't it a crime to move a dead body without reporting it?'

The man pushed out his lips thoughtfully. 'Technically, yes. It points to something not right. There are questions to be asked, that's for sure.'

'Yes.' Thea had only just begun to address some of these questions, most of them beginning with *Why?* 'But meanwhile you think it's OK to remove him now?'

'Probably. Do we have an identity for him?'

'George Jewell. This is his house. Simon next door knows him.'

'When was he last seen alive?'

'*I* don't know.' She began to feel like a fraud, taking over the way she had. 'I'm not really the person you should be speaking to.'

'Oh, I think you are.' He smiled knowingly. 'You're involved in this, Mrs Osborne, right up to the neck.'

An hour and a half later, they drove her back to the top of the lane, regretting that it still wasn't possible to get the car all the way down to the barn. 'Time you got that snow cleared away,' said the constable, who had been unnaturally quiet throughout.

'Tell the council that,' snapped Thea, who was tired and damp. Her feet were unpleasantly cold, and her gloves had been so soggy that she hadn't wanted to put them on again. And she was hungry. Simon had offered her a share of the belated roast, which she had declined.

'Not a public road, is it?' the young man asked. 'Nothing to do with the council.'

She wondered whether Old Kate had found time to bring up her tractor and some sort of implement for pushing snow aside. Too much to hope that she'd have come and done the job while Thea had been out, it seemed.

Everything was quiet at the barn, the sky a heavy grey, and the white of the snow increasingly tainted by tracks and the gradual reappearance of the layers beneath. In the donkey's paddock there were signs that he was losing patience with the altered state, and had been pawing his way through to the scanty grass he had been accustomed to nibbling. The animal itself was standing with his back to the barn and its yard, staring down the hill to the bottom of his territory. Obviously the poor thing was unsettled and probably bored.

She could phone Kate and ask whether there was any prospect of getting her car out. Another day, and she feared she might get seriously worried. Walking to Northleach was not an appealing project, if she was honest. It was bad enough to think of putting her clammy boots on again to feed the animals, let alone walking a mile or more on the slippery road surface.

And she really did not want to walk anywhere. An insistent little voice claimed that it had nothing to do with cold boots or slippery snow. It was good old-fashioned fear that made her want to stay indoors. Something very strange had been going on out there since Friday, and she could make no sense of it. Without a logical explanation, anything seemed possible. Her stomach clenched at the memory of those footprints on Friday morning and her sudden terror at the sight of them. That had been illogical at the time – until she found a dead man, *twice*. Now there was surely every reason to be fearful, and she allowed herself to give in to it, just as soon as she'd got back from a swift visit to the donkey's shed, and the issue of another armful of hay.

Too late now, anyway, to call Kate and ask for some tractor-based assistance. It could all wait for the morning – a Monday, when normal service could be expected to resume as far as possible. Schools would have to open again, snow or no snow, if they didn't want their SATs results to suffer. Shops and pubs and doctors' surgeries would all have pent-up queues wanting their services. Four days was more than enough time to be out of action.

But it seemed the elements had other ideas. When she took Jimmy out for his last toilet break, there were fine flakes of snow swirling in a noticeable breeze. Snow *and* wind equalled a blizzard, and that was the very last thing she wanted. Her bowels churned involuntarily as she imagined how it might be if further heavy snow fell and was banked up by the wind, concealing fences and obstructions even more effectively than before. The sense of isolation became acute, and she returned to the house actually shaking slightly with anxiety.

The wind created sounds that were hard to explain. A sporadic screeching had Thea searching for the cat, thinking it was being tortured somewhere outside. She looked into every room before finding the animal sitting contentedly on a rug beside the warm air vent in Lucy's study. The study door had been closed, or so she thought – presumably the cat had managed to nudge it open at some point. *Don't be so paranoid*, she told herself, as she glanced around at the computer paraphernalia wondering whether some intruder had left the door open. The latch was insubstantial and everybody knew how clever cats could be when they wanted to get through a door.

She worried about the rabbits, especially the babies, with little but their own fur and a somewhat flimsy shed wall between themselves and the cold snow. Was it possible that they could freeze to death? Were they originally from some warm exotic place that gave them little natural ability to maintain their temperatures? Indigenous bunnies had deep burrows to hide in, where the soil retained the heat of summer. So far these tame things seemed to be surviving well enough – but if it got any colder, perhaps she ought to bring them into the house.

She turned on the television, but the uniform banality on all channels only made her feel more at odds with the world. What she needed was a friendly face, an engrossing conversation, with good food and wine. Not a lot to ask, she thought self-pityingly. What stupid mistakes had she made to bring herself to this lonely state? January in a snowbound barn, alone except for a load of dependent animals, and under siege by a menacing lunatic that carted dead bodies across fields for no discernible reason? It was no way to live, she decided with a long unsettled sigh.

Chapter Eleven

Her dreams were full of long chase sequences where she hid behind bales of hay and forgot all about her dog until spotting the soaked spaniel head whirling away on a great flood. She was wearing hiking boots as heavy as lead, which fixed her feet to the ground and made movement impossible. She woke to find Hepzie snuggled against her feet, licking one paw with an urgency that spread moisture around a wide area. The dog had always been a messy licker.

It was dark outside, and still noisy with the wind. Nudging Hepzie with one foot, she hissed at her to stop licking and keep still. She ought to get up and check for snowdrifts, but no way was she going to do that. What would be the point? Time enough in the morning for any really bad news. Everything would seem better in daylight. She drifted off to sleep again, thinking about those hardy human beings who made it through the ice age, without any of the comforts of electricity or oil or underfloor heating. But they did have wolf skins and log fires and each other, she argued to herself. Like the rabbits in their deep burrows, they probably chose the most sheltered caves to colonise, and managed to cope perfectly well.

When morning came, Thea felt no urgency to leave the bed, despite the comfortable background temperature maintained by Lucy's clever system. She could think of no reason to hurry, apart from Jimmy's need to go outside, and he seemed to have an infinitely capacious bladder. The light seemed much as before, but small comfort could be derived from that. All it suggested was that there had not been a dramatic thaw during the night.

Her small travelling clock informed her that it was past eight – not yet late, but close to a dereliction of duty for a house-sitter. She was thirsty, but not desperately so. While she continued to think about it, she drifted back to sleep. When a loud knocking came on the front door, it shocked her awake with a painfully thumping heart. Hepzie gave a protesting yap and jumped off the bed.

She hurried down the stairs in her dressing gown, feeling bleary and confused. What time was it now? Had she slept the morning away? Was it some terrible news waiting for her on the doorstep? Fumbling with the lock, she called, 'I'm coming,' before finally getting the door open.

It was Janina, looking perfectly calm. 'Why is there no doorbell?' she asked. 'I knocked for many minutes.'

'Sorry.' Thea rubbed her hair and tried to blink the fuzz from her eyes. 'I was asleep. What time is it?'

'Nearly nine.'

'So why...? Have you got the boys?' She peered out into the snow, expecting to see a snowball fight under way.

'Benjamin is at school – although I think it wrong to send him. He is very upset about George, poor boy, and Nicky is at his nursery until lunchtime.'

'So early?'

Janina shrugged. 'They go at half past eight, for the working mothers' convenience. Bunny believes Nicky should have social contact, so he attends for three mornings each week. I have him all the other time.'

'Has Bunny come home yet?'

The Bulgarian girl heaved a deep contemptuous sigh. 'I am wondering if she will ever come back. She has gone silent now, and I suspect another man, perhaps.'

Thea belatedly ushered her visitor inside and closed the door. 'They must be desperately worried, then? Simon and the boys. Surely she wouldn't do that?' She spoke to Janina's back as the visitor sauntered admiringly into the main living room.

'This is a pleasant home,' she commented. 'So warm and with good proportions.'

'Do you want some coffee?' Thea's hand went to her hair again, aware of the mess she was in, tousled and undressed. 'I'll have to go and put some clothes on, and see to the animals. Did it snow again in the night? Did you walk here?'

'A bit. I left the car at the top of your track. I like to walk in the snow, but I should have brought my skis with me. I could travel faster then.'

The image of a person skiing across the English fields made Thea smile. 'I doubt if it would have been worth it. This can't last much longer.' She went to the window and looked out. 'It doesn't seem much worse than yesterday, thank goodness.'

'Excuse me, but I came to speak to you about George,' Janina burst out. 'I am disturbed about his dying, and I do not understand some things I heard about you seeing him in a field. Can you tell me the story, the whole thing?'

Thea began to feel harried. 'I suppose I can, but first I really must get dressed.' She could hear Jimmy whining from the conservatory, very much the first priority on a suddenly crowded agenda. 'And before that I have to let Lucy's dog out.' She went quickly through the house to the back, where the lurcher was standing shiveringly by the French window that led out into the garden. This was highly unusual, and Thea felt instantly guilty. 'Oh, Jimmy!' she crooned, 'I'm so sorry. Are you desperate?'

With a vestige of his customary politeness he went outside at the first opportunity and relieved himself as if turning on a tap. He did not cock his leg or squat, but simply stood where he was and relaxed the relevant sphincter. Thea was impressed at the degree of control that had prevented him from doing it indoors. A sizeable area of yellow melting snow was spreading beneath him.

'Good boy!' she approved, giving him a pat. 'Very good boy. Do you want to go for a little walk?' She looked round for her spaniel, but could see no sign of her. 'Hepzie!' she called. 'Where are you?'

'She's here,' came a new voice from a new direction.

Thea's first thought was that it was very bad form to be seen by two different people still in her dressing gown. It was sure to get back to Lucy, and reflect poorly on her showing as a house-sitter.

'Hello?' she called. 'I'm in the garden at the back.'

There was still an unsullied patch of snow around the western side of the house, and it was with a small pang of regret that Thea watched Old Kate stomp vigorously across it towards her in her stout rubber boots.

'Morning,' she said, ignoring Thea's costume. 'More snow in the night, then.' It was a flat statement of fact, requiring no response.

'You didn't bring the tractor.' Thea also spoke factually.

'Too busy. The Herefords need feeding, and one of them looks like calving any time now. I should bring her in, but she's being bolshy about it. I did wonder...' she eyed Thea consideringly '...if you'd give me a hand. Lucy sometimes shows willing when it comes to this sort of thing.'

It felt rather like having to climb up a long ladder, carrying something heavy and needing to get to the top quickly. She remembered her dream, with the lead boots encumbering her movements. 'I've got rather a lot going on, just at the minute,' she said. 'Janina's here, and I haven't done the donkey or the rabbits yet.'

Kate said nothing, merely waiting.

'Hello,' came Janina's firm voice from the conservatory. 'You did not come back.' She fixed Thea with an accusing stare, only flicking a quick glance at Kate.

'Sorry,' Thea apologised, beginning to think it a word she was uttering rather too often this morning. 'And now I really am going to get dressed, and then I must do the donkey. You two can stay and make yourselves some coffee if you like. I suppose you know each other?'

Both women nodded briefly, as if preferring not to make much of their acquaintance. Thea continued, 'Everything's more or less self-explanatory in the kitchen.' And before either Kate or Janina could reply, she had kicked off her boots, carried them through the house and hurried upstairs to her bedroom, Hepzie following her.

'We're not used to visitors, are we?' she said to the spaniel as she quickly pulled on several layers of clothes. The feeling of being invaded was strong, and with it came resentment and some resistance to the demands being made on her. Normally the dog would be delighted to meet new people, and she did seem to have warm feelings towards Kate, but Janina had failed to impress her. She followed Thea back down the stairs, placing her feet carefully on the bare wooden treads.

Without a word, Thea pulled open the front door and went outside, having stamped back into her boots, and grabbed the jacket hanging on the back of the door. This one was hers, not Lucy's, only just warm enough for these wintry temperatures, and not at all waterproof.

The donkey's paddock had clearly been sprinkled with a new fall of snow. The grass that had begun to show through was once again invisible. 'Where will it all end?' she asked Hepzie dramatically. 'I'm fed up with it already.'

This was the fifth day, she calculated, since the first snowfall last Thursday. Less than a week, and she was already wondering how much more she could take. A foolish question, she knew – she, Thea Osborne, had long been rather a specialist in levels of endurance. She lived by the motto that if she was all right at this precise moment, then she was all right, full stop. It had been the mantra that she clung to in the first weeks after Carl's death, focusing on it instead of asking herself how she was ever going to manage, how she could ever hope to recover from such a catastrophic blow.

And it worked, she reminded herself now. She was coping, wasn't she? Carrying water to the donkey, cleaning out the worst of the muck around his stall, giving him fresh hay – all quite normal and efficient. But on another level it wasn't working at all, because she was still quite uncomfortably scared.

What of, she asked herself? What was the source of the unpleasant sensation in her guts, the dry mouth and the semi-paralysis of her thought processes? As she approached the donkey's shed, she had hardly been able to bring herself to go inside, convinced that a crazy attacker would leap out at her with a knife or a gun. Now she emerged again, unscathed, she was sure there must be someone lurking in the snow behind the building. The fact that two women were in the house, within easy earshot, hardly assuaged her fear at all. Ever since those shocking footprints on Friday morning, she had been frightened – pushing it aside for hours at a time, admittedly, but unable to quell it completely. Following those tracks the day before had been a courageous attempt to confront the fear, to discover a rational explanation for the various mysteries, and for a while it had done what she wanted – but since discovering the dead George, with the complete absence of explanation as to who had moved him and why, she had felt the same breathless panic as on Friday.

The unpredicted arrival of Janina and Kate had made it worse: the loud knocking, and then the sudden voice from around the corner of the house – it made her feel that she could be surprised at any moment by anything or anyone. It made her jumpy. It made her see herself as quite unbearably vulnerable to all sorts of ghastly attack.

When she finally got back to the kitchen, it was obvious that conversation had been in full swing. The two heads were close together, the room warm with female revelations and hypotheses. 'Been talking about George, I suppose,' Thea said casually.

'Among other things,' agreed Kate.

'So I was right, wasn't I? He *was* dead, and somebody *had* moved him.' It was less important now that the police had already conceded the victory, but it still had to be said.

'You were right,' said Kate, with a nod. 'I hoped you weren't, but you were. I hope it makes you happy.'

Wrong-footed again. 'Of course it doesn't. But it's horrible not to be believed.'

Janina was looking from one to the other, as if watching a tennis match. 'Did nobody believe you?' she asked Thea.

'Well, they didn't exactly say that, but it was fairly obvious when they decided not to set up a search for him. They definitely didn't think somebody had come along with a sledge and dragged him home.' There was still a warm glow of triumph inside her, at the way she had vindicated herself.

'But *who*?' asked Janina, her eyes wide.

'I thought you might have an idea about that. Haven't you and Kate solved the mystery while I was outside?'

The two restrained smiles were oddly alike on the faces of her visitors, as if she had trespassed on a taboo, and should be politely ignored. 'We have no idea,' said

Kate. 'There's no sense in it at all, as far as we can see.'

'Poor George,' murmured Janina. 'That poor man.'

'Indeed,' nodded Kate. 'Though I have to say my conscience is clear.'

Thea looked at her sharply. It seemed a very odd thing to say. 'Why wouldn't it be?' she asked.

'No reason. What I meant was – we'd given him a roof over his head when he needed it. That's our cottage, you realise. We let him live there rent free.'

'I see,' said Thea, thinking there might be unforeseen consequences to allowing someone to occupy such a prime property for an indefinite period. Perhaps Kate already understood that such an idea might well occur to people. That some might wonder at the convenience of George's abrupt removal.

'I do need to get back in a minute,' Kate reminded herself, and the others. 'About that Hereford...' She cocked an eyebrow at Thea, who was still wearing her outdoor jacket.

'Oh, God,' sighed Thea. 'I'm not sure I'd be much use. And I haven't had any coffee yet. I'm desperate for a drink. And I wondered whether you know much about rabbits. One of them's got babies, and I suppose that means the father is in with them. Does that matter, do you think?'

'Rabbits!' scoffed Kate. Janina laughed with an echoing note of contempt.

Thea found herself tiring of the Bulgarian girl's disdain for everything she encountered. 'Yes, rabbits,' she said. 'They deserve to be looked after as well as anything else. It's what I'm being paid for, after all.'

'If there's a buck in with a group of does, there'll be more babies, won't there?' said Kate, evidently willing to suspend her own priorities for a moment.

Thea smiled for the first time that day. She could feel the pull of the muscles loosening as she did so. 'I hope you're wrong – the shed's not big enough for a whole maternity ward. We could end up with dozens of them at this rate.'

'How many babies are there in this litter?'

'Six, I think. I haven't investigated much yet.'

An impatient *ttchh* from Janina interrupted the cosy distraction. 'A man is dead,' she said sternly. 'And you talk of rabbits.'

'Well, at least nobody killed him,' Thea snapped back. 'We don't have to worry about there being a murderer out there, do we?'

She was speaking without prior thought – voicing the single element of reassurance that she had managed to cling to since Friday. The man had died either from misfortune or deliberate suicide. Sad, but nothing to be alarmed about, she had repeated to herself. So why did she feel so scared? came back the nagging persistent question.

'Simon is hiding something,' said Janina. 'Since yesterday, he has been too quiet and serious.'

'Probably the shock of finding George – or having his children find him. That's enough for anybody to cope with. Not to mention his wife going AWOL.'

'AWOL?' Janina echoed, with a frown.

'Sorry...absent without leave. Shouldn't she have been back days ago? What's going on there – do you have any idea?'

'I suspect another man, perhaps. It is possible that she has phoned him to tell him, and he is keeping it a secret. He never answers me if I question him about her.'

'Lucky kids to have you, then,' said Kate heartily. 'Mind you, Bunny always did exactly what she wanted to, ever since I've known her.'

Thea wanted to ask innumerable questions – how long *had* Kate known Bunny? What exactly was the general view of the woman? What about George – how had he come to be so beloved of the little boys? But she had little hope that Kate would stand for any further curiosity. What did it have to do with her, anyway? Where would it get anyone for Thea, the temporary house-sitter, to gain an insight into the complicated local relationships?

But she did have one question that she thought might elicit a reply. 'Was George a heavy drinker?' she asked.

Kate and Janina exchanged a look, and then Kate replied. 'Not really. He had no money to buy drink.' Then, after a beat, she added, 'Why do you ask?'

Thea shrugged. 'No reason,' she lied. Until then she had given little thought to the empty whisky bottle half buried in the snow. It had disappeared along with the body, and this fact now felt significant in some indeterminate way. Was the person who moved George simply tidying up, she wondered wildly? If so, the bottle must be at the cottage somewhere, and the police wouldn't realise it was an important part of the picture. It might be in the dustbin, or under the kitchen sink with other recyclables.

But the police weren't going to go to any great lengths to examine the house. It wasn't the scene of a crime, after all. They would puzzle over the mystery of who moved the body and why, but she doubted whether they would spend much time or resources on it – not unless the post-mortem revealed something unexpected: a lethal substance injected into George's neck, or signs that he had been asphyxiated. Failing that, they would work methodically down the checklist required by the coroner and conclude that it was a suicide with unexplained overtones.

'I'll have to appear at the inquest,' Thea said suddenly. The thought had not occurred to her until then. 'Whatever happens, they'll need me to do that.'

The other two women looked at her wordlessly. She smacked an annoyed hand on the table. 'And it probably won't be for months. Sometimes it's nearly a year before they get around to it. What a bloody nuisance.'

'And the boys?' Janina said softly. 'Are they to be witnesses, too?'

'Of course not,' said Kate scornfully. 'What an idea! Would they do that in your country – cross-question a tiny child about a dead man?'

Janina frowned. 'I think they might do it in any country, if they believed he had the key to the matter.'

'I can't believe they would,' Thea insisted. She was trying to think whether such a young child as Nicky would ever be required to give testimony, and to remember what a four-year-old's view of the world might be. Her sister Jocelyn's youngest was eight – four was a long-forgotten aeon ago. But she did seem to recall that at four they still hadn't learnt to tell lies or worry about the consequences of anything they might say. In that respect, a child of four would make rather a reliable witness, she supposed.

The kitchen clock gave a shy tinkle to indicate that it was ten in the morning, and Thea was hungry. She was tired of her visitors, who had brought nothing in the way of relief, merely adding to the list of alarming questions and suggestions. 'Rabbits,' she said. 'I have to do something about the rabbits.'

'What about my cow?' Kate asked. For a moment, Thea blinked blankly. 'She's going to have calved on her own at this rate, and I'll lose the calf to hypothermia.'

Only Janina seemed to have nothing urgent to do. Presumably she had time to kill until due to collect Nicky from his playgroup. 'I could help,' she offered. 'I am familiar with cows.'

'Right.' Kate jumped up as if a lever had been pressed. 'That's splendid. Just what I hoped to hear. Come on, then.' And within a minute, the pair of them were marching away towards the lower field and the woods which now held such unpleasant associations for Thea.

Thea went back to the shed, to try to sort out the male rabbits from the females. She examined each animal for a long time, turning it upside down and parting the long hair to scrutinise the genitals. None of the three in the main hutch was male. Fully functioning male rabbits had obvious testicles. She remembered that much with total clarity from Jocelyn's pets. Somehow one of Lucy's does had got itself pregnant immaculately, early in December. 'Oh well, that solves a problem,' she told them. 'You can all stay where you are. Presumably Lucy let Jemima and Snoopy together, either by accident or design, and forgot to tell me about it.'

She yielded to the temptation to peer again into the nest of babies, noting how much they changed from one day to the next. At this rate, they would be out of the nest and playing well before she had to leave Hampnett.

The morning had been so badly disrupted that she could hardly think what she should do next. Five days of snow must be close to a record for Gloucestershire, and she wondered how the world beyond her own little lane was faring. Traffic had to be flowing more or less normally on the larger roads, lorries bringing fresh stocks to the shops in Northleach, children returning to school, all the normal comings and goings of civilised life. But she still couldn't get her car out, and things were still as frightening as before.

With an idea of finding out how things stood, she tuned to the local radio station again. She caught the midday news, which began with a summary of the road conditions and the few remaining closures and cancellations. Then it went on to report the finding of a woman's body in deep snow close to the village of Hampnett. A farmer's dog had made the discovery the previous evening. The police were saying little, but they were pursuing an investigation into the identity of the woman, and the cause of death.

Thea's gorge rose in a wholly uncontrollable surge of alarm. By any measure, this second body must have died only a few fields away. There had to be a connection between this discovery and the dead George Jewell. Two people had died in the snow in the same week, within half a mile of each other. Without even thinking, she reached out for the phone, already repeating Phil Hollis's number to herself.

Chapter Twelve

But before he could answer, she thumbed the stop button. What was she going to say to him? It needed some proper thought first. She winced at the imagined conversation that she might have had. *Phil, there's a murderer out there, killing people and leaving them in the snow. Come and save me.* Was that what she believed and wanted? She remembered his curt dismissal of the day before when she'd phoned him. Detective Superintendent Phil Hollis was too important to run around at the whim of a former girlfriend. And too proud, she supposed. He had shown Thea his weaker side some months earlier, and she had not responded well to it. They had both emerged from that episode with much less certainty about the relationship, and the damage had proved fatal.

And yet he remained her default saviour, she noted. Who else was going to protect her in these alarming house-sitting jobs she persisted in accepting? Phil was probably decent enough to at least listen and reassure, and perhaps send a junior police officer to check her defences.

But there was someone else she could turn to – how could she have forgotten? She picked up the phone again and keyed another number.

'Hi, Mum.' Jess sounded weary.

'Are you all right?'

'Of course. I had rather a hectic weekend, that's all. What's the matter?'

'Did you hear about the second body they've found near here? A woman this time. Have you any idea what's going on? They must have been murdered, surely?'

There was a pause. 'Mum, I've only just got up. I was out all night. You'll have to start again from the top. Is it to do with those footprints you saw on Friday? You never called back, so I assumed it must have all turned out OK.'

Thea struggled to think straight. 'Don't you know?' she said wonderingly. Much of her amazement derived from her own failure to update her daughter on the events of the weekend. Embroiled in George and Janina and the birthday party, she had actually forgotten Jessica completely.

'Mum, why do I keep having to remind you that I'm based in Manchester, not Birmingham? We don't get your stories here. Not unless they make the national news.'

'It was a man, a dead man, who made those footprints. He was called George, and I found his body. Twice, in a way. It was moved. Now there's another one, not much further away. It would be easy to kill someone by leaving them in the snow to freeze, wouldn't it?'

She could hear the deep, slow intake of breath. 'From the top?' Jessica prompted. 'None of what you just said made the slightest sense.'

Thea took a similar breath and slowly recounted the whole story. She concluded by saying, 'I'm really scared, Jess. More than I've ever been in my life. I'm cut off here – nobody can get in or out except by foot.'

'People do die in snow,' Jessica said thoughtfully. 'I mean, they get disoriented and lost and wander around in circles till the cold gets them. Where you are is the worst affected part of the country. Worst for fifty years or something. People have forgotten how dangerous it can be.'

'I know, but even so…' Was she being stupidly paranoid? It still seemed most likely that George had deliberately killed himself. Perhaps this woman had, as well. It did seem quite a handy way to commit suicide – painless and relatively tidy. Maybe George and the woman had made a pact. That was a far more acceptable idea. But the radio report had suggested foul play, without actually saying it.

'Well, you'll probably find the local police want to speak to you again, anyway,' Jessica said. 'You're involved with the first bloke, after all. They'll be able to reassure you better than I can.'

That hadn't occurred to her. Another flurry of anxiety curdled her insides. 'They might think it was me who killed them both,' she wailed.

'Don't be daft,' said Jessica crossly.

'Well, they might.' As happened more and more often these days, their roles had reversed, and Thea felt like the child in the relationship.

'Listen, Mum. There's something I think you should know. Nothing to do with Hampnett or snow or dead people. It's Phil.'

'What about him?' The anxiety burgeoned. Had he had another accident?

'Well, I heard on the grapevine that he's seeing someone. It seems to be fairly serious, from what I can gather. I know you and he have finished, but I didn't want you to make any blunders.'

'It's another police person, isn't it?' Her sudden certainty on this point was inexplicable logically, but it fitted what she knew of the man.

'Right. I met her once. She's uniformed, an inspector. She's called Laura. She was doing some sort of course when I was at college, so I know her a bit.'

'And she's pretty and sweet and kind and young,' supplied Thea.

'No, actually. She's tall with a long face and freckles. Masses of freckles, all over. She's clever, and has a very loud laugh. And I'd say she was a bit older than you.'

Thea felt weak with the surges of ambivalent feelings. 'Good for him,' she said quietly. 'I knew he wouldn't stay single for very long. Men never do, do they?'

'Some do. But no, he's too good a catch to be missed. You've only got yourself to blame, you know.'

'How do you work that out?' Thea flashed, knowing there was quite some truth in the accusation.

'You work it out. I've got to get on,' Jessica flashed back.

'So what do I do about these bodies?' Thea asked after a short pause in which she summoned up the sense not to fight over Phil's emotional life. Jessica had meant well in telling her what was going on, and she supposed she ought to feel grateful.

'Why do anything? Just carry on as normal. The snow must surely be melting by this time, anyway?'

'Thawing, not melting,' Thea corrected. 'And no, it isn't. Not at all. It must be awful for farmers, making sure their animals are OK.'

'Mmm,' Jessica agreed without interest. 'Well, Mum, I really have got to go. You'll be all right, you know you will. I don't know why you're in such a state.'

'Must be getting old,' said Thea, trying to laugh. She wanted to go through it all again – the isolation, the cold and the unavoidable fact that two people really had died. 'Anyway, thanks for listening. I feel better now.' This was a lie, but she owed it to Jess to release her from having to worry.

'Good. And I'm sorry about Phil. I like him, you know. It seems an awful waste.'

Thea made a wordless sound of acknowledgment and said goodbye. Her throat was thick and she found she had to sniff back tears. The year or so she'd spent with Phil had been good. It had shifted her away from the paralysis of sudden widowhood, shown her that there were other opportunities out there, that she was still young enough to embrace them. Men found her attractive, she had no worries about that. And she liked them, with none of the scratchy criticisms of the latest manifestations of feminism, with all the bemused frustration that seemed to grip the modern woman. They'd managed to have it all – career, children, money – and still they weren't happy. That had to be the fault of men, obviously, because they persistently refused to do the shopping or plan the holidays or answer the summons from the head teacher when Little Johnny misbehaved.

And then she thought of Simon, throwing himself into his son's party, because his working wife had better things to do. And Janina, with her scathing contempt for Bunny. She, too, had toed the feminist line and called Simon lazy, which hardly seemed fair from what Thea had seen of him.

She made herself a cheese sandwich for lunch, noting that there was hardly any milk left. A glance through the freezer that Lucy had left at her disposal showed plenty of fancy ready meals but not much by way of basics.

No bread, or simple things like sausages or chicken legs. She didn't like to take the more expensive items, given how much she was being paid. A trip to Northleach was definitely becoming urgent. But knowing how early it got dark, and how unfriendly the afternoon skies could be, deterred her from making the trip that day. She should phone Old Kate, perhaps, and see if she could somehow cadge a ride via the other road, to the south.

She took Jimmy out again for his midday excursion, pleased to see the way Hepzie walked beside him, as if to offer a shoulder to lean on. She was only half his height, but probably weighed more. The lurcher was nothing but bones and sparsely covered skin. Really not a pretty animal by any reckoning, but no less lovable for that. His ready cooperation, and total absence of curiosity, was restful, if pathetic. The place where he peed had turned a dingy beige colour, with a path from the house to the spot showing some mushy grass where Thea had walked. The snow itself seemed more and more grubby and stained, even in places where nobody had trodden on it. The sparkle soon wore off – or perhaps it was all in the eye of the observer. That first morning had been so magical and thrilling. Now it was just a nuisance. She wasn't sure she would ever enjoy snow again, after all this trouble. And that seemed a pity.

It was half past two when a new visitor knocked on the door. Hepzie barked, and the cat, which had been sitting contentedly beside Thea on the sofa where she was reading, streaked away into Lucy's study. Neither animal did anything to calm Thea's nerves.

Opening the door cautiously, she was relieved to see the familiar face of the police sergeant she had met twice before. *I really should remember his name by now*, she thought. He was getting to be quite a friend. With him was a woman she also recognised.

'Hello!' cried Thea with disproportionate pleasure. 'It's you.'

'It is,' agreed Detective Superintendent Sonia Gladwin. 'Fancy seeing you again.'

Thea threw the door wide and ushered them in. It was some minutes before questions began to surface in her mind. 'But...why are you here? Isn't this a bit beneath your area of responsibility, or whatever you call it?'

'You mean two frozen bodies on one weekend is too trivial for a DS?' Gladwin smiled tightly.

'You think they were murdered.' Thea slumped. 'Just when I'd convinced myself it was just a horrible coincidence.'

'You knew there'd been another one, then?'

'It was on the radio.'

'Oh, yes. Well, actually, we can't find any signs of violence on the first one.'

'But...' Thea prompted.

'But the second one was deliberately killed, I'm sorry to say.'

'Did they know each other?'

'We haven't ID'd the woman yet. Forties, well dressed. Nobody's been reported missing.'

A thought flew into Thea's head and out again. Obviously it couldn't be right. The police would know if it was. She tried to concentrate on her visitors.

'Why *are* you here, then?' she repeated. 'I mean... why *me*?'

Gladwin laughed. 'How can you ask that, with your track record? Remember Temple Guiting, only six or seven months ago?'

'Of course I do. And I don't see the connection.' In Temple Guiting, the previous summer, Phil Hollis had been the one to find the body, the heroic figure with a sore back and very little direct involvement in the case. 'You solved that one pretty much on your own.'

'No, Thea Osborne, I did not. I don't entirely understand how you do it, but you have a knack for fingering the right spot when it comes to foul play. You went to the heart of it that time, and I'm hoping you can do it again now.'

'I'm not with you,' said Thea sulkily. 'If we don't even know who the woman is, I don't see how I can help. I never saw George alive, either. Except...' Again she remembered the bearded man in the road. 'I might have done, on my first day here. But I never spoke to him.'

'But you, unlike anybody else I can think of, went off looking for him, and found the trail from the field where he died to his body.'

'So what? Nicky and Benjamin had already found him. I did nothing useful.'

'Thea, don't be stupid. Of course you did. You found him first, in the field, and then tracked him down. You went out on your own to find out what had happened – I don't know anybody else who would have done that. Without you, we'd just have thought he died in his house. You're *crucial* to the investigation, don't you see?'

Thea rolled her eyes. 'Not really,' she said. 'And it would be pretty poor police work to conclude that a man could freeze to death inside his house, wouldn't it?'

'Not necessarily. We might never have been sure how or why he died. The signs are hard to spot after so much time. As it is, you've added about three new dimensions to the case, and I for one am intrigued.'

Despite herself, Thea was hooked. She liked Gladwin, the thin nervy woman with unorthodox methods and dark shadows under her eyes. It would be nice to get to know her a bit better – and much more than nice to have somebody listening and sharing and praising like this.

'So tell me what you want me to do,' she invited, with a smile.

'Show me around,' Gladwin replied. 'Take me to the corner of the field where the body was, and retrace the route to the house.'

Thea looked out of the window at the grey sky.

'Now?' she queried. 'It'll be dark in an hour or two. And it isn't easy walking. The snow's still quite deep.'

'Now,' the detective insisted. 'Robin…you can stay here. We'll be an hour or so.'

The sergeant made a futile attempt to conceal his pleasure at this reprieve. But it was short-lived. 'You could probably make yourself useful with a shovel,' Gladwin went on. 'See how far you can get in clearing the track we came down. Mrs Osborne's probably desperate to get her car out by now.'

Thea swallowed down her instinctive protest. Surely that wasn't police work? But perhaps it was. In a time of such drama, it was back to basics for everybody. With a sigh heaved more for effect than from any real reluctance, she got her boots and scarf and hat and gloves and led the way across the donkey's paddock, and into the infamous field next door.

Chapter Thirteen

They used the gate at the bottom of the field, and walked along to the hollow, where there was little sign remaining of the events of Friday morning. Further snowfall had softened the footprints and tracks made by men and cattle.

'Tell me every single thing you can remember,' Gladwin ordered. 'And show me the precise spots on the ground.'

Thea did her best to recall every detail of her findings on both occasions – Friday morning and then Sunday, when she had tracked the sledge. Gladwin questioned her closely, expertly accessing memories she had overlooked before.

'The bottle,' the detective said. 'Was it empty?'

Thea closed her eyes to re-envisage the object. 'It was half buried in the snow, so I couldn't see. But it was just lying flat, with no top on it, so yes, it must have been empty. I presume he drank it all as part of committing suicide. It would have sent him to sleep faster, wouldn't it?'

Gladwin didn't respond to that. 'So what happened to it?' she wondered. 'Where is it now?'

'Whoever moved the body must have taken it as well.'

'Yes, but *then* what? There was no bottle in George's bin.'

'You searched his bins?' Thea was surprised.

'We did. We need an explanation for what happened to him, and a bin is often a good place to start.'

'The person who moved him must have taken it home with him?' Thea suggested.

'Why would anybody do that?'

'To make everybody believe that George hadn't been dead when he was here. That he got up, collected his rubbish and walked home, where he later died.'

'Possibly. But it raises a few questions, don't you think?'

'Yes,' said Thea. 'I very much think it does.'

Gladwin didn't insist on being led all the way to George's cottage, much to Thea's relief. Having apprised herself of the layout, and the way the fields and lanes all connected, she turned back towards Lucy's Barn.

'There were some tracks down to this gate,' Thea remembered, as they stood looking up the hill to the donkey's shed. 'I think they were only made by Donkey, though. He must have been out that night, or in the early morning, and come down here.'

'Was he wet?'

'Pardon?'

'If he'd been walking in the snow – especially if it was still falling – he'd have got wet when it melted.'

'Only on his legs. I didn't notice. He seemed a bit unsettled, that's all I remember. At that point I didn't think he'd been outside at all.'

'So when did you see his tracks?'

Thea sighed. 'I can't remember exactly. There was too much coming and going. I'm getting Thursday and Friday confused in my mind, now. On Thursday, he hadn't been out. The snow was completely untouched everywhere. Then on *Friday* I saw the human footprints, and they freaked me out. I didn't take much notice of the donkey, I was in such a state. He must have gone out eventually, although his floor was a mess – he'd mucked in there, instead of coming outside which he usually does. He seemed to be just as glum as he was on Saturday. That's all I can remember,' she repeated, helplessly.

'Well I don't suppose it matters what his movements were. But it seems a bit strange that he would walk directly down here and back unless there was something to attract his interest.'

'True. And his normal pattern is just to patrol the upper part, closer to the house. I'd never seen him down here during the four days before it snowed, I must admit. But since the snow, he's been down here a few times. He made quite a path for himself, look.'

Gladwin gave the trampled snow a brief glance, looking back over her shoulder at all the other sites that Thea had indicated. 'I can think of a few scenarios which would fit what you've told me,' she said, 'but they'd all be theories with very little prospect of proof. People, cattle and a donkey walked about in the snow, between the donkey's paddock and those woods. Then you found the marks of a sledge and followed them to George Jewell's house.'

'Where his dead body lay on the floor of his living room. Right.'

'Even if somebody used the donkey to move him, that doesn't help us much.'

'You're looking for a link to the other body,' Thea suddenly realised. 'Where is it now? What's the procedure for identifying her?'

'They'll be moving her about now, I should think.'

'It always takes so *long*,' Thea burst out. 'Why don't you move them more quickly?'

'Because we never get a second chance to understand the context. And there's no hurry, let's face it. Plus, it's sometimes a good idea to let word get around, so the local people can make a contribution. More often than not, some crucial information will emerge in those first hours, while we're doing all the initial scene-of-crime stuff. Somebody will say something, on the edge of the crowd.'

'That's why you tell the media so quickly,' Thea said.

'To give people fair warning, and get them to come out and talk.'

'Something like that. You get a lot more on the spot than pulling them in for questioning.'

'So you think someone who knows her will show up?'

'I'm hoping.'

They walked up the hill, which Thea found uncomfortably steep, combined with the exhausting process of striding through the snow. It was close to a foot deep and clung in claggy lumps to her boots, weighing them down. Pausing at the shed to throw the donkey his afternoon ration of hay, while Gladwin watched, she felt totally worn out. Her feet were almost numb with cold. 'I've had enough of this,' she grumbled. 'I'll never like snow again.'

'Maybe this is the last we'll see,' Gladwin suggested. 'With global warming escalating the way it is, it might never happen like this again. It's just a last freakish gasp before we forget snow ever existed.'

'I doubt that,' said Thea. 'But it's rather a pleasing thought.'

When they got back, they found that the stalwart Robin had made wondrous progress with his shovel. Thea's car had a clear run for a good fifty yards, up a slight incline before the track levelled out. 'You might find you can get out to the road from there,' he told her proudly. 'If you take it slowly, in first gear, it'll cope OK, I think.

It's worth a try, anyway. Do you want to give it a go while we're here? We can give you a push if you get stuck, then.'

Thea was cold and tired. She didn't really want to go anywhere, despite the shortage of milk and easy-cook food. But it would be churlish to refuse the offer. 'All right,' she nodded. 'Thanks very much.'

The car was clammy inside, and the door wouldn't close properly. 'The catch is frozen,' Robin explained. 'The handbrake might be as well. Run the engine for a bit to warm it up.'

It took them half an hour, but they managed to get to the end of the track. Gladwin rode next to Thea, because Robin said extra weight would help, and he walked behind, only needing to push twice. The track had become visible thanks to all the coming and going over the weekend, but it was almost dark by the time they emerged onto the road. 'The shops are going to be shut,' moaned Thea.

'Don't be daft,' said Gladwin. 'They've got an hour or more yet.'

The police car was parked tidily, a few yards away, and the two officers went back to it, leaving Thea feeling bereft. Knowing she could drive out from Lucy's Barn ought to have reassured her, and she tried to imply this in her effusive thanks to Robin – but in reality she felt little better. She still had to go back and take charge of all the animals through the long winter night. She had to drive back along the track in the dark, unsure as to whether further snow might fall to block her in again.

'Leave the car up here,' Robin told her. 'Then you can walk out to it any time you like – whatever happens.'

She smiled weakly. 'Why didn't I think of that?' she said.

She couldn't bring herself to go out again after all that, opting to postpone the shopping until the following morning. The sky had grown thick and dark and ominous. 'Oh, God, Heps, it's going to snow again,' she sighed. 'Where will it all end?'

Jimmy and the rabbits had been overlooked in the visitation from DS Gladwin, and Thea hurried to see to them. It was only half past five, but felt much later. It made her aware of how shielded from the natural rhythms of light and dark people had become, even those living in semi-rural surroundings, as Thea did when at home. Her little house in Witney was in a row, neighbours on either side, and a street light shone until midnight. Now she was thrust back to primitive times when night began at five in the winter, and morning didn't start till after eight. The real surprise was how easy it was to slide out of the twenty-first century, with the help of a bit of extreme weather. What must it be like on Dartmoor, or the Peak District, when snow descended? She could hardly imagine it, suspecting that only the most stoical of old farmers ever ventured out to see. Anybody who could would stay close to home, or rely on their four-wheel-drive vehicles to get them along the roads.

The lurking nervousness that never quite went away had been manageable while Gladwin had been there, but now it returned in full force. She couldn't remember ever having felt so acutely aware of danger before. Fear had been associated with arguments, loss, something unfamiliar. Now it was much more physical. The whole outside world was frightening, in this isolated snowbound barn. There was nothing to protect her, despite the improved state of the lane. A police car could reach her if she summoned it – but how long would it take? And she still hadn't discovered precisely how close Old Kate's house was, despite having glimpsed it away to the south. Not far on a dry, sunny day; quite a bit further in deep obstructive snow.

Two people had died since she arrived in Hampnett. One was definitely local, and the chances were that the second was, too. Something was going on – even with almost no clear facts available to her, she could feel it through her fingertips. There had to be a connection – which may or may not include a third person: the one who had dragged the dead body of George Jewell half a mile over snowy fields. Could that possibly have been the dead woman, who had somehow decided to kill herself after making the trek with George's body? It wasn't too difficult to conjure such a scenario – the discovery of his death by someone who loved him; the struggle to return him to his rightful home; the onset of misery and exhaustion which sent her into her own distant corner of a hidden field, where she too lay down to die in the cold. It made a satisfying kind of sense, and Thea clung to it as a consoling explanation that need contain no threat to her whatsoever.

But Gladwin had been unambiguous in her assertion that the second body had been murdered. She had been searching for signs of that third person, or so it seemed to Thea now. She had created complications where none had existed before, with her focus on the gate at the bottom of the paddock and the suggestion that somehow the donkey had been involved. Did she think the donkey had pulled the sledge bearing George's body? Was that a possibility that Thea had overlooked? Could she have missed the hoofprints that would surely have been made?

There *were* people around, she reminded herself, as she turned up the radio that she had begun to see as her main companion. She could phone any one of a dozen friends or relations, too, and indulge in an hour of gossipy chat. Not something she did often, but always an option. The fear was irrational and unnecessary, and had to be confronted. She found herself listening for a knock on the door, which would turn out to be a friendly face, bringing reassuring laughter.

But no knock came. Instead there was a phone call from a distraught woman whose son's computer had died without warning. 'He *has* to have it for the weekend,' she insisted. 'What's he going to do without it?'

'How old is he?' asked Thea, not averse to prolonging this snippet of human contact.

'Nine.'

'Hasn't he got anything else to play with? Or a book to read? Or friends to go outside with?'

'He has to have the *computer*,' repeated the woman, as if speaking to a mental defective.

'Well, I'm sorry, but Lucy will be away for quite a while yet. I'm sure you'll be able to find somebody else.'

She gave the conversation some thought, afterwards. A nine-year-old boy apparently deeply addicted to a machine, which connected him to an unreal world of fantasy and potential exploitation, with the full collusion of his mother. From what she could glean, this was the norm nowadays. Mothers seemed to welcome the way their male children remained safely indoors, hunched over games where cars were stolen, people dismembered by explosive devices, and immensely long chase scenes culminated in savage violence. When the computer died, the real world intruded unbearably. Thea could see that it might come as a shock to actually have to find something three-dimensional for the boy to do.

All around the barn was silence. When she looked out at seven, there was a light snow falling; small indecisive flakes that could surely not increase the depth on the ground by very much at all. The donkey was snug in his shelter, the rabbit and her babies – which she had almost forgotten for most of the day – were warm in the delicious bed of soft fur. It was still only Monday – almost three weeks to go before Lucy came back. It seemed impossible to continue here for so long: the time stretched infinitely ahead, each day an ordeal of worry and trouble. But she had to do it. She had promised, and Lucy had paid her half her fee in advance. There was absolutely no choice about it, and besides, it could only get better from here on. Couldn't it?

Chapter Fourteen

Tuesday arrived after a restless night, in which the silence had seemed deeper and more terrifying every time she woke. Without the spaniel on the bed with her, she didn't think she could have borne it. She spent a whole hour, between three and four, listening for some sound, however faint. She heard one motor engine – or so she told herself – out on the main road, less than a mile away. But there was no fox or owl or cat out on such a night. Hepzie was disturbed by this unfamiliar wakefulness, and kept crawling up to lick her mistress's face and thump a consoling tail on the duvet.

The snow had not perceptibly deepened, but it had a fresh whiter appearance, with the footprints and tyre marks blurred and partly filled by the new sprinkling during the night. There was no sign of anything alarming or different, and Thea went out with her shoulders squared, determined to shake off her foolish fears, and behave like any unimaginative farmer.

The baby rabbits were alive, their mother and aunties all seeming eager for their breakfast. The long hair that grew between their ears and sideways from their cheeks made them look raffish and carefree, as if life was too short to keep hair under control. They fell on the carrots that Thea gave them, nibbling one each, in identically neat patterns from the middle outwards, which was very entertaining to watch. 'Simple pleasures,' Thea murmured to herself, thinking she ought to take some photos of these odd-looking creatures.

The donkey needed more water, and she lugged two full buckets across the paddock for him, puffing and panting from the effort. He was standing peacefully in his byre, the hay all gone from the previous afternoon. Remembering the questions from Gladwin, Thea gave him a close examination, wondering whether he had ever been required to work in his life. Had anybody ever ridden on his back, or harnessed him to some sort of equipage? There was no sign of rubbed hair on his back or head; no traces of a bridle or straps. Except, she belatedly noted, on his chest. As she stroked a hand down his neck, she encountered a rough patch on the breastbone. He flinched when she touched it, and she found a scabbed abrasion when she parted the winter coat for a better look. It proved nothing, she told herself. He could have done it to himself in any number of ways. But the picture of him pulling a sledge containing a heavy body would not leave her mind. All the pressure would be exactly on that spot, and a careless buckle might easily scratch him and make just such a sore place. But a harness would surely have been found with the sledge and raised just such questions.

The need for essential groceries had become urgent, so the moment she had completed the morning work, she took the dog and headed for the car at the top of the lane. The snow was increasingly friable, the top crust turning to ice, the lower parts growing hollow. It was briefly entertaining to step onto those areas which had not yet been trampled, and feel the initial crunch, before her foot went through into nothingness. No wonder that some communities had several different words for snow: this stuff was nothing like the dense chalky substance of the first day or two, where a spade could carve through it like a cake knife through thick icing sugar. Now it was little more than brittle white ice.

Her car started obediently, and she turned towards Northleach and its well-stocked shops. She drove slowly, taking note of the long street of modest terraced houses before coming into the market square, watched over by the big Cotswold church. Another over-large display of affluence, financed by profits made from wool. Profits, perhaps, so embarrassingly big that they had to be donated to the clergy to assuage some lurking sense of guilt.

The air was less hostile than it had been, and she took her time, walking around the square to view it from all angles. Even so, there was little to detain her.

She could go into the church, which she could see had a handsome stained-glass window that could only be appreciated from inside – but the prospect did not much appeal. So she returned to the car, where the dog waited for her, wondering whether liberation was imminent.

Two men were standing near the war memorial, their backs to her. They were not speaking, and seemed to have no motivation to move. This was oddly unusual and, her attention caught, Thea paused to watch them. One moved a little way, and she recognised the profile of Simon Newby. From there it took no time to grasp that the other man was his brother – the photographer, Tony.

It did not occur to her to continue on her own business as if she hadn't seen them. The presence of even faintly familiar people was a cause for celebration, and she trotted over to them without a thought.

'Hello, you two,' she said. 'Remember me?'

The bright tone, the smile and little laugh, all died away as they both turned to face her.

They were clearly brothers. Of precisely the same height, with similar hair and stature, they stood shoulder to shoulder and looked at her blankly. 'The house-sitter,' said the photographer, eventually, in a slightly husky voice. 'How're you doing?'

Only then did she begin to understand that *they* were not doing well at all. Simon gave her a look that was like that of a drowning man. 'I'm all right,' she said slowly. 'Has something happened?'

'Bunny,' said Tony, the younger brother. 'We've just been to identify her.' He glanced at Simon, as if for permission to say more. When there was no reaction, he added, 'She was frozen in a field.'

'My God!' She knew instantly that they were talking about the second body, that the mother of those two little boys was dead. That Simon had been widowed, and the shock was still so fresh that he had not learnt any of the expected responses or reactions. 'I heard about it on the news yesterday. I'm *terribly* sorry.'

The fact that she had undergone the same annihilating experience herself made it no easier to come up with useful words. All she could think of were questions, and she did vaguely recall that these could become burdensome very quickly.

'We had to go and talk to Ben's teacher,' he continued. 'Funny, the things that take priority.'

'Those poor little boys,' Thea uttered, entirely in agreement that their needs must come first. 'What a dreadful thing.' The dreadfulness was beyond her imagining, until she remembered that their mother had been absent for several days already, without any undue trauma, as far as she had been able to see. 'Will Janina stay on longer now?' The Bulgarian girl was suddenly crucial, surely – the mother substitute that couldn't possibly be dispensed with now.

'Somebody *killed* her,' said Simon, speaking for the first time. 'They murdered my wife. How is that possible? I thought she was in Bristol.'

Thea experienced a painful jumble of emotions at this. A surge of anxiety, just when she'd begun to think there was nothing to fear; pity for Simon and his boys; weariness at the prospect of the investigation that would now ensue and which she would probably find herself involved in. She thought of DS Gladwin, and that other body in the snow.

'So…George…' she stuttered, unsure of what she was trying to ask.

Tony reared back as if she'd spat at him, and then turned to Simon with an expression of alarm. Simon merely closed his eyes in a slow bewildered blink. 'George?' he echoed.

'Nothing,' she said. 'Just that…well, that's two dead people, isn't it?'

'They're not connected,' said Tony. 'Obviously.' He gave her a look of pure rage. 'Why did you have to bring that up?'

If little Nicky had been with them, she could have understood his attitude. Perhaps he felt equally protective towards his brother, worrying about overload of some sort. But she didn't like being reprimanded and stood her ground. 'They might be connected,' she argued. 'How do you know they're not?' She had a thought. 'The police are already taking a view that they probably are.'

'What? What are you talking about?'

'Well, you should know. You work for them, don't you?' The events of the previous Friday returned to her

– the group of men floundering down her snowy track, Tony himself examining the empty spot where George's body had been. She frowned as her thoughts began to take more shape. 'It can hardly be a coincidence, can it?'

'George?' said Simon again, more loudly. 'Was he murdered as well, then?'

The others said nothing, but Thea met his eyes with a meaningful nod that said *maybe he was*. Then she caught herself, and gave a self-conscious little laugh. 'I'm sure he can't have been.' Her head felt thick with new implications, new questions, all wrapped in a stifling sense of shock.

'It doesn't make any sense,' moaned Simon. 'I thought she was in Bristol. She sent a *text*. They said she must have come home days ago. Why didn't she come to the house? Where has she *been*?'

His bewilderment was painful to witness. Thea turned to Tony for support, but he was still looking at her angrily. She reviewed what she had just said, and could hardly blame him. What had she been thinking of, to launch into half-baked theories about Bunny and George, when she knew nothing of the background? She had also been careless, talking as if she were party to the police investigations.

'Well, I'd better go,' she said weakly. 'If I can do anything...'

Tony's look clearly said, *Haven't you done enough?*

* * *

She and Hepzie drove back to the barn, across the main road where traffic was flowing fast enough to make it seem a normal winter's day, despite the white fields on all sides. She dithered about whether or not to take the car down the track, risking it becoming stranded again. The snow might be altering its nature, but it was still there, and the way would be unpleasantly slippery. There could also be further snowfall to come. With a sigh, she opted to leave it at the top, and carry the shopping the last leg.

Her head was full of thoughts about poor little Nicky and his brother. Whatever Janina might have said about their mother, they were bound to be badly damaged by her death. Simon might need a more permanent mother substitute than the au pair, who would inevitably disappear before long, her own professional life calling to her more and more insistently. There would be more changes and disruptions, in the short term, and the debilitating lifelong loss that would never allow them to be the secure and confident people they might otherwise have become.

She thought about the unhappy reclusive George and the probability that his lonely death would become sidelined by the far more significant murder of a young mother. Whatever the connection between the two may or may not have been, Bunny was sure to become the more newsworthy, earning more police time and media attention. It seemed unfair – from what she could gather, George had been a nicer person. His loss was another blow for the two little boys. At least they had Uncle Tony, she remembered – it seemed to be a good sign that he had gone with Simon to see the school people.

Disjointedly, her mind flickered from one observation to another, images and theories jumbled together with an awareness of how little she really knew about the people involved. The only one who had made any real disclosures had been Janina. On that first Sunday, outside the church, she had seemed eager to pour everything out to the first person she met – her disapproval of Bunny was still vivid in Thea's mind. Unbidden, there arose ideas about this: had Janina fallen for Simon, and opted to remove Bunny permanently from the picture? Had she wanted the children for her own, having determined that she, Janina, would make a much better mother to them than the absent Bunny? Or had Simon himself taken the fatal action? After all, the husband was generally the prime suspect in such cases. The subsequent remorse and trauma were apparently easy enough to simulate. She ran through the scanty cast of characters she had met in Hampnett since she arrived. Old Kate, the vague parade of parents collecting children from the party – that was it. Kate had an aged parent living invisibly with her, and Simon had a few scattered neighbours who might be central to the story, for all Thea knew.

If it hadn't been for Gladwin's unsettling visit the day before, she might have been able to sit back and let somebody else worry about who killed Bunny, and what might happen next. As it was, she feared she would be drawn in, whether she liked it or not.

The day before had seen importunate visitors interrupting the routine, which Thea had found irritating. Now she rather wished for a repeat, instead of the eerie silence and blank snowy wastes. Even with the cleared track and liberated car, she felt isolated and forgotten. The animals were all subdued and undemonstrative. Jimmy performed his routines with his usual lack of emotion. He and Hepzie rubbed noses, but nothing more than that. It was all rather mundane and repetitive and the remaining two and a half weeks at Lucy's Barn stretched uninvitingly ahead.

Time drifted on to midday, and a glimpse of blue could be found between the clouds. Hope was raised for a bright afternoon and a possible thaw at last. The local radio had stopped talking about the snow as an impediment to normal life, and instead brought in old timers who could remember 1947 when the whole of the West Midlands had been covered for weeks on end. There were climate experts attempting to reconcile this traditional winter weather with the scare stories about global warming. It all amounted to a lot of pointless prattle, as far as Thea was concerned.

She ought to go out again, and attempt at least some sort of exploration of the area. It was what she always did when house-sitting – it had been a lot of the reason for taking on the work in the first place. Her subject was history, and she had discovered numerous interesting old stories and events from the various villages she'd briefly inhabited. Hampnett had a famous church, with a small mystery as to precisely who had performed the remarkable claim to fame inside it. Thea had read about it, but not yet seen it with her own eyes. She really should go and have a look before much longer.

But an unfamiliar lethargy had her in its grip. She did not want to put on boots and gloves again and thick confining coat and either walk or drive to the village centre. Even if she did force herself to do it, she might not meet anybody to talk to, and it was a need for human company that she felt more powerfully than any wish to do a bit of sightseeing. And by the same token, she didn't suppose that anybody would feel inclined to come and visit her. Yesterday had been an aberration, obviously. The day would soon be over – only another four hours or so of daylight, and then it was on with the lamps and across with the curtains, forgetting the hostile world outside for another long, long night.

The thought was somehow shameful. How could she fritter away a whole day doing virtually nothing other than a bit of shopping? It went against her nature, although she knew plenty of people who barely understood the concept of frittering time. They watched daytime television, phoned friends for long fatuous conversations about nothing, cleaned things that weren't dirty and made not the slightest contribution to anything. They were, Thea sometimes thought, literally a waste of space. They were consuming energy and food without paying anything back. Carl, a deeply benign person, had raged at the mindlessness of so many people who lived in this way. He and her father between them had trained Thea into other attitudes to life. Sometimes the high-mindedness made her feel rebellious – more often it left her weak and pessimistic. But mostly she was thoroughly convinced that she should earn her place on the planet, and that meant getting involved, paying attention and trying to do a bit of good here and there.

Chapter Fifteen

Jimmy seemed unusually stiff when she took him out for his midday airing. He took much longer than normal to get up, and then his back legs were quivering as he tried to walk. Worriedly, Thea examined him, unable to think what could be wrong. 'Probably just cold,' she concluded. He followed her out to the garden with a determined expression, but his head drooped and he failed to produce any urine. Hepzie kept her distance, as if embarrassed by him.

The conservatory was quite chilly, with the wind gusting against the glass and the minimal heating in that part of the house. Even the plants looked pinched, after so many cold days. Should she move the dog into a warmer area? Would he settle in a different place? Perhaps some warmer bedding would be enough, at least until the evening.

Mindful of the cold, she went out to the rabbits' shed, to inspect the babies again. Earlier, she had done nothing more than give them all some food and water, knowing it was risky to interfere too much with a nest of young ones. But if they were at risk of freezing to death, she ought to do something. The wind was strengthening, reducing the temperature considerably. Her hands were chilled, despite the gloves, and her feet inside the boots lost much of their feeling after a few minutes. Tentatively, she poked through the covering of soft rabbit hair to the little bodies beneath. It was as warm as any bed could be, as cosy and safe as the most cherished infant could wish for. Trying to see them in their shadowy corner, she noted that the babies were acquiring more and more hair, with different colours emerging delightfully. The mother sat nervously by, her nose working busily as she seemed to mutter to herself. 'Sorry to disturb you,' Thea murmured. 'I'm just checking.' She gave the rabbit an apple she had brought out with her, and the animal seized it with enthusiasm.

Another visit to Jimmy only increased her worries. He still shivered, lying awkwardly with his neck stretched out. Thea knelt beside him, and stroked him for a minute or two. It struck her that she would have difficulty getting him to the vet, with her car a quarter of a mile away. He was light enough to carry, in a real emergency, but she wasn't eager to try it. For one thing, the dog would only get more chilled, and for another the strange procedure would probably traumatise him. Besides, what good would a vet be, anyway? If Jimmy's problems were emotional or psychological, there was no cure for them, other than keeping him quiet and safe as Lucy had said. The conservatory was on the north side of the barn, exposed to the bitter wind that continued to blow. The temperature inside had to be close to freezing, even by day. It couldn't possibly be healthy for any creature as thin and hairless as this one to remain in such a cold place. Decisively, Thea set about moving him into the heated living room.

Gently she led him by the collar to one of the sheepskin rugs that were scattered over the floor. Leaving him standing obediently where she put him, she went back for his bedding. Beanbag, fluffy woollen blanket and a piece of colourless felt that he treated much as a child treats a familiar scrap of cloth – she brought it all through and arranged it in a corner, where the floor felt comfortably warm. 'Come on, boy,' she coaxed. 'This is your new bed, OK?'

In reply, the dog released a stream of yellow urine directly onto the white sheepskin beneath him. Thea shrieked, unable to restrain herself. The dog flinched slightly, but stood his ground. Hepzie, from her place on the sofa, gave a short yap of echoing reproach.

'Oh, God,' Thea moaned. 'This is impossible.' Evidently Jimmy associated being moved from his bed and spoken to encouragingly with relieving himself. Would it happen every time she said anything, if he was relocated to the living room? And how was she supposed to deal with the soiled sheepskin, in this weather? Wasn't there something about laying them

out flat in weak sunshine on a mild day? Would it be
all right to put it in the washing machine? Would it be
ruined if she just left it for Lucy to deal with?

The combination of urgent need for action with a
basically trivial problem irritated her. Outside, people
were dying. Two children had been left without a
mother, and the police were going to be mounting a
determined investigation. Inside, she was in a panic
about a sad and difficult dog. The dislocation was
uncomfortable. But Jimmy undoubtedly required the
bulk of her attention, and she had to find a way to keep
him as healthy and contented as she possibly could.

She was not being paid to get involved in murder
inquiries – she had to remind herself of that. Her duty
lay with Jimmy and the rabbits and the donkey. She was
perfectly justified in forgetting all about Bunny and her
family; about the dead George, too, despite having been
the person to find his body – twice. She meant nothing
to Simon or Janina or the boys; she was just somebody
passing through, who would soon forget them and leave
them to gather up their lives as best they could.

It was a rational decision that ought to have brought
some relief in its wake. But Thea Osborne was not a
totally rational person. She was curious by nature, and
liked to get involved with people, if only temporarily.
She became enraged by cruelty or stupid selfishness.
Killers, in her increasing experience, were generally
unimaginative solipsists who could seldom see beyond
their own short-term self-interest. They murdered for

money, or in the hope of maintaining a shameful secret, or even for the preservation of some misguided ideology. And in the process they caused appalling distress and misery. She could no more let it all go than she could bring her own dead husband back to life. Somehow, in the murky illogical depths, there was a connection. The sudden stupid death of the innocent Carl meant that further sudden stupid deaths had to be confronted and given the dignity of resolution – not just for the sake of the families, but for the sake of Order itself.

Nonetheless, Jimmy had to be cared for. He certainly couldn't be allowed to freeze to death under her watch. The incontinence had been understandable, under the circumstances. She would just have to take more care from here on, and stick as closely as possible to the routine that Lucy had managed to establish. At least he wouldn't need to go outside again for a while. His bladder must be quite empty.

She had forgotten to have any lunch, she realised, on noticing that it was past two o'clock. The light was fading dramatically, and when she looked out it was to see renewed snow falling, blowing diagonally in the ever-increasing wind, already piling up against obstacles in the yard. Her insides lurched, and her mouth felt oddly dry. *I'm scared*, she thought. *Really scared, just because it's snowing.* She tried to analyse the cause of her fear, which was worse than she could remember feeling for years. The isolation, she concluded, and the responsibility, were part of it. She would have to slog through drifts and ensure the donkey was all right. She might not be able to get to the car, if it snowed all night. She might have to summon help from people too busy to bother with her. But an image was forming insistently in her mind's eye: the image of the man, curled stiffly in the snow, his hair and skin so cold that snowflakes didn't melt on contact. It had looked so easy to die out there in the icy white world. You merely lay down and let yourself fall asleep. It would be quiet and painless and imperceptible. As she let the picture develop, the sensations of fear increased. *That* was what she found so terrifying, then. The appealing ease with which you could kill yourself; the vivid presence of death just a few seductive yards away brought with it a horror that wouldn't go away. Thea, who had known pain and love and triumph and even some moments of nobility, was unexpectedly staring into the jaws of death and finding them dreadfully attractive.

Desperately, she sought for handholds that would return her to the normality of wanting to live, whatever the circumstances. There was Hepzie – her spaniel would be distraught without her. Except she wouldn't really. She would go to live with Jessica or Jocelyn or Thea's mother, and carry on with remarkable equanimity. But there was a future of forty years or more, in which she would meet new people, and love them. She would become a grandmother, in all probability, and see herself perpetuated down the generations. She would be useful and creative and caring.

As if waking from a nightmare, she shook herself and looked around at the solid world. What had all that been about, she asked herself? It had begun with George, the apparent suicide in the snow, and the slide into too close an identification with him. She had almost been possessed by him for a few moments, and the experience had been frightening. But it had also brought a moment of enlightenment that she should hold on to. A valuable insight into the appeal that death could offer. Did all suicides glimpse that same allure? Did they go into oblivion with a sensation of relief and gladness in those final seconds? Nobody was encouraged to think so. It was almost a taboo to regard suicide in a positive light. Now Thea was not sure this was right. If life had become so untenably distressing, then why not simply leave it?

Not that this applies to me, she told herself sternly. I am a different case entirely. I might feel abandoned and aimless just at this moment, but I have plenty to live for. And for a start, I ought to go and feed that donkey before it gets too difficult to cross his paddock.

She needed human company – without it, she was liable to sink back into the same dark place again. Too much solitude was clearly a dangerous thing, especially in such hostile weather conditions.

But the day was closing in, and people everywhere would be huddled indoors, or forcing their cars through the blizzard to reach the shelter of home. They would not be available to a lonely house-sitter who merely wanted to chat. And then, with a thump that seemed to affect every internal organ, she understood exactly where the problem lay.

The woman with the freckles and the loud laugh who had replaced her in Phil Hollis's life. Everything sprang from that overlooked detail, so carefully imparted by her daughter. Phil and Thea had agreed to part, in a mature and unemotional exchange, and left it at that. They had spoken on the phone a few times since, in polite tones, about nothing much. When Jessica gave her the news, she had swallowed down the jagged feelings of rejection and jealousy, sternly labelling them as unjustified. But feelings seldom did as they were told. They simmered persistently, emerging in disguise, sometimes so powerfully that you were undone by them. You thought you were going mad with the irrationality of it all. Why feel so afraid of a fall of snow, when it couldn't possibly hurt you? Because it wasn't the snow at all that was the problem – it was the terror of remaining single and unloved for the rest of your life, and a neat symbol for that state might easily be a featureless expanse of snow stretching as far as you could see.

When a very sweet and trusting little boy lost his mother to a violent and senseless death, that too represented abandonment and rejection. Plus the pathetic dog, similarly abandoned on the roadside, with whom it had been all too easy to identify – it all added up to a cold, lonely universe in which there was very little comfort.

Not to mention poor George, she added to herself, wryly. As the pieces all slotted into place, she found herself feeling much better. There was sense in her alarmingly dark musings after all. Anyone would have reacted the same way. And it was all quite readily soluble. She would meet new men, make new friends. She only had to settle herself into the right frame of mind, and they'd be flocking to her door.

But it would never come right for George, or Nicky or even the wretched Jimmy. They were the truly tragic victims in this particular story, and she owed it to them to do all she could to offer at least some consolation.

She passed the rest of the day playing games on her computer, watching a long film on a DVD, cooking herself a generous quantity of spaghetti bolognese, with real ingredients, including two carrots that were strictly intended for the rabbits, and which had gone somewhat rubbery. She took Jimmy out, and then led him back to his new corner, trying to convince him that it was exactly the same as the old one. She added a small quantity of cooked mince to his dinner – as well as to Hepzie's – hoping they would regard it as a treat. When the two dogs curled up together on Jimmy's beanbag, she felt she had accomplished something important.

Chapter Sixteen

She awoke to Wednesday with a sense of trepidation. Had the snow deepened again? Would Jimmy be all right? Had it got even colder than the day before?

She pulled aside the curtains. Light bands of white cloud gave the sky a festive appearance. Water dripped past her window, and as she focused on the buildings and trees around the barn, they all appeared to be wet. Streaks marked the vertical surfaces, and the ground was patched with dark colours between the areas of snow.

Thawing! It was all thawing. Like a miracle, the snow was turning to water, even at this hour of the morning. The normal world was returning, shaking off the unnatural white covering and getting itself back to business. As she listened, she could hear drips and gurgles as it all turned to liquid.

She turned on the radio just in time for the weather forecast at five to eight. The wind had veered to the south-west, raising the temperature by seven or eight degrees overnight. The fast-melting snow might cause flooding in some areas, as it rushed down the hillsides and into rivers that might not cope with the sudden influx.

Only in England, thought Thea, could one weather-related drama switch so abruptly into another. Should she now3 be worrying that Lucy's Barn could be inundated with floodwater? She went outside and tried to assess the lie of the land, and where the snow melt might go. It seemed that the barn had been built on a slight rise, which was only to be expected from those sensible farmers of a century or two ago. To the left, the slope was obvious, leading down to Old Kate's. Ahead, where the donkey had his paddock, the ground also fell gently away at first, and then more abruptly. Behind the barn was a level stretch, but a ditch had been dug twenty yards away, which would surely divert any run-off water. Only to the right, where Gladwin had helped her to get her car out, was there a little uphill slope. And anything running down there would surely maintain the course of the track, and head off down towards the next farm.

So she could allow herself an inward whoop of relief. She could collect her car and bring it back to the yard. She could open one or two windows and let some milder air into the house. She might go for a walk across the fields behind the barn, where she had not yet ventured. There should be snowdrops growing, and catkins on the hazel. Regardless of it still being the middle of January, she felt stirrings of spring already. Six days of snow had been winter enough, surely?

She fed the animals quickly, her toes still unfrozen inside the boots, and gloves quite unnecessary. The baby rabbits remained invisibly in their luxurious nest, and the donkey had already come outside for a look at his changing world. Jimmy was at least alive, and there was no sign of further incontinence. After his visit to the garden, Thea put him back in the conservatory, making up his bed as close as possible to how it was.

Then she got the dog lead and wallet and took Hepzie out to collect the car. There was still a lot of slushy snow on the ground, but it seemed to disappear on contact with her feet. Water lay in pools all along the track, and trickled musically on all sides. After the silence of the snow, this evidence of movement and life was a delight to the ears.

The car was where she'd left it, which seemed like another cause for relief. 'We'll go to the shops in Stow,' she told the dog. 'And get something nice for supper.'

The car was facing north, and rather than turn it round in the still-slushy and possibly slippery road, she drove off in the direction it faced, towards the centre of Hampnett. The road was very wet and splashy, the trees on her left looking drenched in an oddly different way from usual. A rainstorm left its own patterns of drips and rivulets. Melting snow was quieter, more gradual and more penetrating. The world looked as if it had been dipped in a large pool and brought up again, streaming with water. The water came from below, not above, and it looked nothing like rain. Thea drove slowly, savouring the oddness of it all.

At the village centre, she paused, wondering whether she might see someone familiar. Then it occurred to her that the only people she knew were directly involved in a murder, and were unlikely to be in any mood for chatting to an ephemeral house-sitter. All the same, she drew the car to a halt, thinking it was high time she investigated the famous church. It was there to her right, with its own parking area. A slightly sloping path led through a small gate and along to the porch and big old door.

Glad of her sturdy boots as she trod through the puddles, she approached the building. Hepzie stayed unprotestingly in the car, which Thea had not bothered to lock.

Inside, the church was light but chilly. At first glance it seemed unremarkable, until she turned east and was abruptly dazzled by the stencilled decorations on all the walls of the further end, where the altar stood. Slowly, she approached, noting the arch between the two sections, carved and painted with such exuberance it felt nothing like a place of Christian worship. The patterned walls were more like those of a papered sitting room than a chancel, or whatever it was. There was a joyful decadence to it that struck her as defiantly nutty. She had read of the arguments many years ago, in the parish, and the near victory of those who wanted it painted over and decorum restored. That it had survived for something like one hundred and fifty years was amazing, and glorious. Now, of course, it attracted tourists and anything that did that acquired a sanctity all of its own.

The archway was as flamboyant as the stencilling, with crinkly stonework and stylised little carvings of men who were probably saints. There was also an intriguing pair of birds at the top of a column, drinking from a bowl, their wings half open. She stared at it for a full minute, wondering about its age, and the motivation behind the choice of subject.

But it was the stencilling that gave the place its character. There was something foreign and pagan about it that Thea found mildly unsettling, here in the heart of rural England. But then she remembered that William Morris had once lived close by, and that the very architecture of the area stood witness to the spirited imagination of people who had lived here. They might have been shepherds for the most part, and stolid merchants, but they had not been immune to beauty, both natural and man-made.

A sound amongst the scanty rows of pews attracted her attention. She had walked past them with her eyes fixed on the painted walls, seeing nothing else. Now she looked back, and saw a small head close to the floor. 'Hello?' she said quietly, half convinced that it was something insubstantial that would vanish on closer inspection.

It didn't vanish, but neither did it move. She went closer, bending down to look between the pews. 'Who's that?' she asked. There was a little body crouching on the floor, parallel with the seats, its bottom towards her. 'Hey...come on out of there,' she persisted. 'It must be cold on that stone floor.'

Awkwardly, the child shuffled backwards, before standing up and turning to look at her.

'Nicky!' Thea cried, in recognition. 'What on earth are you doing here? Where's Janina? Or Daddy? What's been happening to you?'

The little boy said nothing, simply staring at her with eyes full of unshed tears. Thea sat down beside him and pulled him to her, fighting back her own urge to weep. 'Oh, Nicky,' she moaned. 'It'll be all right.' But it wouldn't. How could it be? Nicky shivered and stood stiffly in her encircling arm. He was wearing a thin shirt, with no coat or jumper. Only then did Thea wonder just how he had got there, and why nobody had missed him. Why was there no frantic search party out there calling his name?

'I want George,' whispered the child. 'I'm finding George.'

Chapter Seventeen

She carried him back to his house, which was after all only two or three hundred yards away. But he had crossed a road, albeit a very little-used one, and got inside the church through the heavy oak door. He gave her no enlightenment as to where he was meant to be and how he had evaded the adults who should have been looking after him.

The house was deserted, and Thea assumed that Janina and perhaps Simon were, after all, combing the area in search of the missing child. The front door was closed but not locked, and she took him inside, anxious to get him warmed up. He was still shivering, and when she settled him into a corner of a big red sofa, he looked horribly pale and drawn. The room was warm and tidy as if waiting for visitors to arrive.

'I need to wee,' said Nicky suddenly, and rolled off the sofa. He headed for a door next to the kitchen, and Thea let him go, trying to remember the usual level of competency of a four-year-old in that department. Her sister's youngest was eight, and it didn't seem too long ago that he had regularly wet his pants in times of excitement. She considered herself lucky that this one had waited until she put him down, rather than let go while still in her arms.

She heard the flushing of the loo, and then the pale child returned slowly, a frown on his face. 'What's your name?' he asked.

'Thea,' she told him. 'I came to your party, remember?'

'Oh yes,' he nodded, with no sign of recognition. It was impossible to guess what was going on inside the little head, but it was easy to believe that events since Saturday had completely obliterated all memory of his birthday. 'You came when George was dead.'

Even harder to grasp just what a four-year-old understood of death. They played games about killing on the computer, watched it in TV cartoons, heard references to dead animals and perhaps people. But to see an actual dead person at that age was beyond the realms of comprehension, in this society at this time. Fears about the damage it would do must run riot amongst his family and teachers. Why, then, had he apparently been abandoned to lose himself in a church? How in the world could such a thing have happened?

'That's right,' she said. 'And you've been looking for him today, have you?'

'Janina said he would go to the church,' he nodded.

She must have meant his funeral, Thea supposed. The au pair had presumably been trying to explain the process, in an effort to reassure and inform. People these days believed it was important to keep children abreast of events, not to exclude them and lie to them. Thea approved of this, herself, but in this instance she suspected that Janina had gone too far. Or had failed to anticipate the effect of her explanations. And what, if anything, had Nicky been told about his mother?

She began to feel awkward in her role as rescuer, making free with someone else's house, and in sole charge of a traumatised little boy. She should summon somebody – especially if there was in fact a desperate search party out there looking for Nicky. But the only call she could think to make was to the police, and that seemed ill-advised, until she knew more. If Nicky had not been reported lost, then there might be repercussions for those who had allowed him to wander away unnoticed. It would be doing Simon no favours to add this charge of neglect to his other worries.

But as she sat beside the child, having found him a sweatshirt and made him a drink of warm milk in the microwave, she began to wonder about Simon. What father would be so careless, whatever the circumstances? She thought about her own father, always so mindful of his children's welfare, and Carl, who had devoted himself to Jessica when she was Nicky's age, taking her for long country walks and carrying her home when she was too exhausted to move another step. She might have heard stories of men who forgot to collect their kids from school, or left them for hours in a car – but she had never experienced one of them at first hand.

After half an hour, she knew she had to make a move. Her dog would be restless, she herself was getting hungry, and Nicky was in obvious need of a familiar pair of arms around him. She had switched on the TV and they were watching something mindless as a distraction, when the doorbell rang.

Carefully, with her heart thumping nervously, Thea went to answer it. A woman she recognised stood there, with a small girl at her side. 'Dorothy!' Thea remembered. 'Aren't you Dorothy?' The argumentative child from the party – one of Nicky's little friends. It explained nothing, but she was very glad indeed to see them.

'Have you got Nicky?' the woman burst out, before Thea had finished addressing the little girl. 'He hasn't been at nursery all morning. Bernard was supposed to collect him.' She grimaced with that familiar look of wives who found themselves saddled with unreliable men.

'Yes,' said Thea shortly. 'But there's nobody else here.'

'Thank God for that.'

'I *told* you, Babs,' said Dorothy. She looked at Thea, woman to woman. 'Daddy forgot all about it. He doesn't listen, you see.'

Dorothy was at least six – old enough to be in school.

But a closer inspection revealed a crusty nose and red eyes indicative of a nasty cold.

'Can I have a quick look at him, do you think?' asked Barbara. 'I was *aghast* when I realised what must have happened. I would have sent Bernard to abase himself, but what's the point. He's had Philippa on the phone to him half the morning, God help us, so he's in no state to deal with nursery matters.'

'Come in, then,' said Thea, with an exaggerated version of the odd pang she always had when making free with other people's homes.

Nicky was still on the sofa, his eyelids flickering as he dozed off to sleep. Barbara took one look at him and retreated back to the hall, Dorothy following her.

'I really am terribly sorry. Where's the au pair? Have you been here with him all morning?'

'I found him in the church,' said Thea brutally. She gave a brief account of events, experiencing afresh the shocked alarm at finding the small child all alone in the cold. 'Heaven knows what would have happened if I hadn't gone in there. I'm not sure he could have opened the door again by himself. He might have been in there for *days*.'

Barbara shuddered. 'Let's hope someone would have thought to look for him there, once they realised he was missing. And where *is* that girl?'

'I have no idea. I suppose I'll have to stay here until somebody comes back. I assume Ben's at school as normal?' She still had no clear idea of what the original plan had been that day, or how Bernard had so comprehensively failed to play his part in it.

Barbara shrugged. 'I suppose so. I've been concentrating on Nicky. Bernard took Wilf to nursery this morning, and apparently should have taken Nicky as well. But he got distracted somehow, so I only heard about it later. Then he had to go and see someone, so I was left with madam here.' She shook her head impatiently. 'It never occurred to me that kids could be so *complicated*,' she complained. 'I thought I'd escaped all that business. All my own fault, I know, for falling for the silly old sod. Terrible what a moment of weakness can lead to.'

Thea laughed, liking Barbara more by the minute. 'I expect there are compensations,' she said, eyeing the self-possessed Dorothy.

'Oh, Dottie and I get along marvellously. She makes everything worthwhile.' *And she calls you Babs*, Thea thought. Somehow that did suggest a good relationship.

'You do seem rather alike,' she observed, wondering about the absent Philippa.

'So Bernard says. Well, we'll go, if that's all right. Dottie's not supposed to be out, by rights. She's got a stinking cold.'

At the door, Barbara turned back, and said in a low voice, 'You have heard what happened to his mother, I assume?'

'Mmm,' Thea nodded briefly, reluctant to speak about Bunny in front of the little girl. 'I assume that's what all this is about. Simon and Janina must be – I don't know, helping with investigations, or something.'

Barbara widened her eyes. 'Appalling thing to happen. That's what Philippa was on about to Bernard, apparently. Ranting about nowhere being safe, and were we looking after her children properly. Bloody nerve! If she cared all that much, she'd look after them herself.'

This was definitely not for Dorothy's ears, and Thea put a quick stop to it by ushering her visitors out to their car, and closing the door on them. After they'd gone, she arranged a rug over the sleeping Nicky, and briefly considered running back to the car to rescue her dog. How stupid of me, she thought, not to ask Barbara to at least do that for me. As it was, she had no way of knowing how long she might have to stay in post – minding a little boy, when she was being paid to mind a dog and a donkey and a barn.

It was clear that somebody had dropped poor Nicky in the process of handing him from one person to another earlier that morning. Had he been sent outside to wait for his lift, all on his own? Why had he not been wearing a coat, if so? And where on earth *was* Janina?

Part of her wanted to punish the useless Bernard for sheer criminal incompetence, but a larger part simply wanted to forget all about him, so she could concentrate on Nicky.

She sat down on the sofa with Nicky and tried to think. The apparent neglect of the child was much less culpable than she had first thought. Bernard had been trusted to do as asked, and if Nicky had been allowed to stand by himself at his own front door for a few minutes, that was hardly a crime. When the man never arrived, the little boy had walked up to the church, and stayed there all morning. At some point he had shed his coat, but no real harm had come to him. Janina or Simon had been unavoidably delayed somewhere, and would have assumed that Nicky would be taken home with Dorothy and given some lunch and kept safe until collected. Sorted!

At least...a scenario that would have made perfect sense fifty years ago was no longer so convincing in an age where children were obsessively supervised for every second of their lives; where everybody phoned everybody else on a mobile phone, to impart the vital information that they had just walked from the kitchen to the living room, that one person had eaten a slice of bread and the other was wearing a bright blue jumper. None of this had happened that morning, and it seemed inadequate to simply remind herself that Janina was Bulgarian and maybe they did things differently there.

Thea herself would have dearly loved to make some phone calls that would resolve everything, but she could think of no one to call apart from DS Gladwin, and that seemed excessive. She considered taking Nicky with her back to Lucy's Barn, and might have done if he'd been awake. As it was, it seemed unkind to disturb him, or to transport him while asleep and then let him wake in a strange place with a comparatively strange person. And soon there would be the additional problem of his older brother. School would be finishing in a couple of hours, and there would be another little boy to worry about.

Perhaps she could phone the school. Simon and Tony had been there the day before, discussing how the news of his mother's death might affect Benjamin. It had left an impression of a sensible caring establishment that might have good advice to offer. And if this was a remotely normal family, there would be a piece of paper somewhere prominent with the phone number on it. She got up and went into the kitchen. There, as hoped, was a small crowded noticeboard above the telephone, boasting a sheet with Northleach Primary School's letterhead. Without pausing to rehearse what she would say, Thea lifted the receiver.

A friendly sounding woman responded, and Thea found herself unable to form a lucid sentence. 'Oh, yes, hello,' she stammered. 'My name is Thea Osborne, and I'm phoning about a little boy called Benjamin. He's six. I'm afraid I can't remember his surname.' Then her eye caught another piece of paper on the board, addressed to a Mr S Newby. 'Oh, I think it's Newby. Yes, yes, Newby. Sorry – I've only met them recently.'

'Ben Newby…yes,' said the woman carefully. 'What about him?'

'Well, you know about his mother being killed, of course.'

'Uh-huh.'

'Right. Anyway, I'm here at the house with his

brother. There's nobody else here. I need to go soon, actually. It all happened by accident – Nicky's lift didn't come to take him to nursery, so he went up to the church, and I found him. I need to contact his father or the au pair.'

The woman was admirably calm, given the stream of irrelevant information she had just been treated to. 'Janina usually collects Ben. We have no note to say today will be different.'

'Good. That's a relief. But I think you might find she doesn't appear. What would you do then?'

'Phone Mr Newby, I suppose.'

'Yes! So do you think you could phone him now, and tell him there's a problem with Nicky? I'm not sure you can rely on Janina.'

'All right, Mrs...um...Osborne. Thank you.' The wariness was palpable, and Thea could hardly blame the woman for it. The murder of the mother of one of her charges had to be considerably outside her comfort zone.

Thea felt little better afterwards. The question of Janina loomed largest in her mind. Had the girl simply bolted at the news of Bunny's murder? Had the involvement of the police scared her away, for complicated reasons of her own? Perhaps she was working illegally, or in possession of hard drugs, or simply scared of the forces of the law. And yet she had seemed unfazed by the earlier attentions devoted to the death of George, Thea remembered. Hadn't Janina simply stood by, seemingly quite relaxed? All of which suggested rather insistently that the Bulgarian girl might just have been responsible for the death of her employer.

It was half past one, and she was hungry. Both the dogs under her care would be needing her. She went to the front door and listened. Yes…Hepzie was yapping, up in the car. It was more than Thea could manage to leave her there any longer, and taking great care not to lock herself out, she trotted quickly up to the church parking area and threw open the car door. The spaniel climbed out with dignity, ignoring the cold water underfoot. She went to a patch of grass and relieved herself, as if she'd been confined for twenty hours, not one and a half.

'Come on,' said Thea. 'We have to get back.' Then she noticed a small blue coat hanging on the gate into the churchyard. It could only be Nicky's, and she could not imagine how she had failed to see it earlier. With a feeling of having collected another useful piece in a puzzle, she unhooked it, and led her dog back the way she had come.

Before she reached the house again, a car had come up behind her, and was drawing into the space in front of the Newby home. The passenger door opened, and Janina emerged, looking anguished. She slammed the car door impatiently, and ran to the house. Not once had she glanced at Thea or her dog.

Thea followed her determinedly, ushering the spaniel into the house with no ceremony at all. 'Janina!' she called. 'Wait a minute.'

The au pair was on her knees in front of the sleeping Nicky before Thea could catch up with her. No mother could have shown more agonised love, more debilitating relief than this foreign girl was showing to a child she had only known for a few weeks. 'He's all right,' Thea said quietly. 'He's fine.'

Only then did Janina acknowledge her presence. 'Why are you here?' she asked, with a frown. 'Did Bernard ask you?'

'Not exactly,' she said. 'I found Nicky in the church. He never got to nursery.' There had been a momentary temptation to shield the forgetful Bernard, but the prospect of introducing lies and evasions at this stage was untenable. 'He was very cold, but I think he's OK now. He'll be hungry, I expect.'

Nicky was stirring, roused by the lavish devotion coming his way. He opened his eyes and smiled. 'Hello, Janina,' he said, like a model English schoolboy. His long eyelashes fluttered, and his rosy cheeks glowed. He was a really beautiful child, Thea noted again. The sort that made people go soft and doting.

'Where have *you* been?' Thea asked. 'What was that car?'

'Police,' said Janina shortly. 'They kept me too long. Simon too.'

'Oh?'

'They have kept him still there. Questions about Bunny.' Too late, she lowered her voice, hoping to avoid Nicky hearing what she said.

'Mummy?' he mumbled, still sleepy. 'Is Mummy coming?'

'No, darling,' Janina told him. 'But soon we can go and get Benjamin, and we can have some sandwiches and cake, and watch one of your DVDs.'

'With Daddy?'

'Perhaps.'

Thea was profoundly impressed by this scene. Janina's calm tone seemed to be pitched precisely right, the stress on normal schedules and routines designed to reassure a confused child. She took a step back, feeling her own work was done. 'I'll be going, then,' she said.

Janina did not turn round, but said over her shoulder, 'Thank you very much. You have been wonderful. I don't understand about the church, but it doesn't matter now.'

Without warning, Thea felt her throat constrict, and her eyes grow hot. She was going to cry if she didn't get away quickly – and that was sure to be the wrong thing to do in front of Nicky. The sadness of it all could not be ignored, but he needed the adults to maintain some equilibrium. 'Oh, I phoned the school,' she remembered to say, in a thick voice. 'They'll be trying to get hold of Simon. You might call them and say there's no need to worry.'

'Yes, I will. Thank you,' said Janina softly. It was impossible to know what she was thinking, as she gently stroked Nicky's hand. 'No need to worry,' she repeated, in a crooning voice.

Hepzie had been exploring in the kitchen, but reappeared at Thea's call. They walked back to the car, over increasingly sodden ground, and drove back to Lucy's Barn, all thought of shopping or exploring quite abandoned. The track down to the barn still had vestigial snow along the sides, but it was not difficult to manoeuvre the car over the wet ground, suddenly soft and yielding where before it had been treacherously icy.

She thought about Janina, and her volatile temper, remembering the savage criticisms of Bunny at their first encounter. Was it too much of a leap to suspect that Bunny's death had been brought about by the au pair? Given her profound solicitude for Nicky, it seemed very unlikely. Except...perhaps Janina believed herself to be a big improvement on the children's natural mother. Perhaps she saw herself as a better mate for Simon, too. Bunny had clearly been a part-time mother, but Thea knew better than to draw from that any conclusions concerning Bunny's relationship with the boys. They probably worshipped her, and treasured every second spent in her company. Images of Princess Diana and her sons intruded, although with no obvious insight. As far as she knew, Diana had been a fairly useless mother, the princes left to nannies and less prominent relatives. But she knew better than to judge such matters. Families were by definition inscrutable. Things were seldom as they seemed. All she could think was that if Janina and Simon had conspired to kill Bunny, and if they were caught and imprisoned, that would be far more desperate news for

Nicky and Ben than she cared to imagine. So desperate that she, Thea, wondered whether she might be tempted to conceal any evidence against them, if pushed into a situation where she had to choose. She liked Simon and admired Janina, and found herself wanting everything to go well for them and the two little boys in their care.

Chapter Eighteen

She was hungry. Jimmy would need to go out. She ought to check the roofs and gutters possibly damaged by the weight of snow. There was plenty to do, and with the sudden accessibility opened up by the disappearance of the snow, she could walk the dog as far as she liked. The air had lost its bitter chill and was back to how it had been two weeks earlier – thick enveloping clouds sucking away the light.

She calculated, with a little shock, that it was already 17th January. It seemed impossible that she had passed such a chunk of the month at the barn, with only two weeks and two days still to go. She tried to imagine how she would look back on this record-breaking long stint, with the snow and the sadness of the bodies left to freeze outdoors. Tempting fate, she admonished herself. It was far from over yet, and it was impossible to predict what would happen next. She would remember the magical little church merely as a backdrop to the unhappy discovery of a shivering child seeking his dead friend. She would remember the witless Jimmy as another figure of misery, abandoned by those who should have protected him. But she might also remember the sweet little rabbits, born so surprisingly in the middle of winter. The soft warmth of them in their impossibly cosy nest, demonstrating that it was possible to remain safe and oblivious, so long as your mother followed the rules that instinct ordained.

Hepzie had been cheated of a decent walk by the events of the morning, and this, combined with the sudden liberation of the weather, sent Thea outside again, as soon as she had given herself some lunch and tended to Jimmy. For a change of scene she turned left, down the incline to Old Kate's premises, where she vaguely hoped for a chance to download the events of the morning.

The yard gave an impression of hard work and organisation, with a great tumbling stack of root vegetables the first thing she noticed. The objects were more or less spherical in shape, piled into a three-sided compound, from which they were escaping and spreading a few feet onto the concrete yard in front of the stack. 'Mangel worzels,' Thea murmured to herself, with a smile. She went to gather one up for closer inspection. It struck her as entirely alien – she had no concept of how it would taste, or any method by which it needed to be processed for consumption. There were ridges and knobs all over it, unlike a turnip or a swede, which she might have recognised. She sniffed at it, but could only detect the smell of damp soil, with all its unsettling associations.

'Caint eat that, my lovey,' came a husky male voice from behind her. 'Not 'less you'm starving, anyhow.'

This had to be Kate's old father, Thea remembered, as she met the rheumy gaze of a very old man. He wore rubber boots and a tweed jacket that looked too big for him. 'Hello,' she said.

'House-sitter,' he nodded. 'And dog.'

'That's right. I was hoping to meet you.'

He cocked his head and treated her to a searching gaze through tiny deep-set eyes. 'Were you, now?' he said. 'And why should that be?'

'I like to meet people when I'm house-sitting. It gets lonely otherwise. And boring.'

'Hmm.' She thought she detected a twinkle, a glint of amusement at the follies of people who had not yet reached half his age. Not for the first time, she found herself wondering how it must be to achieve such an accumulation of years. Surely it had to be burdensome to the point of torment? The physical weaknesses and failings, the loss of independence – all the usual clichés swarmed in on her. But this old man looked contented enough, at least at first glance.

'The snow's going, then,' she said foolishly.

'It'll be back again yet, though,' he said. 'Reminds me of '47. Lasted till March that year, it did.'

'So I gather. But the world's got warmer since then. I must admit I've had enough of it for one year.'

'Doubt it'll mind what you think, all the same.'

Ouch! 'That's true,' she smiled. 'Well…I was wondering whether Kate might be around?'

'Working,' he said shortly. 'Busy time. Using the chance of the thaw to get some patching done.' As he spoke, a loud hammering filled the air, and Thea looked upward towards its source. Kate was kneeling on the roof of a large barn, the far side of the yard. It looked alarmingly high.

'Gosh!' she said. 'Is she safe up there?'

'Not fallen off yet,' the careless father observed. 'Always been a good climber, that girl has.'

All Thea's instincts were to go and help – to hold a ladder, or pass nails up as required. 'What's she doing?'

'Fixing a hole where the snow broke through. If the hay gets wet it'll be no use. Wasted.' He shook his head. 'Naught worse than wasted hay.'

The banging persisted, and Thea could see the woman wielding the hammer with impressive vigour. Moving closer, she understood that the barn beneath was more than half full of large hay bales, and that if Kate were unlucky enough to fall through, she would have a soft landing. The roof was comprised of sheets of galvanised iron, some of them looking rather rusty around the edges. From where she stood she could not see Kate clearly, but could only assume that she had somehow carried a replacement sheet up a ladder and was using it to patch a hole. Such competence filled her with admiration and she waited for a chance to say so.

With a final flurry of hammering, Kate withdrew, crawling backwards to where there must have been a ladder. She had ignored Thea's presence throughout, despite it being obvious that she was there. Kate had almost certainly heard the conversation between Thea and her father, as she hoisted her iron patch up a high ladder.

'I could have helped you,' Thea said, as Kate finally reappeared on firm ground. 'I make a rather good assistant.'

'Best working on my own,' said the farmer shortly. 'Quicker, generally.'

Ouch again, thought Thea. 'Well, I must say I'm very impressed.'

'Why?'

'Having such a head for heights,' said Thea quickly. 'I'd have been terrified.'

Kate shrugged, and looked towards her father. 'Dad...you need to get back in the house. I'll be in for tea soon.'

The old man made a sound like a low growl. Had his daughter just humiliated him by highlighting the reversal of roles between them? For how long had he been confined to domestic duties while Kate wielded hammers and drove tractors and made stacks of alien vegetables? Kate heard the unspoken question, and said, 'He's had pneumonia for most of the winter, and isn't meant to be out. It's the devil's own job to find him something to do, mark you. Making a pot of tea is about his limit. Isn't it, you old pest?' she added, with an exasperated grin.

So that was all right, Thea concluded. They loved each other, just as a father and daughter should. She thought of her own father, recently deceased, and felt a pang.

Then she thought of Bunny Newby, who would never know the love of a grown-up son, and a complicated grief seized her.

'Did you hear about Bunny, the mother of those two little boys?' she said. 'I suppose you must have known her.'

Kate grabbed her arm and shook it violently. 'Be quiet!' she hissed. 'Mind what you say.'

But it was too late. The old man had heard and was visibly crumpling. 'Is it true?' he croaked. 'Kate, you told me it wouldn't be her. You *promised* me.'

Kate rolled her eyes skywards, and shook Thea again. 'See what you've done,' she snarled. 'Bloody hell.'

'But... But he would have found out eventually,' she defended. Then she turned towards the old man, reaching out a hand to him. 'But I'm terribly sorry if I said the wrong thing – I mean, who was she to you?'

'My wife's daughter,' said the old man softly. 'Beatrice was my stepdaughter.'

Thea struggled to grasp the chronology – Bunny

surely had to be ten or fifteen years junior to Kate. So Kate's mother must have taken chronological precedence over Bunny's in the old man's life. Confused alternative scenarios flickered through her mind, whereby Bunny was born to another man whilst her mother was married to the one standing here in the yard – but the primary thought was that her image of Bunny failed utterly to cohere with life on this farm, in any shape or form.

'I knew, anyway,' continued the old man. 'I knew when you said the telly was playing up, and when you made such noise in the news on the wireless. Dropping that pan,' he stared accusingly at Kate. 'Think I'm daft, don't you?'

'Did they give her name out, then?' Thea asked. 'When did they do that?'

Kate shook her head irritably. 'No, they didn't. But I didn't want him worrying.'

'So how did you know who it was?'

'And just who might you be, to ask so many questions? What business is it of yours?'

'I'm sorry.' Thea could hardly deny the justice of the question. She must seem outrageously nosy and intrusive. 'But I have met the family, and I'm dreadfully upset about those poor little boys.'

'Hm. Me too,' muttered Kate, still eyeing her father with concern. 'Dad? Come indoors and we'll talk about it.'

'She was *killed*. Isn't that what they said? A woman

killed at the weekend, in the snow. Poor little fool. She might have been stupid, but nobody deserves that.'

Thea's eyebrows rose and she threw Kate a look of wordless enquiry. Kate shook her head impatiently. 'It's not like it sounds. He's no blood relative of hers. Hadn't even seen the woman for a year or more.' She gave her father a fierce look. 'Don't you go all soft on me, you hear? She was nothing to you – not really.'

'But the boys,' Thea persisted. 'Wouldn't they have loved to come here, and get to know their… stepgrandad? I mean, they live barely a mile away, for heaven's sake.'

'They came,' muttered the old man. 'George brought them.'

George? Thea's insides began to churn. This was beginning to sound alarming. If George had secretly brought Nicky and Ben to the farm, without the knowledge of their parents, then something wasn't right. Besides…how did you ensure that a four-year-old kept it quiet? Nicky was too young to understand about secrets and things you shouldn't say. Unless the au pair was part of the conspiracy, and somehow an alternative story had been created, to make Bunny think the child was describing something else.

Her mind raced through all this, as she looked from father to daughter and back again. 'I'm sorry,' she said feebly. 'I shouldn't interfere.'

'Bit late for that,' said Kate.

Thea knew when she'd outstayed her welcome, and calling her dog from where it was nosing after rodents in the heap of beets, she turned back towards Lucy's Barn.

As had happened before, Thea found herself wondering whether she was ahead of the police investigation, or behind it, or simply running along a parallel track. The clear fact was that there had been no police visit to Kate and her father, which suggested that their relationship to the murder victim had not yet emerged. And until it did, there was little likelihood of the police discovering that the connection was closer than might first appear.

Carefully, she rehearsed a possible conversation with DS Gladwin in which she passed on the information she had just gleaned. Who, if anyone, would she be betraying? Janina emerged as the most probable name, and that depended on a lot of unfounded supposition on Thea's part. It was perfectly likely that Simon had known about the visits to the farm, but kept it from Bunny, due to some long-founded animosity between her and her stepfather. So...would it make any difference what she did? If ancient feuds between the old farmer's two wives emerged into the light, so what?

So perhaps Kate herself would be put under the spotlight. If the stepsisters had not been speaking, and yet the children had been visiting the farm, did that not suggest a possible motive for killing Bunny? Kate herself showed no sign of having any offspring of her own – perhaps these were the only grandchildren and therefore in line to inherit the farm. Plainly there had been some kind of conspiracy going on behind Bunny's back, if only a very small and innocent one.

And what about Simon? He was becoming increasingly enigmatic. His brother had been called on for support in the initial shock of losing Bunny; Janina was his stalwart deputy where the children were concerned, while he worked all kinds of unsocial hours at his smart hotel. Did Bunny work because she thought it preferable to being at home with young children, or because she earned irresistibly good money? What did she and Simon actually want out of life? Thea had found it helpful at times to ask this question, when tracing out the past histories of the people she encountered in these villages. Sometimes it was easier to answer about somebody she had only just met – their goals and obsessions were often nakedly apparent. But with Simon Newby, she was stumped.

The afternoon tasks were upon her, and she sloshed across the donkey's paddock, melted snow creating squelchy indentations with every step. There was water everywhere, on surfaces both horizontal and vertical. It dripped from the trees and trickled down fence posts. The donkey came out to greet her, his ears pricked forward, his eyes bright. 'Good afternoon, Donk,' Thea trilled at him, reaching out to stroke the soft nose. 'This weather more to your liking, then?'

She examined the abrasion on his chest, which seemed to be healing nicely. She resigned herself to never knowing exactly what had caused it. It was possible that he had slipped over in the snow and caught himself on barbed wire or a sharp stick, although such an accident was difficult to envisage. It was more of a denial of the real probability than a genuine hypothesis, since George had crossed this paddock during Friday night, and had died just over the fence. Had the donkey witnessed this final trek through the snow? Had the man's last act been to pause and fondle this velvet nose, just as she was doing now? If the donkey had brayed, would Thea have heard him, and got up and discovered the man in time to avert his suicide?

If...if...never a useful word, and one she consciously fought to avoid as much as possible. 'If' could lead to defensive living on a grand scale. *If I let my daughter go out with that boy and he has a drink, he could smash up the car and kill her. If I don't put away a hundred pounds a month in high-performance shares, I won't have anything to live on when I'm old.* In Thea's experience, the effort of trying to predict and thus avoid the worst-case scenario led nowhere. Things happened that you could never have foreseen. Your precious savings evaporated under severe mismanagement by the banks. Your daughter ran away from home because you were impossibly repressive. Better by far to expect the best, and let the *ifs* look after themselves.

It was an outlook you devised in early infancy, she had concluded. Her brother Damien regarded her as almost criminally feckless in her refusal to worry about the future. He had, it seemed, listened to his mother's worries and resistance to risk from his earliest days and accepted her world view as right for him. Thea, on the other hand, had adopted her father's trusting approach. The other two siblings, Emily and Jocelyn, had constructed their own variations on the theme. And once established, it was never going to change. That, Thea sometimes thought, was the true tragedy of the human condition.

Chapter Nineteen

Gladwin was turning out to be something of a mind-reader. Her car splashed down the track at half past three that afternoon, just as Thea was kicking off her boots and thinking about a large mug of strong tea.

'Brilliant timing!' she applauded. 'On your own?'

The detective nodded. 'Not too early for tea, I hope?'

Thea laughed, finding herself unreservedly glad of the visit. 'Follow me,' she said.

The two women settled down in the kitchen, the spaniel under the table at their feet. 'George,' said DS Gladwin firmly. 'I want to talk about George.'

'Me too,' Thea nodded. 'Very much so.'

The post-mortem had failed to find any suspicious cause of death, apart from the confirmation that the body had been moved some hours after he'd died. Calculations had been made on the basis of low temperatures, the effects of alcohol, and George's low proportion of body fat. 'Skinny as a rake,' said Gladwin, with a pitying sigh. But there had been no wild guesses as to the exact time of death. 'If you hadn't found him, we'd never even have managed to pin it down to a given day,' said Gladwin.

'Does it matter?'

The other woman shrugged. 'Everything matters,' she said. 'And it would be extremely useful to know whether he died before or after Mrs Newby.'

'Oh?' Thea frowned. 'But surely she was *ages* later?' She tried to remember the sequence of events. 'She wasn't found until Sunday, was she?'

'Right. The operative word being *found*. We think she was there for two days or more. She was well covered with snow.'

'When was she last seen alive?'

'Thursday morning.'

'My God! Hadn't she phoned her family since then? Weren't they *worried* about her?' Then she remembered. 'But she did send a text. That was Saturday morning, I think. Benjamin said something about it. She sent a text to say she couldn't be there, and Ben was sarcastic because Nicky couldn't read it.'

'Anybody can send a text,' said Gladwin, with an air of having uttered something significant.

'Would they know if it was from her phone?'

'Probably. Most people have caller ID come up automatically.'

'Then someone took her phone, after she was dead?'

Gladwin exhaled with exaggerated patience. 'If she was dead by the time the text was sent, and if it was sent from her phone, then yes.'

'Sorry,' said Thea. 'I'm being obvious, aren't I?'

'Not really. It helps to talk it through.'

'But could Bunny still have been alive on Saturday? Could she have sent the text herself?'

'It seems not.'

'Can you tell me exactly how she died?' She knew she was pushing the limits of Gladwin's easy goodwill and comradeship. She had already heard a lot more than she expected.

'Blows to the head with something heavy. It's not entirely clear-cut, which is nothing new.' She sighed. 'Unless someone's shot point-blank through the back of the head, there's generally scope for alternative explanations.'

Thea sighed in sympathy. 'Tell me about it,' she said feelingly, thinking of a recent experience of her own. 'But can you tell whether she died in the place where she was found?'

'Near enough. The pooling of the blood shows she didn't lie anywhere else for any length of time. All the snow under her had melted, so she would have been warm when put there.'

'Have you been interviewing loads of people?'

'We only got a definite ID for her yesterday. Give us a chance. But yes, a few. They're ongoing as we speak. I've seen a handful of the interview reports.'

'And...?'

'She was a law unto herself, off around the country on her campaigns, meeting clients, selling ideas. Whatever it is that advertising people do. She worked her socks off – everyone agrees about that. Made good money, which is amazing in itself, these days.'

'Did people *like* her?' Thea wondered.

'Admired. Envied. Were intimidated by. One or two disapproved.'

'Like Janina,' said Thea without thinking.

'Oh? You think she disapproved of her employer?'

'Well, yes. I don't know how deep it went, but she didn't seem to have much regard for her. I met her two Sundays ago, outside the church, and she was full of how stupid Bunny had been to pursue such a useless career when she could be looking after her own kids. Something like that, anyway.'

'She told us that she had great respect for both her employers. That it was a model family, fully functional and happy in every way.'

'Hmm,' said Thea. 'And she had a best friend – Philippa something. Have you spoken to her?'

'Lives in Stow with a bloke twelve years younger. Children taken on by a stepmother.'

'I'm impressed,' said Thea.

'Don't be,' said Gladwin. 'She approached us. She has theories. Which brings us back to George Jewell,' said Gladwin.

'Does it?'

'A lot of quite unsavoury unfounded ideas about him, in fact.'

'Surely not.' Thea was shocked. 'Those little boys were very fond of him – they went looking for him. People saw him with them. He took them for walks.'

'Oh?'

Thea chose that moment to tell her about the visits to Kate and the stepfather of the boys, without Bunny's knowledge or consent. Then, for good measure, she described her encounter with Nicky in the church. 'So what?' she added when she'd finished. 'I think it sounds rather nice that George took such an interest in them.'

'You would,' said Gladwin with a shrewd look. 'You're living out of your time, Thea Osborne – you do realise that, I hope?'

'No I'm not.' She felt surprisingly annoyed at the accusation. 'It isn't old-fashioned to trust people and believe the best of them. It's you police people who've put everybody against each other and sown suspicion on all sides. All this talk of crime and security and the need for everybody to be surveilled – or whatever the word is – every minute of the day. It's all rubbish. People are the same as they've always been, and you need to just let them get on with their lives in their own ways.'

'Phew!' Gladwin rocked back in her chair, exaggeratedly. 'Where did that come from?'

Thea took a deep breath. 'It's something I feel strongly about,' she muttered. 'The only thing wrong with this country is the spineless way we've let it turn into a police state.'

'Steady on.' Gladwin's eyes were wider, her thin nose sharper. 'No way is this a police state. That really is rubbish.'

'It isn't far off. Anyway, what were you going to say about George?'

'I wasn't going to say anything. We have no reason to think he was doing anything wrong. As you say, the kids loved him. They'd never have felt like that if there'd been any funny business.'

'Right,' said Thea, feeling as if she'd somehow tilted at the wrong windmill. 'Good.'

'But it's not that simple. He has a police record – vagrancy, disturbing the peace, getting on the wrong side of neighbours. Treated with suspicion everywhere he goes.'

Thea frowned. 'A scapegoat,' she summarised.

Gladwin met her eyes. 'In the old-fashioned sense of the word, yes. The outsider, shouldering all the guilt and shame of the community. Unfortunately, there are members of my team who see this sort of thing differently. *No smoke without fire*, they say. *A lone man like that, maybe not quite right in the head, stands to reason he's got something to hide.*' She put on a growly voice to quote her colleagues' remarks.

'So you think he killed himself because people were being horrid to him?'

'It's a thought. If you'd heard that Philippa woman, you'd understand.'

There was a short silence, during which Thea wondered about the cruelty of village life, and the undercurrents she was having difficulty in ignoring.

Gladwin spoke first. 'How much contact have you had with Janina? How frank do you feel she's been with you?'

Thea had to think about it. 'I've seen her four times in total. First time was outside the church. Then I met her in the road and went to Nicky's party. Then she came here at the same time as Kate, and they talked to each other, mostly, while I was outside. Then yesterday, when I found Nicky and took him home. She always seems quite open and friendly. I didn't get any impression that she was hiding anything or worried. She was cross, the first time, and there's a kind of cynicism about her – an air of knowing better than other people. She is very highly educated, isn't she? She must feel a bit demeaned, doing what she does. I don't expect she gets the recognition she deserves.'

'Except by you,' said Gladwin, still in shrewd mode.

Thea brushed this aside. 'And I think she liked George,' she added, remembering the fresh news of that morning. 'She must have done, to go along with him taking the boys to the farm.'

'Yes, I want to come back to that. Who are these people?'

'She's called Kate. I don't know the surname. Her

father is Bunny's stepfather. Second wife must have already got her when she married him. Doesn't sound as if she and Kate had any time for each other.'

'And they live just down the track from here?'

'Right. This used to be their barn.'

'Bloody hell,' Gladwin groaned. 'How are we meant to keep track of these convoluted families? There isn't even a proper computer program for it. We've got names for both her parents, of course, but not how they connect to everybody in the area.'

Thea was reminded of the earlier murder inquiry, in Temple Guiting, where the complications of families formed a background that confused everybody. Gladwin had sorted that one out ahead of everyone else. 'You could go and see him – he's quite a character.'

'Sounds as if I should, if there's a George connection. Well done, you,' she smiled. 'Never miss a trick, do you?'

It was a barbed accolade, which Thea did not much like. 'I just get bored all on my own, and go out to find people to chat with, that's all.'

'OK, OK.' Gladwin held up her hands in surrender. 'I'm not knocking it. I don't know where we'd be without you. Is that better?'

Thea drained her tepid mug of tea and rubbed her shoeless foot against the soft side of her dog. 'So why did he kill himself?' she asked. 'What made him so desperate that he did that?'

'Precisely,' nodded Gladwin. 'That's what I have to find out.'

Thea half expected that to be an end of it, the detective's valuable time consumed, along with the tea. Instead there was a portentous pause, which threatened to take them into far deeper waters.

'Do you have any idea what it's like to freeze to death?' asked Gladwin.

'I suppose I assumed it must be fairly pleasant, as methods of suicide go. You just fall asleep and never wake up.'

'Oh yes...that's the easy part. But you don't just sit down in the snow and fall asleep. You get very, very cold first. It makes the marrow in your bones scream with pain. It always finds some part of you to attack – the long thigh bones are a favourite. Or the feet. Your body begins to suspect what it is you're planning to do, and it resists. It fights and pleads and *hurts*. You've got to really mean it, to force yourself to stay there and let the cold win the fight. It helps to take sleeping pills or something of that sort. Alcohol might dull the agony a bit, for a while, but not as much as people think. You know...it makes me furious, the way people pretend that there are painless ways to kill yourself. Suicide is, by definition, an expression of immense suffering.'

This time it was Thea who rocked back. 'Good God,' she murmured. 'You really know about this stuff, don't you.'

'I grew up in Cumbria. I know about cold,' was the brief reply.

'And about suicide,' said Thea, insightfully.

'Right. My sister lay down in front of the Kendal to Carlisle express. That was probably painless, too, once the train arrived. But can you even begin to imagine those endless minutes beforehand?'

Thea shuddered. 'I'm not going to try,' she said.

'No. But sometimes I find I have no choice. And when there's a suicide involved in my caseload, I need to stop and think about it a bit more than some others on my team. I try to find out just what it was that was so unbearable in that person's life, and why they've chosen this particular moment.'

'In George's case, maybe he was just waiting for the right weather. Maybe he'd planned it ages ago and needed a freezing cold night to put it into action.'

Again Gladwin surprised her. Instead of the anticipated disdainful snort, she inclined her head in agreement. 'That's entirely possible,' she said. 'And if it wasn't for the other death, I might have accepted it as the most likely answer. As it is...well, let's say that nobody in the police really believes in coincidence.'

The silence that followed was filled with the same sort of melancholy acceptance of the darker side of life that Thea had experienced with Lucy, as they'd contemplated the fate of the pitiful Jimmy. Life could go so *wrong*: for no reason, people would opt for the callous act, creating ripples of damage that spread further than anyone might have predicted. She wondered why Gladwin's sister had reached such a desperate point; why Jimmy's people had abandoned him; why George Jewell should have been so alone and dispossessed.

'But somebody moved the body,' she remembered, with a leap of logic born of her incorrigible optimism. 'Somebody couldn't bear for him to be left out in the snow like that.'

Gladwin gave her a look from under her brows, sceptical, questioning. 'Or they were trying to hide the evidence,' she suggested.

'What evidence? If it was a suicide, why would anybody be looking for any evidence? And why would they leave such obvious tracks in the snow, if they wanted it all to be hidden?'

'You think it was a caring act, then?' It seemed that this interpretation had not occurred to the senior detective. 'Something essentially innocent?'

'Well, I suppose I did, until now. Are you thinking it might be the same person who killed Bunny?'

'I try not to theorise,' said Gladwin primly. 'We're still at the stage of assembling facts.'

It felt like a full stop. Whatever the woman had wanted, it seemed she had found it. She began to look round for her coat, and glance outside at the darkening sky. 'Strange how impossible it is to imagine long summer evenings, isn't it? And yet it's only a few months ago. I don't think I'll ever really get to grips with the changing seasons and the way it all happens so *fast*.'

Thea nodded in full agreement, before another logical leap took place in her mind. 'Do you know Phil's new woman?' she asked. Perhaps it was the idea of change, the need to keep up, and accept whatever came next. 'I can't remember her name. Jessica did tell me.'

'Laura. Yes, I know her. She's a really nice woman. I think she'll be very good for him.'

The shock was not so much in the words as in their effect on her insides. If Gladwin had produced a gun and pointed it at her, she couldn't have been more stunned. Did she still care about Phil that much, then? Enough for this surge of jealous rage to grip her, quickly followed by a return of the chilly fear of previous days. She wanted to turn back the clock by a year or so, when they were easy and happy together, and there had never been the slightest chance that she, Thea Osborne, would ever do anything to jeopardise the comfortable relationship she and Phil had had.

'Oh, dear,' she said weakly.

'Why? Don't you want him to be happy?' The detective's look was full of challenge – challenge to speak the truth and avoid the usual foolish female games.

'I don't want him to be miserable. I think that's as far as I can go, just for now.'

'I'm sorry, Thea, but I did see you two together, remember. You weren't right for each other. I shouldn't say it, but Phil's not strong enough for you. Laura wants something different – something you hardly even believe exists.'

'And what's that?'

Gladwin shook her head, with a little laugh. 'I'm not sure I can put a word to it.'

'Try,' Thea insisted.

'Couplehood. Something like that. Nothing very surprising – it's what all men want.'

'But that's what I had with Carl,' Thea objected. 'Why do you say I don't believe in it? Of course I do.'

'But you never wanted it with Phil, and he understood that only too well. He wanted it and you didn't. End of story.'

The sense of betrayal was acute. 'But he said he didn't,' she wailed.

'Because he knew that's what you wanted to hear,' said Gladwin, patting her hand.

Chapter Twenty

It was a bad time to be left alone with turbulent thoughts of suicide, abandonment, cruelty and failed relationships. Even Thea's tendency to see the bright side was inadequate to the challenge of such an overwhelming onslaught. She had to get herself through another endless evening before she could decently give up and go to bed. It was these evenings that would drive her to find another source of income, she feared. They could be alternately tedious, depressing or frightening. The burden of keeping a house and its contents safe grew heaviest at the end of the day. If it hadn't been for the dogs, she wasn't sure she could have borne it.

As it was, the needs of Jimmy and, to a lesser degree, Hepzie, gave her a focus. The lurcher continued to shiver, but the conservatory was no longer worryingly cold. He ate a substantial supper, and permitted the spaniel to lie down with him while

Thea cleaned up the kitchen and ran a quick inventory
of the contents of the fridge and freezer. She had
the radio tuned to Classic FM, for a change, and a
bracing aria from *La Bohème* belted out, filling the
barn with the manageable emotions of other people
long ago and far away. Music had never had a very
high rating in Thea's list of pleasures, apart from a
few obligatory teen years. But there were times when
it could grip her and provide a useful diversion. She
found it blanked out all conscious thought, much as
swimming in a stormy sea might do. You simply let
some outside force take you where it wanted, and
relinquished all pretence of being in control. It didn't
stir her emotions as she knew happened for some
people, but it created its own shapes and colours,
that had nothing to do with the here and now of her
personal preoccupations.

Then the phone rang, barely audible beneath the
warblings of Mimi and Rodolfo. Muting the radio,
Thea heard her daughter's voice. 'Mum? Can you hear
me? What's that awful noise?'

'Opera.'

'Good God...where on earth are you?'

'The same place I've been for the past two weeks. I'm
listening to Classic FM.'

'Nice,' said Jessica with dubious irony. 'So you're
OK, then?'

'Yes thanks. Why wouldn't I be?'

She could hear her daughter's sigh, loud and clear.

'No reason, except you seem to be in a funny mood these days. At least the snow's melted. That must make it easier, I imagine?'

'The old man on the next farm says it'll come back. He seems to think it's going to snow until March.'

'I expect he's bonkers.'

'It's possible.'

'Meanwhile, you can get your car in and out, and there won't be any scary footprints. That has to be an improvement.'

'You're right. It's all much better now.'

'You don't really *sound* better.'

Thea made a major effort. 'I'm fine, Jess. I was just getting carried away by the music when you phoned. I can't think of anything to say.'

'You're not helping Sonia Gladwin with her murder, then? I rather thought you would be.'

'She was here earlier on, as it happens. She seems to have everything under control.'

'Really? That's good to know.'

'Have you heard anything to suggest otherwise?'

'No, Mum.' The patience was much exaggerated. 'I keep telling you, I'm in a different region. I don't hear any of the West Midlands stuff.'

'Except the gossip about who's shagging DS Hollis.'

'Oh-h-h, I get it. You're upset about Ms Freckles. Has anybody else said anything?'

'Not really. Gladwin knows her, apparently.'

'And?'

'And she seems to think she'll be a lot better for him than I was.'

'Oh-oh,' said Jessica, with audible embarrassment. 'Honestly, Ma, this isn't really my territory. I hardly know the woman. She seems OK as far as I can see.'

'She sounds wonderful,' said Thea glumly.

'Well, I hate to say it, but—'

'Yes, yes. No need to go on. Too late now, anyway, to start saying you told me so. Besides, I'm not upset at all. Just…adjusting.'

Jessica made an inarticulate sound. Somewhere not far away another person was speaking. There was a muffled exchange before she spoke again to Thea. 'I really phoned about Sunday,' she went on. 'I wondered whether I could come down and spend the day with you. Would that be all right? And…um…I might bring a friend as well. We could go out for lunch, maybe?'

'A *boy* friend?'

'Wait and see,' giggled Jessica.

Sunday was three days away – a length of time in which anything could happen. Thea wondered at her own lack of enthusiasm for the suggestion. 'Well, that sounds very intriguing,' she said. 'And there's plenty here to show you. There's a nest of baby rabbits. They're ever so sweet.'

'Mum, I'm not nine any more, you know. I'm not terribly turned on by baby rabbits.'

'Oh…I thought everybody was, whatever their age.

Well, there's a remarkable church, as well – though Sunday isn't a good day for seeing it, I suppose.'

'You don't have to think of things to show me. We can just sit around and chat, maybe take the dog for a walk. I haven't seen you since Christmas.'

And then only for one day, Thea wanted to add, but stopped herself in time. How quickly one turned into one's own mother, she thought ruefully.

'You're quite right. I'm looking forward to it already. Shall I give you directions?'

She described the track down to Lucy's Barn, and where it turned off the road into Hampnett, thinking how far in the future Sunday suddenly felt.

Jessica rang off distractedly, the other person evidently claiming the bulk of her attention. Thea was left wrestling with her role as mother to an almost-grown-up daughter. It was often following an exchange with Jess that she most missed Carl. He had been a better parent than her, in many ways. He had never ceased to feel and express wonder at the miracle of the creation of life, until Thea had felt ashamed of her resistance to producing more children. Somehow she had found her child less interesting than she ought to have been. Where she could feel profound curiosity about other people and their lives – people in different times and places – she found her own daughter mostly rather predictable. The fact of Jessica did not impinge on her own life in the deep visceral sense that other mothers seemed to feel. It had been a simple biological event, and while she had no problems physically – the feeding and cuddling and protecting; the singing and chatting and joking – Thea never felt that her very identity depended on the little girl. She had been more of a wife than a mother, and to lose Carl rather than Jessica had seemed the larger of the two possible torments. This led to an insidious little thought that she always quashed before it could take root; a stupid fate-tempting thought that no worthy woman would ever entertain for a second. After all, it didn't work like that – you weren't given any choice, and even if you were, it would be impossible to let one survive at the expense of the other.

All of which made her think about Bunny Newby and her apparently poor showing as a mother. Never having met the woman, she could contemplate her death only through its effects on those she *had* met. The consequences of the murderous act were, in any case, arguably more important for her family than for Bunny herself. It was a terrible thing to do, and the idea that the killer was still 'out there' somewhere, in the fields and woods of Hampnett, made her shudder. It was no wonder she felt so scared, in the circumstances. Unlikely as Phil Hollis had always insisted it to be, there really were psychopaths in the world, who enjoyed murdering women, simply because they *were* women. An undefended female house-sitter in a remote spot might very credibly be regarded as a likely victim.

It had, after all, taken place horribly close to the barn. She should lock the doors and keep her phone within reach, and trust no one.

The house phone rang while she was in the middle of frightening herself with dark thoughts. She grabbed it quickly, before she could further scare herself with predictions as to who it might be. Even a phone call could be threatening and fearful, after all.

It was Lucy, sounding so cheerful that Thea suspected she might be slightly tipsy. 'Everything OK?' she trilled. 'Has it stopped snowing?'

'Yes and yes,' Thea replied shortly.

'And?'

'And there have been two people dead found in the fields just over the hill.' Her earlier determination to shield her employer from bad news had evaporated, as she envisaged Lucy's carefree sojourn in the sun. There was an unfairness to it that she found hard to swallow.

'What? Who?'

'The first one was a man called George Jewell, which looks like suicide – and the second's his neighbour, Bunny Newby. She was definitely murdered.' There was relish in this stark telling, this dumping of ghastly news. She should have done it sooner.

Lucy was gratifyingly appalled. 'Good God! What on earth happened to them?'

'It's under police investigation,' said Thea stiffly. 'Actually, I found George, over a week ago. I didn't say anything about it last time you rang, but since then it's all got a bit more...stressful.'

'*You* found him? When?'

'Last Friday. The second day of the snow.'

'And Bunny, did you say? Bloody Bunny.'

'Right.'

'She's Kate's stepsister. George was friendly with her boys. I suppose they are neighbours, now you mention it. Funny I never thought of them like that. George is – was – such a recluse. Damn it, I don't know what I'm burbling about. I can't take it in. You poor thing! No wonder you sound so...disenchanted.'

The word was so entirely apt that Thea's mood instantly lifted. She remembered that she liked Lucy and had willingly enabled her to take herself off to the sunshine. 'Jimmy's fine, by the way. I'm sure that's what you called to find out. He got a bit cold one day, but there haven't been any ill effects.'

'Is he still in love with your spaniel?'

'No, not really. She cuddles up to him now and then, but I think they've cooled off a bit. Oh, and one of the rabbits had babies. I tried to tell you about that before, as well.'

'No! Are you sure? I mean...*how?*'

Thea laughed. 'The usual way, I suppose. There are six, in assorted colours, and they seem to be doing very nicely.'

'It must have been that day when I was cleaning them out, and put them all in a box together, for about forty-five seconds. I never saw anything going on, though. Cheeky little beasts.'

'So everything's fine, as far as the barn and all the animals are concerned. The donkey eats everything I give him.'

'I bet he loved the snow, didn't he?'

Thea wasn't sure whether or not this was meant ironically. 'I don't think he did,' she said. 'He didn't come out of his shed for about three days. I had to muck him out.'

'Well, the soft thing. I'd have thought he'd find it fascinating.'

'Not as far as I could tell.'

They both knew there was more – much more – to say about Bunny and her sudden death. Thea was curious to know how well acquainted Lucy had been with her, for one thing, and whether she had any theories as to what could have happened. 'The police never contacted you, then?' she said, already fully aware of the answer. She hadn't told them where Lucy was, and she doubted that they would know who else to ask.

'Certainly not. Why would they worry *me* about it? Obviously *I* didn't kill her. How was it done, by the way? Knife, gun or garotte?'

'Blow to the head, I gather. I'm probably not supposed to tell you, so keep it to yourself.' It was, after all, perfectly possible that Lucy would phone half the people in Hampnett, once this call was finished.

'It'll be that foreign girl, I expect,' said Lucy carelessly.

'I shouldn't think Bunny was very nice to her.'

'So what was she *like*?' Thea burst out before she could stop herself. 'Nobody has said anything about her as a person.' Except Janina, who had labelled her employer as stupid and a rotten mother.

'Gosh – well, I suppose she was typical of her generation and class, if I'm allowed to say that. She did something like business studies at college, and worked her way up the management ladder by mastering the jargon and getting on the right side of the people who mattered. I never thought she was very bright – never caught her having an original thought, anyhow. Actually, she's rather bigoted in a lot of ways. The sort of person who believes everything they read in the *Daily Mail*. Simon's not much better, of course. They seemed pretty well matched, as far as I could tell. She bossed him about, of course, but he never seemed to mind.' She paused. 'Perhaps that's a bit unfair. I think he's a lot *nicer* than her, as a person. She has – had – this awful friend, Philippa, who got her going on all the usual prejudices. Foreign workers, child molesters, people evading their taxes. She can rant for Britain, can Philippa. I always run a mile if I see her coming.'

'So what does she think about Janina?' Thea wondered.

'Oh...probably rationalises that into being OK, because it helps Bunny cope. After all, Philippa managed to unload her kids altogether. Have you come across the sainted Barbara?'

'Once. She was in a bit of a tizzy. Dorothy's got a cold.'

A muted squawk from the other end suggested that Lucy had suddenly realised how long the phone call had become. 'Gosh, I must go. At least it sounds as if you've got plenty to occupy you.'

Her voice contained all the detachment of a woman who had got away, and had no reason to particularly care what cataclysms were taking place back home. So long as her animals were alive, she was content to let everything else go to perdition.

'Yes,' said Thea. 'It's the children who'll suffer, of course,' she could not resist adding.

'Not really,' came the astonishing response. 'She was never there for them. Now if it had been *Simon*, that would be very different. Some women never ought to have kids, and Bunny was one of them.'

Thea's internal defences rose automatically as she heard this judgement. Once or twice she had accused herself of being just such a woman. 'Maybe,' she said coolly.

'At least they're young enough to avoid the worst of the turmoil. I mean…I don't suppose they'll be taken to the funeral or anything of that sort.'

'I don't know.' Thea's mood had darkened again during this exchange, and her opinion of Lucy had similarly changed. She allowed an audible sigh to escape. 'But don't you worry about it. Your dog's fine, and the baby rabbits will be at their most adorable when you get back. Oh...one last thing.'

'Yes?'

'Why do you call your neighbour *Old* Kate? She's not old at all.'

Lucy giggled. 'Oh, that's just my little joke. She's a week older than me, you see. Nobody else uses it. You haven't been calling her that, have you?'

'Not to her face, obviously.' But, yes, in my own head, she added silently. She felt disproportionately cross about the explanation, as if she'd been deliberately misled. 'You and she are friends, then?' she went on.

'Not really. We began well, when I first got there and bought the barn off them, but we don't have much in common, to be honest.'

'Oh. Well, she's been all right with me.'

Lucy seemed increasingly eager to curtail the call. 'Just so long as the weather bucks up by the time I get back, I'll be happy,' she breezed. 'I'm beginning to wish I'd signed up for two months, instead of one. Do you realise it's almost halfway already?'

'Yes,' said Thea. 'I did realise that.'

It had to be the time of year, she assumed, that caused the repeated bouts of self-analysis. That, and the hours of solitude, and the imminence of her birthday. She found herself wondering just how nice a person she really was, and how other people perceived her. Only once or twice in her life had she experienced the blind terror that came with loss of regard from a social group. The first had been at school when she had objected to a collective decision to boycott one teacher's lessons. She had stood alone, stubbornly solitary, and suffered agonies in the process. Some of her fellow pupils had never spoken to her again. The second had been when she and Carl had unwisely joined a local babysitting club, only to discover that there was a branch devoted to wife-swapping. Several of the husbands made no secret of their attraction to her, and she had turned deeply puritanical, telling an assembled group just what she thought of such practices. Pulling moral superiority was never a good idea, she had discovered, and again there had been frosty ostracism from all sides. Her stomach churned as she remembered how frightening it had been to stand alone. Carl had supported her, but he didn't have to meet people in the shops and outside the school gates as she did.

The fear came from a mismatch between the person she knew herself to be, and the one other people thought they saw. It was like Bunny Newby, who had apparently seen herself as a successful businesswoman, adequate wife and even perhaps an acceptable mother. Janina's accusations had implied that her employer was too stupid and blind to understand what she really was. The air of frustration in the au pair surely arose from this failure to make Bunny understand the error of her ways. Not for the first time, Thea wished she had at least met the woman. Getting to know a person after they'd died was a futile exercise – and yet she could not prevent herself from trying.

She had spoken to four very different women that

day. Only two of them had actually known Bunny, and
they seemed in some sort of accord as to her essential
character. But the people who knew her best – Simon
and Janina – had actually told her very little. Was that
because they had conspired between them to kill Bunny?
The situation pointed strongly to that scenario; it was by
far the most obvious solution to the investigation, and it
seemed that the police were acting on that assumption.
But then what about George Jewell? George who had
killed himself, or at least allowed himself to die in the
snow without a struggle. What had brought him to such
a point?

It was time for bed at last, after a day that felt
interminably long, looking back on it. The late TV
weather forecast warned of abrupt falls in temperature,
with resulting ice. All that melted snow outside would
freeze over and transform the world into a skating
rink. Thea sighed and tried to dismiss images of her
car sliding into ditches, and herself slithering across the
yard, trying to carry water to the donkey.

Tomorrow would be Thursday, and Thursdays
were often good. In the illogical way of it, there were
still associations with a school timetable that offered
all her favourite subjects. The memory came back
trailing all the feelings of thirty years ago. Something
about the calm organisation of it all had delighted her
beyond expression. There had been double history
after the morning break, which most pupils had found

outrageous, but which Thea had loved. On Thursdays she had been able to spread herself, immersed in the attempt to transport herself back in time. History for her had always been the ultimate romance, the glimpses of events and people long gone like flashes of paradise or fairyland.

Tomorrow, then, she would seek to assist the admirable Gladwin in her investigations.

Chapter Twenty-One

The forecast had been right, and the first thing that happened when she went out the next day was that she fell over. It was so close to the scene she had imagined the night before that she wondered for a moment whether she might be dreaming. But no – her wrist was hurting where she had landed on it, and she was definitely sitting on a hard concrete surface that was glazed with ice. Hepzie was nuzzling her in concern, while Jimmy, who had been on his way to his toilet patch, merely stood patiently waiting for instructions.

The slippery surface was worse than she had imagined. Ice coated almost everything in sight, making progress even more difficult than it had been in the snow. 'This is ridiculous,' Thea muttered, as she scrambled to her feet, looking around for something to hang on to. The donkey would be waiting for his fodder, likewise the rabbits. She had no choice but to get on with it, sliding her feet over the ground as if wearing skates.

Keeping her balance required great concentration, until she reached the paddock, where the winter grass broke up the ice and made things easier. Hepzie loyally accompanied her, not understanding the difficulty. So what if a foot slithered sideways every now and then?

To get the donkey fed and watered took at least as long as it had on the snowy days. The ground was hostile beneath her feet, frozen into uneven lumps and bumps that threatened to turn her ankle if she didn't take care over every step. It was exhausting and annoying. This was not the life she had imagined for herself, even three years ago. Something had gone wrong somewhere, and she found herself getting cross at this realisation.

But then she went to see the rabbits and her mood changed. This twice-daily visit had become a small treat that she looked forward to more every time. The babies were now fully covered with hair, and she could see their colours clearly: mostly white with patches of bluey-grey, like their mother, but one a delicious meld of black and brown and another that reminded her of butterscotch pudding – brown with hints of ginger. Their dense furry nest was slowly disintegrating as they became more active, making it possible to watch them without disturbance. There were even moments when Thea wondered if she could adopt one of them as her own – until she remembered that she was so often away that the poor thing would need a sitter itself, while she was sitting other people's animals.

The cat was becoming increasingly friendly as the

days passed. Initially very wary of the spaniel, it had kept mostly aloof on the upper surfaces of the furniture. But this morning it had followed Thea outside, and was delicately tiptoeing around the yard before disappearing into the field to the south. Gone for a bit of hunting, Thea supposed, admiring the independence of the creature.

By ten o'clock, she had finished her work, including a thorough clean of the kitchen. Her wrist was still sore from the fall, but it worked normally, and she chose to ignore it. Persistently, ever since she had got out of bed, her thoughts had been on George Jewell and Bunny Newby. She tested every imaginable connection between them that might have led to their deaths within, it seemed, a few hours of each other. They had lived in adjacent houses; George had been friendly with Janina and the boys; and somebody had moved George's body for reasons that remained exasperatingly obscure.

There were too many holes in the story for a thorough analysis. She had not been able to get a close view of how people reacted to the news of a murder, other than Simon and Tony's appearance in Northleach. And, she remembered, Simon and Janina's behaviour on Sunday when George had been found. She paused to rerun that scene, wondering for the first time at the relative calm the two had displayed. Had it been for the sake of the children, or had they in fact already known George was dead? Neither had shown any real sorrow – but she knew that this was often the case. Shock tended to obliterate everything else, for the first few hours. It was as if the truth had to work its way through several layers before it reached a nerve. And then, before that could happen, the news of Bunny's murder must have overlaid all thought of George, especially for Simon.

She wished she knew where exactly Bunny had been found. It was unfair of Gladwin not to share the full facts with her, she felt, when she'd been acknowledged as an important element in the investigation. She knew that modern policing relied more and more heavily on forensics, tracing microscopic clues back to one database or another, pinning down the killer by a relentless scientific process that took a lot of the guesswork out of the whole business. Soon the need for detectives would disappear completely, if the new generation of computer geeks had their way. But in George's case at least, the forensics had to be ambivalent, if not completely useless. Evidence would have melted away along with the snow. Whoever had moved his body had done a fine job of confusing the whole case. George could have been very cleverly murdered, but if so, there was little chance of it ever being proved. But the killing of Bunny had not been especially clever, from the sound of it. Only the presence of the snow had concealed the body for two or three days, where it might otherwise have been found almost immediately. The killer had been lucky, then.

She missed Phil. He was the real gap in the story. If they had still been together, he would have shared the details with her, unable to resist her eager interest, content to allow her into the investigations. Without him, she was just a confused bystander, contributing nothing because she was restricted to the sidelines. And that was a waste. She was sure she could help in some way. Hadn't she unearthed the detail about George taking the children to Old Kate's farm? Wasn't that immensely important in forging a link between the two victims?

Which left her with two options: either shut up, sit back and forget the whole thing – or find a way to get more involved. Obviously there was no contest. How else was she to get through another two weeks in this desolate place?

But how was she to do it? She thought back over earlier experiences, where she had marched boldly up to the door of suspected killers and confronted them with her suspicions. At least, she amended conscientiously, she had *sort of* done that. Generally she had found more circumspect methods of persuading people to admit their guilt. More than once she had been completely wrong in her conclusions, anyway. She had even been tempted to help the guilty person to conceal the truth from the police, now and then. It was no light matter, after all – not a mere puzzle placed before her to while away the time. Murder carried with it a large dose of horror, despair, trauma and fear. It ought not to be something she relished – and yet a part of her responded in just that way. She had discovered a knack in herself which had more to do with an absence of squeamishness than any great desire for justice. And until she arrived in Hampnett, she had believed herself to be unusually fearless. Where most people would dive for cover and block their ears, Thea Osborne had waded into the fray. But ever since that morning last week when she had seen the footprints in the snow, she had been undeniably frightened. From feeling apprehensive and nervous in the first moments in the isolated barn, she had progressed to real gut-wrenching fear. And once one thing had scared her, many others flooded to join it, until the churning in her insides had become almost constant. As soon as one fear had been tackled and allayed, another arose in its place. That too, she believed, was due to Phil. Phil not being there behind her, covering her back, folding her in his arms, laughing at her and listening to her – that made all the difference in the world.

She had made the acquaintance of two households: the Newbys, and Old Kate and her even older father. She tried to visualise her reception at each of these if she paid a social call that morning. The Newbys were in shock and grief at the loss of Bunny – a situation that might work in Thea's favour if she arrived offering practical help and advice. But there was still the unpleasant reality that Janina and Simon might actually have been responsible for Bunny's death. They would, if so, have to pretend to feel sorrow when they had actually got exactly what they wanted. Thea did not wish to be at the receiving end of such deception and betrayal. She would make a rotten detective when it came to this particular family, because she *liked* them. And she hated the idea that the two remaining adults in the lives of Nicky and Benjamin might be incarcerated for a decade or more. Yet again, her bowels spasmed at the prospect of witnessing such complications that could only result in misery.

Kate and her father were busy. All day, every day, there was work to be done. The very briskness of it made Thea feel weak and useless. What would be her reception if she turned up again with no adequate pretext? It was not an appealing idea.

All of which left a blank, until she recalled Tony Newby, the photographer. He who had a cold and was self-employed and lived in Turkdean and might be susceptible to a visit from a friendly female bearing... bearing a basket of calves' foot jelly and fresh figs under a red-chequered cloth. Not quite, but she might be able to construct an offering that would justify paying him a call. After all, his chill was in part her responsibility. She had called him out in the snow on Saturday morning, which was apparently the source of his illness. He'd looked as if he was catching a cold then, now she came to think of it.

She found 'Newby, AJ' in Lucy's telephone book, which gave the name of his house in Turkdean as 'Forsythia Cottage'. Precise location could be left until later. She noted the telephone number and added it to the directory in her mobile. If she couldn't immediately see the cottage when she got to Turkdean, she could phone him for directions then. How simple it was to find people, she mused, even in these paranoid times. There had been previous occasions when she had needed to pay calls on people involved in village conspiracies, without warning, and it had seldom presented any real difficulty.

She remembered being with her father on a drive to Leicestershire, when she had been six or seven. He had often taken just one of his children along for the ride when he had to go on one of his trips. The ostensible purpose had been work related – something wrong with a machine, he would say, vaguely, leaving nobody much the wiser. But this time, he also planned to pay a surprise call on a cousin he hadn't seen for years.

The cousin's name was Lancelot Jones, which helped considerably when it came to finding him – necessary because he had moved house and nobody had thought to keep a note of the new address. All they'd had to do was call in at the post office in the small town they remembered he had gone to, and within moments a full set of instructions had been provided by the delighted woman behind the counter. No hesitation, no suspicions that Dad was a hit man or someone set on long-harboured revenge. Probably the presence of a small girl made a difference. In any case, Lancelot had been happy to see them, and gave them sandwiches with oily fish in them that Thea could never remember without feeling sick.

The Internet had replaced the post office in recent times, but with much the same levels of usefulness. Anybody called Lancelot Jones would almost certainly jump out, with email address, or even a landline phone number. People *wanted* to be found, on the whole – especially if they had a service to offer or something to sell.

And so she finally got herself there. Forsythia Cottage was readily located at the end of a short row of houses; small, neat and set back some way from the road. Without pausing to consider how intrusive her sudden appearance might seem, she walked up the path and rang the doorbell. It was almost eleven in the morning, on a Thursday, and most people would be at work. If Simon hadn't mentioned that Tony was laid up with his chill, she might never have taken such a step.

But it turned out to be justified. The man she remembered from the main street of Northleach, telling her that his sister-in-law had been murdered, was standing in the doorway, the door only partly open, wearing a red dressing gown. His feet were bare. 'What do *you* want?' he said, making no effort to conceal his awareness of who she was and where he had seen her before.

'I heard you were poorly, so I came to see whether

I could do anything for you.' It remained an oddly Victorian notion, even now she was here. 'I would have brought you some calves' foot jelly, if I'd known where to find it.'

He did not laugh, or even smile. 'I don't get it,' he said. 'What am I to you?'

'A distraction,' she flashed back.

Still no smile, but he did roll his eyes in an exaggerated way. 'I see,' he said. 'Well I guess I'll have to let you in.'

The interior of the house was bare of any superfluous decoration. Unlike most dwellings, it seemed larger on the outside than the inside. A main living room evidently served for eating, relaxing and working. Thea sought in vain for displays of the photographer's work. The only area of untidiness was a large computer desk with an expensive-looking A3 printer standing next to it. Catalogues, packs of paper, ink cartridges and several cables formed a small pool of chaos in an otherwise pristine room.

'I'm not especially ill,' he said, as he offered her a place on a cream-coloured two-seater sofa. 'I just didn't think I should go out again in the cold for another day or so. I'm working.'

'Any more police commissions?'

He went very still, and looked away. 'No,' he said. 'I'm not doing that any more.'

'I don't blame you,' she assured him. 'Not when you might have to take pictures of your own dead sister-in-law.'

'They wouldn't have let me, anyway. I'm too closely related.'

'Oh.' Of course, he was effectively part of the Newby household. Hadn't he been taking care of his wretched brother when the news of Bunny's death had emerged? Hadn't she discussed him with Simon? And yet, all along she'd imagined him as detached, on the outside of the intimate circle of the bereaved. This had to be because her first encounter with him had been as a member of a police team – she associated him more with Gladwin and Phil than with the murder victim.

'So...coffee?'

'Thanks,' she nodded, beginning to feel slightly foolish. 'But listen...exactly where was Bunny found, do you know?'

He reared back, chin high, revealing a thin vulnerable throat. He was very pale, she noticed, with long fingers and narrow shoulders. 'What's it to do with you?' he spluttered.

'Well, nothing, officially. But I did find George Jewell's body, and then the detective superintendent came to see me, and I have got rather attached to sweet little Nicky. I just want to help,' she finished weakly.

'I don't know the precise answer anyway,' he said. 'She was hit, I think, and then dumped in a ditch just down the lane from the house.'

Thea's head began to buzz. She had envisaged a spot rather further away. 'You mean somewhere near that clump of trees, where I thought George might have gone?'

'So it seems. There's a path that runs the other side of the trees from where you're staying. It connects with the road they live in. The snow had covered her almost completely, as I understand it.' He spoke hoarsely, steadfastly avoiding Thea's gaze.

'Did she die before or after George? That seems really important, don't you think?'

He shrugged tightly, edging slowly towards a door she assumed led to the kitchen. 'Not my problem,' he said. 'They're both dead – isn't that enough?'

'Did you know George?'

'Of course. He lived next door to my brother.'

'Yes, I know he did. I've been in the house, remember.'

'Have you?' He frowned at her.

'Yes,' she said with patient emphasis. 'I followed the trail back from where I saw him in the snow, and it led to his house.'

The adam's apple in Tony's throat bobbed and dipped as he digested this information. 'Oh,' he said, still trying to escape to the kitchen. 'Nobody told me that.'

She frowned, trying to untangle who knew what, and whether she could trust Tony to be telling the truth.

'That seems quite odd,' she said. 'After all, you must have been there since they found Bunny. You were with Simon on Tuesday in Northleach.'

'Be quiet,' he ordered her fiercely. 'Stop *telling* me

things. Isn't this bloody mess bad enough without some ghoulish little house-sitter making everything worse?'

It was an accusation she had heard before, and it always touched a nerve. She said nothing more as he finally got out of the room and started noisily to make coffee. *At least he's not so angry he's throwing me out without a drink*, she thought ruefully. She might be a ghoulish little house-sitter – it was the *little* that rankled most sorely – but he seemed prepared to endure her presence for a while longer.

She always hoped that she could resolve nagging questions simply by asking people to supply the answers, and was generally disappointed. Either somebody volunteered an important fact without prompting, or they told lies. Or they just remained silent and tried to keep out of her way. It made her tired to realise that she would have to be devious and clever with this man if he was to disclose pertinent details – assuming he knew some. Perhaps he was a mere onlooker with a cold and a very ordinary horror of death, violent or otherwise.

Except he had applied for the position of police photographer, and that suggested a stronger stomach than that possessed by an ordinary person. So maybe he was lying, after all.

He came back five minutes later with two mugs of instant coffee. She was surprised by the speed, and the downmarket beverage. Should she detect a subtle insult in his failure to make something better? She sipped it with a display of satisfaction, and sat back on the sofa.

'Did you believe me?' she asked, chattily. 'On Friday morning? What did they say about me afterwards?'

'I...I couldn't see why you'd invent such a story. But I thought you'd got it wrong – that he was only sleeping or unconscious, not dead. The others said the same.'

'They had to believe that, didn't they – to justify not carrying out a proper search for him.'

'The sergeant wasn't happy about it. He wanted to order up a search party. But they got a call, at the top of your lane, about a big accident near Stow. You probably heard about it.'

'No,' she said absently. 'Did it take the full team to deal with, then?'

'Obviously not. But the weather created quite a bit of chaos. Two plods were off sick, and one couldn't get his car out. Usual sort of thing, never enough bodies for the work.'

'You seem to have picked it all up very quickly. I thought Friday was your first assignment?'

He flushed, showing some colour for the first time. 'I was in the force for a bit, ten years ago. I packed it in.'

'Really? My daughter's a probationer, you know. I keep expecting her to call it a day, but she insists she loves it. She's coming here on Sunday,' she remembered. 'For a visit.'

'Women and gays still have a hard time,' he said,

as if repeating a line that had the truth of a well-worn platitude.

Thea looked at him, slowly understanding that he had just told her something. 'You're gay?' she queried.

'Yup. Not that it makes a lot of difference to anything – not had a partner for years now.' A flicker of sadness crossed his face, a contraction of his features, and a slow intake of breath. 'Did you get a good look at his face?' he continued in an apparent non sequitur.

'Who? George?' Tony nodded. 'Well, not really. Hardly at all in the field, but a bit more in the house. Long grey hair and a straggly beard.'

'He had beautiful eyes, and a *glorious* voice. Deep, with a creamy Oxford accent.'

'Ah.' The story was shifting, expanding into some new revelation that sat at odds with what had gone before. 'Well...no, I'm afraid I didn't get any sense of that. Although I think I did see him a fortnight ago, when I first got here. Tall, and somehow *loose*. I thought he might have been a ghost, which is quite weird, given what happened afterwards.'

He looked at her with the first sign of genuine interest since she arrived. 'Good God,' he said.

'I know it seems like idle curiosity, and an almost rude interference, but I really care about what happened to him.' She clutched the mug with both hands. 'And Bunny.'

'You never met her, did you? What can you possibly care about her?'

'I've met her children, and Simon and Janina. I care quite a lot about them, especially Nicky.'

Tony snorted cynically. 'Yes, you would,' he spat. 'Everybody cares so *immensely* about that kid. Just because he has long eyelashes, everyone worries for his emotional welfare. Not Ben, you notice. Nobody ever talks about Ben. It was just the same with me and Simon – everybody favoured him because he had nice eyes.'

'You're right,' she said contritely. 'I'm sorry.' She clutched at a faint notion that she was missing something, that Tony had obliquely told her more than he intended, if she could only interpret it.

'Well, I should get dressed,' he said pointedly, when the coffee was finished. 'I'll have to go out later to get some milk and a paper.'

A phone began to trill, playing a rapid version of 'Jingle Bells' and they both looked round the room for it. Thea's eyes landed on the mantelpiece, over a tiled fireplace, where two mobiles sat side by side.

Tony grabbed one of them, and thumbed a small button, causing the phone to fall silent. 'Not answering any calls today,' he said. 'There's nothing that won't wait.' She was reminded of Lucy's agonised computer customers, desperate for someone to repair their beloved machine. But she supposed that a photographer could turn away work without too much resulting disappointment.

She looked at his narrow body, wondering whether

another man would find it any more alluring than she did. There was something melancholy about him, living in his little cottage all alone.

'Thanks for talking to me,' she said, as she left. 'I'm sorry if I've been a nuisance.'

His answering smile was brief and superficial. 'I probably ought to thank you for your interest. I'm not sure of the protocol for a situation like this.'

'There isn't one,' she said. 'You just have to make it up as you go along.'

It wasn't until she was almost back at the barn that the obvious parallels between Tony Newby and George Jewell struck her. Both men lived on their own in small Cotswold cottages, keeping themselves neat and apparently quiet, carrying an indefinable whiff of failure about them. At least, George's failure had been more overt, relying as he did on the charity of Kate's father. How unusual for a property to be squatted, as it effectively was, if she had understood correctly. Tony had hinted at feelings for George, with his eulogy about the man's eyes and voice. Had George also been gay, then? Presumably not – otherwise why wouldn't Tony have made advances to him? For the two of them to get together would surely have solved several problems. Tony was in his thirties, and George in his fifties; would such an age difference matter? Perhaps Tony did reveal his feelings and received a rebuff. The hypotheses multiplied in her fertile imagination, until she dismissed them all. The only thing that she had really gleaned was that Tony had a closer involvement with what had happened than she had first appreciated.

Yet there had still been no elucidation about Bunny, other than the location of the discovery of her body. With the distances so much shorter than she had first assumed, a wholesale revision of the timescale seemed to be called for. The two bodies had effectively been on either side of a relatively small patch of woodland – probably well under half a mile apart. As soon as she got back indoors, she grabbed the ubiquitous Pathfinder map, and checked her mental picture of how the points were related.

She had been right – it was about a third of a mile from the spot where she had first found George to the place where a path led up to the northern side of the trees. On a dry summer's day, the dumping of either body would have been impossibly close to habitations, with walkers and dogs certain to see them within hours. So…had the snow been a fortunate accident, making everything easier for the killer, or had it been an integral part of the whole plan? In the case of George, it had been the means of his suicide – but a sharp frost would have served the same purpose.

Had it been a foolish mistake to go and talk to Tony? Would he immediately report her snooping to his brother, or another person Thea had never met – a person known to Tony as the probable killer of Bunny? It seemed all too possible that connections existed between local families that she could never hope to unravel. Even more possible that her transparent interest in the events of the past week had been noted, rendering her unpleasantly vulnerable in the isolated house where nobody would ever hear her scream.

Without thinking any further about it, she called the mobile number that Gladwin had given her. She had no opening line ready, no pretext for disturbing a busy detective, other than a need to hear a competent voice. She could think of no one else who might satisfy the same need.

The phone was answered by a recorded voice telling her to leave a message. Doggedly, Thea told the machine her name, with a request that DS Gladwin get back to her. 'It isn't really urgent,' she added, 'but I would like to speak to you.'

Then she prepared herself an omelette for lunch, spending extra time on sautéed potatoes and peas to go with it. The cat, increasingly friendly with every passing day, sat on the kitchen table watching closely. At one point, as Thea passed it carrying the empty eggshells to go in the compost bin, the animal reached out a deft paw and swiped a shell onto the floor. A sharp claw snagged in Thea's cuff, and for a moment the two were linked. 'Hey, let go!' she told the cat.

It seemed the claw would not retract easily, and she had to detach it by force. Spirit hissed at her, and the moment the paw was free, gave another swipe, this time catching the bare skin on the back of Thea's hand.

'For heaven's sake,' she protested. 'What's the matter with you?'

Flicking its long black tail, the cat jumped down from the table and left the room without a backward look. Thea sucked the beads of blood from the scratch and wondered about the odd behaviour of other people's pets.

It was – as far as she could recall – the first time an animal in her care had deliberately hurt her, and it added to her sense of insecurity, here at Lucy's Barn. Danger seemed to be in the air, hanging over her, waiting to pounce. Awful things had happened already, but she could not shake the conviction that something even worse was about to strike.

Forcing the omelette down, against her body's inclination, she contemplated the afternoon ahead with a profound lack of enthusiasm. She could clean out the donkey and give him a fresh new bed of straw. She could inspect the baby rabbits, and perhaps even pick one up for a cuddle. She could sit with Jimmy and talk to him, communing with a creature that appeared to share her current frame of mind. Indeed Jimmy was a permanent example of melancholy. Perhaps it was his presence in the house that was doing such damage to her own mood; a lowering reminder that life could go dreadfully irreversibly wrong at any moment.

But then, Jimmy had been rescued, and Thea too had begun to function again a year or so after the abrupt death of her husband.

She got up and went back to the living room, followed by her own dog, who also seemed rather subdued, only to see the front door opening.

Chapter Twenty-Two

It was a weird horror-movie moment, despite the fact of it being broad daylight. She had left the door on the latch, never for a second thinking to lock herself in, despite her gathering anxieties. In the tiny moment before the intruder could be identified, Thea's natural optimism asserted itself and she found herself expecting to see Lucy Sinclair, home early for some unfathomed reason.

She was at least right about the gender. Janina, the Bulgarian nanny, came flying into the house, bringing cold air and hot panic with her. 'Quickly!' she cried. 'You have to help me. It's Ben.'

Ben? For a second, Thea could not remember who that was. Instead, she heard it as Nicky, the little boy who had a habit of wandering off and getting himself involved in situations where he had no business. 'Ben?' she said. Then she got it – the other boy, Nicky's brother. Of course.

'The school called, and said I should fetch him. I did, just now, and tried to take him home. But he screamed and said he couldn't go into the house ever again. He is crazy, like I never saw before. And strong. He is six, and I cannot manage him. So I came here. I thought perhaps Kate would help, but no – you are better.'

'Where is he?'

'In the car. Just here.'

'Should we take him to a doctor? It sounds like a sort of breakdown.' Did six-year-old children *have* breakdowns, she wondered?

'Listen to me. I am trained in child psychology. I know him better than a doctor would. I believe he must be obeyed in what he wishes. His house has become horrible to him.' She was agitatedly swaying in and out of the house as she spoke, staring back at the car, which she had driven across the slippery yard, almost to the door. 'Come now, will you please?'

Thea had nothing on her feet but socks. Her boots were at the back door, and she could not remember where she'd left her shoes. It seemed an insuperable problem. Her dog had gone out, and was jumping up at the car, trying to get a good view of the child inside.

'Let me find my shoes,' she said, struggling to remain calm. 'I won't be a minute.'

Her trainers were in the kitchen, and she fought her way into them, tempted just to get them half on, the laces undone and the backs trodden down, but a small voice of good sense told her she might need to move quickly, and loose shoes would be a real hindrance.

'What did the school say exactly?'

Janina shook her head. 'They said a child ought not to be sent to school so soon after such a trauma. That he was emotionally unstable and could not stop crying. He has not cried before today. That is quite normal. He is not able to understand what has happened, not fully. It is better to keep quiet and still, and wait for everything to make sense again.'

'But that isn't what's happening to him, is it?'

'Maybe it is. But I have to find him somewhere warm and safe, before I can work out what he's feeling – and thinking. He is afraid of something.'

Join the club, thought Thea.

They persuaded the little boy into the barn relatively easily. He looked around suspiciously, his face smeary with tears and mucus. He really was so much less appealing than Nicky, Thea noted. It had to affect the way people treated them. As if reading her thoughts, Ben muttered, 'Is Nicky here?'

'No, no. He's still at nursery,' Janina assured him. 'He's there all day today, remember?'

Ben gave an uninterested twitch of his shoulders, but seemed relieved to be the only child present.

'Shall I get you a drink or something?' Thea asked. 'Have you had any lunch?'

He shook his head. Janina sat close to him on the sofa. 'It was lunchtime when the trouble started, wasn't it?' she said. 'Can you say what happened?'

A firmer shake of the head.

'Was it about your mummy?'

'No!'

Janina took a deep breath, and threw Thea a look of despair. Thea responded cautiously. 'Ben, did somebody say something? I remember when I was at school, there was always some silly person who would upset me by being rude about somebody I loved. Usually it was my little sister, Jocelyn. They used to say she was fat – well, she was, quite – and that made me so angry.'

It was moderately successful. The child was watching her face, listening to her words. 'Yeah,' he said heavily. 'People say things.'

'Was that what made you cry?'

He nodded reluctantly. 'They said George was a tramp.'

Aha! The two women exchanged triumphant glances, despite their surprise. 'You're upset about *George*?' echoed Thea. Then she remembered that both children had seen their friend's dead body, whereas they had no actual evidence of their mother's permanent loss. It made sense that the first death would make the greater impact.

'Yes, that is dreadfully sad,' she sympathised. 'And he was your friend – is that right?'

'Yeah,' muttered Ben. 'He was our friend.' The words felt hollow, mechanical, repeated for convenience rather than from any sincere feelings.

'George was kind to the boys,' Janina supplied. 'Especially Nicky.'

A bad mistake. A look of revulsion and rage crossed Ben's face. '*I* was his favourite,' he said firmly. 'Not Nicky. Nicky's a baby, can't keep a secret.'

Thea's heart thumped. Surely *secret* had to be one of the great buzzwords of the age, when associated with children. Dark suspicions came crowding in, alien thoughts that Thea had so far successfully kept at arm's length.

'You mean going to see Granfer Jack, don't you?' said Janina, leaning forward, pushing her face urgently close to Ben's. 'We were supposed to keep quiet about that, because Mummy would be cross with me and George. Nicky didn't tell her, did he?'

The little boy slumped, as if under a great weight, his head drooping hopelessly. 'Yeah,' he agreed. 'That's right.'

Janina wouldn't drop it. 'But *did* he? Did Nicky tell her?'

Ben shook his head. 'No, he didn't,' he said. 'I wouldn't let him. He just said he was George's favourite – when he *wasn't.*'

Janina showed no signs of the same dawning suspicions that Thea was experiencing. Perhaps the paranoia in Bulgaria was directed somewhere else entirely. More likely, Thea hoped, she knew the people concerned and had every reason to be relaxed. Except, she was not relaxed at all – she was still pushing herself too close to the child, as if trying to control his very thoughts.

'Where's Simon?' asked Thea, from a growing sense that Ben needed additional protection. From the little she had seen of his father, there were no grounds for thinking he would fail in this duty. Other than his habitual absences, of course, his job removing him when he was most urgently needed.

Janina flapped a hand, brushing away the man she had characterised as lazy and useless, nearly two weeks ago.

'So what happens now?' Thea persisted. 'He'll have to go home eventually. And you have to collect Nicky, I presume?'

'Not till five. Simon is at his work. They had a problem.'

'Good God…aren't there rules about bereavement leave or something?'

Janina rolled her eyes. 'I suppose so, but he says they cannot manage without him, and he cannot afford to lose his job, and he has no choice in the matter.'

Again, the way Janina had described Simon sat totally at odds with Thea's impression of the actual man. How could he be lazy, if he could hold down a job that demanded constant vigilance, attention to detail, control of a large staff and a dozen other necessary talents? It also, she supposed, required a lot of play-acting. You had to be polite and cooperative to an endless parade of fools and hysterics. Hotel guests were famously unreasonable and capricious, and the management had to smile and apologise and rectify, whatever they might be feeling inside.

'I wouldn't think they'd be very busy this time of year,' said Thea.

'There is a conference this weekend,' Janina told her. 'They cannot manage without Simon.'

Thea wanted to be useful and involved. She was worried about both the little boys, and increasingly concerned that they were not being adequately cared for, given the circumstances. Benjamin's 'breakdown' had demonstrated how needy they were. 'Are there any other grandparents?' she wondered aloud.

'Oh yes,' said Janina nastily. 'In South Africa and Spain.'

'So what about getting Granfer Jack to pitch in? Or Kate?'

Ben squirmed, uneasy at losing his place at the centre of attention. But at least Janina had backed off a little way, and his tears had dried up.

'It is not for me…' Janina sagged slightly in the face of her limitations. 'I have no authority…'

'No. Except you did bring him here. Why not carry on down to the farm, where they know him?'

'They are strange people. I cannot understand their minds. You are easier. And nicer,' she added disarmingly.

And unlikely to be busy with animals and barn roofs and mangel worzels, thought Thea.

'So let's all have a drink, and a biscuit, and see what's

what,' she offered brightly. 'Things are going to start looking better after that, I'm sure. Do you know, Ben, I have a motto. Shall I tell you what it is?'

The child frowned at the unfamiliar word. 'Motto?'

'Yes…something I say to myself when things get difficult or sad. It's a bit long, compared to most mottoes, but it does work.' She sat up straight and declaimed, 'If you're all right now, this very minute, then you're all right, full stop.' She laughed. 'Well, it varies a bit, but that's the basic idea. It's all about the present moment. The thing is, you're almost certain to be OK at any given moment. It's worrying about what comes next that brings you down.'

'But I'm not OK,' he said, as if this was perfectly obvious. 'I'm *desperate*.' And he burst into fresh tears, turning to hide his face in the cushions behind him.

'Oops,' muttered Thea. Maybe all that had been rather too grown-up for him. Janina gave her a look of reproach.

'Come on,' coaxed Thea. 'I'll go and get that drink. Do you like milk?'

'Noghh,' came the muffled response.

Janina snorted. 'They are not allowed milk. Do you have fruit juice – without any E-numbers, of course.' The habitual scorn was back, presumably directed somewhat callously at the deceased Bunny.

'Pineapple juice?' Thea offered. 'I brought some with me that I haven't opened yet.'

Janina shrugged. 'OK. Or water. Do you want a drink, Ben?' she asked, her voice raised.

Thea remembered the warm drink she had given Nicky after his chilly morning in the church. Warm drinks was something she could do.

There was no response, and Thea hesitated. She was reminded of the younger boy, shivering after a morning in a cold church, every bit as pathetic as his brother. The ghastly glaring fact that their mother was dead hit her with fresh force, rendering futile any attempts at reassurance. You couldn't say, *There, there, everything's going to be all right* – because it wasn't. They would be marked for life, not only because of the loss, but because of the ineradicable taint of murder. And if it turned out that their father had been the killer, then their fate grew even darker. She felt chilled at the prospect ahead for them. Foster care, boarding school, adoption – anything was possible once their parents left the picture.

'Poor little boy,' she murmured. 'No wonder he's desperate.'

Janina was hovering, more and more agitated as the lack of decision expanded. Neither woman had any idea what to do, each wrestling with a jumble of resentment, pity, and helplessness. Thea still made no move to fetch drinks, anticipating that Benjamin would simply ignore anything she offered.

And then an unlikely rescuer came slowly into the room.

'Jimmy!' Thea exclaimed. She moved to intercept him, afraid that he would repeat the performance of a few days ago, and soak another rug with malodorous urine. But he pushed against her when she laid a hand on him, evidently intent on his goal – which was the sofa on which the snivelling child huddled. Thea backed away, some instinct telling her she should trust him.

The cold nose found Benjamin's hand, and he raised his head to see what it was. With an inarticulate cry, he stared at the scruffy animal as if at an angel. 'Oh!' he cried.

The dog wagged his tail slightly, and nestled his face against the boy. Ben gently stroked him with both hands, following the line from neck to shoulder to ribcage, then back to the top of the head. Jimmy made a noise of contentment and hauled himself up onto the sofa, where he curled himself around the child.

'My God!' squawked Janina. 'What is that?'

Thea braced herself for a struggle if the au pair chose to try to remove the dog. But it seemed that Jimmy's force of character had affected her as well.

'That's Jimmy,' she said. 'He was a stray, and Lucy rescued him. Now I think he might have rescued Ben.'

'Jimmy?' crooned Benjamin. 'Are you Jimmy?' He looked up at Thea. 'Why's he so thin?'

'That's just the way he is. He's half greyhound, and they're always thin.'

It hadn't actually resolved anything, of course, but it brought considerable relief to have Ben no longer crying about his own desperate situation. She remembered how Ben had petted Hepzie on their first encounter, and Janina had said something about a special liking for dogs. Why hadn't the spaniel had the sense to cuddle up with the kid, twenty minutes ago, instead of remaining antisocially in the kitchen, where she had established a favourite warm corner during the daytime?

'Ben,' said Janina, aiming for a firm tone, 'we have to go home soon. Daddy will be back any time now, and then Nicky. It will be the same as always.'

'I don't want to talk,' said the child, hugging the dog to him. 'I want to stay here with Jimmy.'

'You don't have to talk. And you can come and see Jimmy again at the weekend. But we must go now.'

Benjamin pouted exaggeratedly. 'Nicky will talk and be annoying.'

It had all become much more normal, Thea realised. Whatever dreadful terror had seized him had withdrawn again, leaving the far more manageable sibling antipathy. 'I will tell him not to,' said Janina. 'You can be in the playroom by yourself, if you want.'

'Can I have supper in there?'

'I expect so.'

Ben looked at Thea. 'Can I really come and see Jimmy again?'

'Of course you can. And the donkey, if you want. *And...*' she held up a finger, insisting on his attention '...there are baby rabbits in the shed outside. They're absolutely gorgeous.'

He clasped the lurcher closer. 'I only want to see Jimmy,' he said.

'Oh, well,' Thea shrugged. 'That's fine.'

The shift in atmosphere seemed to leave all three of them limp and inert. 'Home,' said Janina. 'Come on home now, Ben.' There was just enough authority in her voice to penetrate the child's defences. Or perhaps it gave him the courage to trust her and do as she said. Thea had often thought that modern children were cruelly denied the discipline and authority their elders owed them. It was pleasant to be told what to do, at least some of the time.

The visitors departed, leaving a miasma of sadness and fear. The real reason for Ben's distress remained obscure, as was frequently the case with children, Thea recalled. There had been episodes when Jessica had been discovered crying in a corner, quite unable to explain why. 'Cosmic misery,' Carl had called it. 'She's weeping for the woes of the world.'

It was less than ten minutes before another car arrived at the barn. Thea sighed, as she heard the slamming door. 'What now?' she muttered to the dogs, both of whom were settled on the sofa, woven together like conjoined twins. They ignored her.

She opened the door to Gladwin, feeling no surprise. 'I got your message,' said the detective. 'Are you OK?'

Thea went blank, forgetting entirely what she had wanted to impart. 'Um, yes,' she said. 'Come in. I'm fine. It's Tony. I went to see Tony Newby this morning. Then Janina turned up with Ben. It's all a bit of a muddle, actually.'

'So it sounds. Well, if it's any help, we're more or less straight at our end.'

'What? What does that mean?'

'It must have been the husband. It's always the husband. We've got ten officers trawling through Mrs Newby's computer and papers, looking for a motive. But it has to have been him. Everybody's been telling us what a cow she was. He'll have lost it, last week. Probably something snapped over Christmas – that's usually it.' She had moved into the main room, and stood gazing at the tangled dogs, as she spoke. There was an air to her that Thea hadn't seen before. A tension that contradicted the confidence in her words.

'Simon did it? You really think so? I can't believe that. Have you got any evidence?'

'Nothing concrete. I was kinda hoping that's what you were offering. If I know you, you'll have picked up a whole bagful of important clues since I last saw you.'

'Well, no, not really. I don't feel very clued up at all, quite honestly. For instance, was Bunny hit from the back or front?'

'Back.'

'Without any warning? So she wouldn't have had time to scratch or hit her attacker?'

'That sort of thing, yes.'

'Do you think somebody lured her down a snowy

lane, to a ditch beside a field, coshed her from behind and left her there? Is that the picture?'

Gladwin was restless, walking around the back of the sofa and leaning over it, then jerking upright, swinging her arms. 'Oh, shit, it isn't very convincing, is it? There's some massive factor we haven't got hold of yet. I always want to go for the simplest answer, but it's not working this time.'

'Maybe it is. You might be right. Except, I just can't see Simon doing anything so violent. Not to the mother of his children. I know lots of men do it, but he seems so *docile*.'

Gladwin huffed a small laugh at that. 'Docile? The man manages a busy upmarket hotel. He keeps a staff of twenty or more under control. I don't think either of us has seen what he's capable of.'

Thea pondered for a moment. 'It's no good – I honestly don't think Simon Newby could do such a thing. He's not passionate enough. There's no hint of temper in him. And what about *George*? Everybody keeps talking about him as a bigger loss than Bunny. Tony loved him. The boys loved him. Janina hatched a conspiracy with him – and the people on the farm. He's at the centre of everything. It's as if Bunny was just some kind of distraction. I swear Nicky and Ben are more upset about him than their own mother.'

Gladwin held up a hand. 'Stop, stop. You've left me way behind here. Who's Tony, for a start?'

Thea gave vent to a delighted little snort of laughter.

'Your own police photographer, as it happens. Tony Newby, Simon's brother.'

'Uh-huh,' said Gladwin doubtfully. 'I'm not sure I've met him. He'll have been interviewed, of course, and I must have seen the report, but...' She frowned and scratched at a rough patch of skin on her chin. Looking at her more closely, Thea observed signs that the senior detective had been out in the cold and got herself chapped. Thin and bony, Gladwin carried little natural protection against extreme winter weather.

'He's gay, and he had a thing for George Jewell – which I gather was not reciprocated. He seems rather a pathetic figure, especially at the moment. He's caught a chill and is working from home in a dressing gown.'

'You're saying he might have killed George in some sort of jealous fit? And Bunny as well, for reasons that escape me?'

'Not at all,' Thea almost shouted. 'I'm saying he knew both of them very well, lives a couple of miles away and was here on the morning I found George's body.'

'And he's Simon's brother? Are they alike?'

'Fairly. I think Simon's older, but Tony took charge when the news came about Bunny. I met them both in Northleach soon after. Simon was more or less useless with shock, and Tony was shepherding him about – seeing the people at the boys' school, for one thing.'

'Useless with shock? You thought that was genuine, did you?'

'Very much so.'

'He has to present a front as a matter of course, you know, at his hotel. Probably very good at hiding his feelings.'

'I know, but even so...' Why am I defending him, she asked herself? 'I just don't want it to be him,' she admitted miserably.

'Nor me,' Gladwin agreed. 'I hate to think what it'd mean for those kids.'

'Right,' said Thea. 'The kids. It all comes down to them, in the end.'

'I'm still not entirely sure why you called me,' Gladwin resumed after a short silence.

'Nor me,' smiled Thea. 'I think I just wanted somebody sensible to talk to. It used to be Phil, you see...' she tailed off helplessly, resisting the slide into self-pity. 'I used to be much more *included*. I suppose I miss it.'

'You could still sign up for the force, you know. Even if you don't qualify as a uniformed, you could be a special, or admin, or clerical. There's loads of openings.'

For a moment, Thea considered the prospect of such a life change. A real job, with regular income, with all the paperwork and commitment and a desk and colleagues. Things she had never in her life experienced. She'd worked at a succession of indifferent jobs after graduating and before Jessica was born, but that period of her life had been very short and inconsequential, overshadowed by Carl and the thrill of being married. 'I doubt if they'd have me,' she said. 'I haven't got anything you could call a CV, for a start.'

'Phil's not on this case, anyway,' Gladwin went on, dismissing Thea's objections with a flip of her hand. 'There's something up in Broadway that he's focusing on.'

'Anyway...you think you've cracked this one, then? Done and dusted?'

'I wouldn't go as far as that. Very strong suspicions, yes. Evidence, motive, means – no. And about a dozen loose ends.'

'Such as George.'

'Exactly.'

Chapter Twenty-Three

Gladwin stayed for a mug of tea, and then went with Thea to feed the donkey. 'I'm intrigued by this animal,' she admitted. 'What does it *do* all day?'

'Not a lot in this weather. Dreams dreams, I guess. Lets the time pass. What do most animals do?'

'Work. Breed. Socialise. This poor fellow gets none of that. It's cruel, if you think about it. Has he ever worked in his life?'

'I have no idea,' Thea shrugged. 'I can't imagine there's much call for donkey work any more. It's a surprise, really, that there are any left. Don't they say that once we all turn vegetarian, that'll be the end of sheep and cows and pigs? Donkeys are obsolete already.'

'And I'd say their days are numbered, at least in this country.'

'Pity. He's an inoffensive creature. They deserve to exist for their own sake, same as everything else.'

'Of course he does, in theory. But it depends on rich philanthropists like your Lucy. She's got all this land just for one useless animal.'

Thea sighed at the familiar turn of conversation. The donkey tore at his fresh hay, nodding his head up and down as if agreeing with the sentiments being expressed. 'He goes for regular little walks as well, though I haven't seen him down by the big gate since last week. He definitely went down there in the snow, because I saw his tracks.'

'Ah yes. Tracks.' It was as if she had been summoned back to work after a break. 'I knew there was a good reason why I came out here with you. I wanted to check all that again. We need to draw diagrams, to get it all straight. It might be needed as evidence, if this business ever comes to trial.' She spoke distractedly, her eyes flickering from one corner of the paddock to another. 'It would be great to have a complete picture of what must have happened. I hope you can still remember it all?'

'I expect I can,' said Thea, mentally running through the events of the previous week. Seven days ago, the whole area had been blanketed with snow, pristine on its first day. 'Though I'm slightly hazy about what happened on which day, now. Let me think. It was Friday morning I saw the footprints, wasn't it?' she asked herself. 'So it was Friday when I called the police about the body in the field?'

Gladwin said nothing, just giving a slight nod. Thea continued, 'Saturday I went to Nicky's party. Sunday

I found George and you found Bunny on Monday night. Then you identified her and I met the Newbys in Northleach. It was still snowy then.' She looked up in triumph. 'That's right, isn't it?'

'As far as I know, yes. Does it suggest anything to you, timing-wise?'

'Not really. Do you mean that Simon might have been acting innocent all the time we were playing games and eating ice cream for Nicky's birthday? That Bunny was already dead then, and he knew it? When did anybody last see her alive?'

'Thursday. She was in Bristol at a meeting, that morning. Said she was going straight home afterwards.'

'But she couldn't because of the snow.' The effort of keeping it all in her head was starting to cause Thea some trouble. There was definitely something amiss with the story, where Bunny's movements were concerned.

'Maybe,' Gladwin agreed. 'The roads were cleared by the middle of that day. The motorways were never really affected, anyway. She could have got to within a few miles of here, with no trouble.'

'But instead she phoned them and said she couldn't manage it.'

'She didn't phone. She texted. We saw the messages on Simon's mobile.'

'So?'

'So he could easily have sent it himself from her phone, to cover himself.'

'She didn't call Nicky about his party?'

'Nope. Nobody spoke to her after Thursday morning, so far as we can gather. We've been trying the number of her phone every now and then, just to see if someone finds it and picks it up.'

Thea was still focusing on the timing. 'But she *did* come home, because she died here. When?'

Gladwin shrugged. 'That's the big question which we can't answer precisely. From the amount of snow on top of her, and the state of her insides, it looks like Friday, but we can't be certain.'

They were walking back to the barn, the light fading rapidly. Thea wondered at the apparent lack of urgency in the detective's demeanour. Was this, then, a crucial interview – something she had planned to conduct in any case, regardless of Thea's earlier phone call? 'Do you want to see the baby rabbits?' she asked. 'They're so sweet.'

'OK,' said Gladwin with a girlish grin, and Thea found herself rejoicing in the femaleness of her companion. Gladwin had twin boys of her own. She understood baby things and the minor miracles of motherhood. If it had been Phil, she'd have felt foolish in doting over such unimportant scraps of life.

The babies were growing fast, their eyes open and tiny ears just starting to lift from their early flat position. Thea fished one out and handed it to the detective superintendent. 'Aaahh!' she sighed.

'Lucy was amazed when I told her about them.'

'Why? Was it an immaculate conception?'

'Not at all. She's a bit naive about it, if you ask me. She left the buck with all the does while she mucked them out. She's lucky they didn't all have babies.'

'Do you think I could have a couple of them for my boys? They're old enough now to do some of the cleaning and feeding.'

Thea hesitated. 'Not for me to say,' was her reply, covering herself. It was true, of course, but her resistance was much more due to the idea of the vulnerable little rabbits being consigned to the care of two growing boys. 'Would they treat them properly?' she couldn't refrain from asking.

Gladwin gave her a look. 'Of course. They're as soft as anything, real cissies. We've deliberately gone that way with them – which shouldn't surprise you, if you think about it.'

Thea thought. 'You've seen too much of feral urban youth, knifing each other for no good reason,' she summarised. 'So yours resolve any arguments by rational discussion and a warm hug.'

Gladwin laughed delightedly. 'That's the idea,' she confirmed. 'And being in charge of two adorable little bunnies is just the thing to cement that approach.'

'You'll have to ask Lucy, then. I expect she'll be more than happy to find a home for them so easily.'

It was a stolen interlude from the serious business of investigating murder, and they both knew it couldn't last. The detective was skilfully concealing the stress of her work, showing no overt sign of urgency or anxiety.

Her skinny figure suggested a busy life with little time for food or idleness. Her dark eyes habitually darted from point to point, suggesting constant thought, her brain never resting. But she seemed to have a fair balance in her life, as far as Thea could ascertain. She was a good listener, and in Temple Guiting had shown herself capable of taking short cuts in her work which ran counter to the official regulations. She trusted her own judgement, and thereby earned the trust of others. Her parting remark accurately acknowledged Thea's feelings. 'Don't worry about not being involved in this one,' she advised. 'You don't want to get yourself murdered, now do you?'

'Not really,' Thea muttered, to the detective's departing back.

But it was too late, of course. She was involved, like it or not. She had heard disclosures from people close to a murdered woman, and in so doing had quickly come to care about them. She had let Janina and Ben leave without knowing what happened next – would Simon be at home to watch over Ben while Nicky was collected from nursery? Such minutiae of family life acquired great importance, essential for a sense of normality and security on the part of the children. She wished she had told Janina to call on her if help was needed, as she was increasingly convinced it would be.

If evidence was found against Simon, he would be arrested and kept in custody for the lengthy period before the trial. *If.* Thea tried to assemble everything she knew of the case, searching for possible indicators that Simon had in fact murdered his wife, only to find herself hampered by the many gaps in her knowledge. Nobody had told her where Simon was on Thursday or Friday or Saturday, nor how he felt about Bunny. She knew nothing of his feelings towards George – or George's towards him, or Bunny's towards anybody. Janina was hypercritical of both the boys' parents, but seemed well disposed towards George, and very good with Nicky and Ben. Other people such as Tony, Kate and Granfer Jack appeared to have a part in the picture, none of them with a good word to say about Bunny.

The phone rang, and again her instant thought was of Lucy. It was time for another check-in from her employer, but this was somewhat earlier than her usual calls. And she was wrong again. At first she did not recognise the voice, which began hesitantly. 'Yes, hello? I'm sorry, but I forgot your name. This is Kate, down the track.'

'Oh! My name's Thea. What can I do for you?' Why were telephone conversations still so stilted, after all these years? There were times when it felt like a frightening new invention, even to someone whose great-grandmother had used it. Perhaps because it continued to carry associations of bad news or intrusive attempts to sell you something.

'We thought you might like to come and eat with us. You must be lonely, up there by yourself.'

'How kind of you. When?'

'Well, we generally start about six, if that's all right.'

Six! It was already five-fifteen. No time for a bath and a hair wash, then. 'Today?'

'That's right. Do you like liver?'

Did *anybody* like liver? 'Um...' she said. 'I don't think I've had it since I was little.'

'You'll like it the way I do it,' she was assured. 'With bacon and onions and thick gravy. Just the thing for a cold winter evening.'

'I'll walk down, then, shall I?' The track would be slippery and dark, and coming back would be even worse. But you couldn't drive such a short distance – that would be stupid.

'Granfer can come and fetch you. He knows every inch of the way. That barn was ours, you realise. Used to keep the big implements in it, when I was a girl. There were owls roosting in the beams.'

The nostalgia was palpable, the usual sweet mixture of regret and rose-coloured memories. 'I'd love to hear more about that,' she said, stilted again. 'I'll wait for your father to get here, then, shall I?'

'He'll be half an hour or so. I told him he has to shave first.'

Chapter Twenty-Four

The old man crooked his arm gallantly, and Thea willingly took it. They walked slowly down the track, which was lit by a great moon that Thea had not previously noticed, to her shame. The silvery light glittered on the frost forming on every surface, and she groped for the lines of a poem she had learnt at the age of six or seven. 'With silver paws there sleeps the dog' – something like that. But her dog had been left behind in the barn with Jimmy, and she was not aware of one at Kate's place.

In that, however, she turned out to be wrong. A chubby corgi greeted her at the door, wagging its non-existent tail and grinning. 'This is Beryl,' said Kate. 'She's a curmudgeon most of the time, but seems she's taken to you.'

'I'm good with dogs,' said Thea immodestly. 'Hello Beryl.' She bent down and rubbed the animal's shoulders in both hands, enjoying the thick creamy coat. But she was also wrestling with an avalanche of associations, due to the fact that Phil Hollis also had a corgi. Claude was its name, and it was virtually identical to this Beryl. She hadn't known how much she missed the Hollis dog until this moment.

The house was brightly lit, with unreconstructed high-energy light bulbs, at least a hundred watts apiece. She was ushered into a large kitchen with lino on the floor and painted wooden panelling on the walls. Everything was immaculately clean. There was a sense of openness that stood in utter contrast to what Thea had been expecting. Something about farmhouses suggested dark secrets in her mind: grubby corners containing dying lambs, stacks of neglected DEFRA paperwork and overheated kitchens where the Aga was king.

There was no Aga here, just a faintly battered electric cooker, on which two bubbling saucepans sat. A table was laid for three, covered with an oilcloth boasting pictures of large red flowers. Beryl's basket stood near a back door, lined with clean bedding. There was almost nothing on any of the surfaces – tidiness taken to a disturbing extreme.

'Right...now you're here, I'll get frying,' said Kate briskly. 'It doesn't take long. Can we get you a drink?'

That was another thing – farmers were famously abstemious when it came to drink. If you found a dusty bottle of sherry in the back of a cupboard you were doing well. Where, Thea asked herself, did these stereotypes come from? *Cold Comfort Farm*, probably. 'Thanks,' she said cautiously.

'Gin? Wine? Apple juice? Sherry?'

With a wry inward smile, Thea opted for sherry, only to be offered a choice of sweet or dry, and Granfer poured a generous glass from a new-looking bottle of Amontillado.

The smell of the liver and bacon frying was undeniably appealing. Then Kate added onions and it became irresistible. 'Wow!' Thea inhaled. 'I can't wait.'

Deftly, the woman produced mashed potato and sprouts, served from a large, warm dish onto large, warm plates. Then, with a flourish, she doled out three slices of liver and two rashers of bacon per person, returning to the cooker to make gravy from the fat and juice left in the pan. Granfer fetched a bottle of rich red wine, which had been previously opened, and poured it out without being asked.

'This is fantastic,' Thea approved, after her first mouthful, which did not include any liver. 'Incredible.'

'Well, we always say if you can't enjoy the fruits of your own labour, then what's the point of it all?' said Kate. 'This is from our own lambs, of course. They were a good lot last year. Pity the price was so poor. We reckon we made about fifty pence on each one.'

The moment had come – she could not defer it any longer. Cutting a small piece of liver even smaller, she coated it with gravy and popped it in.

It was so different from her expectation that she

closed her eyes for better concentration. Soft, and with a taste she could never remember experiencing before, it was as if her whole body had been waiting for this moment for years. Quickly she took a larger piece, impatient to repeat the miracle. 'Fabulous,' she sighed, when her mouth was empty. 'I've never tasted anything like it.'

'Full of goodness,' Kate nodded carelessly. 'Most likely your body's been starved of the vitamins and minerals it needs. Liver's the best source of iron, for a start. Plus all sorts of other things.'

It was easy to believe. The two remaining slices on her plate seemed far less than she wanted and needed, and she had to force herself not to gobble it down. 'People forget how to cook it, these days. Keep it simple – that's the thing.' Kate was plainly gratified by Thea's response, but equally plainly she did not intend to spend the whole meal discussing food production.

'We've been talking about you,' she said frankly.

'Oh?' Thea took a gulp of the wine, aware that it was something rather good.

'Funny way to live, we thought – moving around from one house to another, never really coming to know anybody. Getting into things you don't understand. Made us curious, to be honest.'

The old man, sitting opposite Thea, met her eye and gave her a friendly wink. It made her feel very young and naive and rather vulnerable. These people were so firmly settled, *rooted*, with their self-sufficiency and long memories. They were normal, in a way that Thea suspected she could never be. They knew a few people very well, watched the same things on telly as everyone else, visited the sick and kept a clean and tidy house. And they recognised a troubled soul when they saw it.

'Oh, well…it suits me very nicely,' she said, resisting the sense of being attacked.

'Have you no family, then? No home of your own? Just that dog?'

'My husband died,' said Thea, slightly too loudly.

'Shame,' said Granfer Jack with his mouth full. Thea wondered whether he was reproaching his daughter for the interrogation as much as he was sympathising with her loss.

'I see,' said Kate, giving every indication that she really did. She saw how it might be – the empty house with the painful associations; the need for distraction and to feel useful. The serial escapes from her own life and concerns. Thea could see it all in the woman's eyes, and she remembered how she had dashed straight from her own father's funeral to a house-sitting commission in Lower Slaughter.

'And I meet new people, make new friends,' she added, increasingly on the defensive.

'You never knew George Jewell, though, did you?' Kate continued, in the same light chatty tone. 'You only found his dead body, poor bloke.'

'I followed a set of footprints that appeared out of

nowhere. I was scared, and I wanted to find out who had made them.'

'I saw you, as it happens.'

'Pardon?'

'From the barn roof. When you found me up there, it wasn't the first time. I was trying to clear the snow off, that Friday morning, and I saw you go down into that hollow and then come stumbling out again. It was obvious you'd found something.'

'You knew he was there?' Thea's blood was pounding in her head. Was Kate about to confess to murder, and then silence her for ever?

'No, of course I didn't. Not till I went over for a look.'

'You moved the body into the woods?'

'I did not. If poor old George wanted to die peacefully in the snow, what business was it of mine? Or yours?'

'Your cattle trampled all around, hiding the tracks.'

'So what if they did?'

'You drove over there on your tractor, saw the body and just left it where it was? That's very hard to believe.'

'I did no such thing. None of *my* business,' repeated Kate. 'We keep ourselves to ourselves around here. Besides, you'd done whatever you had to do – I knew there'd be officials on their way. Took a time coming, though. Best part of two hours.'

'In which time, *somebody* moved the body into the woods. Were you watching then as well? Did you actually *see* him?'

Kate shook her head. 'I saw no more than my cows milling around, after you'd gone back to the house. Wasn't sure it was anything more than a touch of needless panic on your part. Wondered why there was no helicopter or ambulance or the like. Made no sense to me till I heard later.'

'Who told you?'

'That Bulgarian girl. At your house. Filled me in nicely, she did.'

'I don't believe you,' said Thea flatly. 'You must have seen who moved him.'

Kate flared up. 'You think I've got time to stand about watching what goes on in a field when I've got a hundred jobs to do every morning? Don't be daft.'

'It was *your* field. You must have tipped somebody off, if you didn't move him yourself. How else would anybody know he was there?' The tangled story was winding itself in muddled loops around her mind.

'All I did was get on with the work and leave it to you. I didn't want the police down here, did I? If I'd have gone to see what was up, and found a dead man, I'd have felt obliged to bring him here on the link box. Then they'd have come down to us, after him, and started all kinds of searches, like as not.'

'They wouldn't. What a stupid idea. Besides...what have you got to hide?'

Kate sneered, 'Shows what you know about farming. One dead sheep is enough to fetch a fine of hundreds of quid. Medicine book, movement book, ear tags, tax returns, farm assurance – it just goes on and on. You can't move for red tape these days. There's always something wrong. They only pay those officials if they find a mistake. It's like something out of Kafka.'

'But none of that is the *police*,' Thea bleated weakly. 'My daughter's a police officer. So is my brother-in-law.'

Kate shrugged, implying *say no more*.

The delicious meal was spoilt, leaving Thea confused and sad. Somehow it felt like her fault, as if by her very character she had failed or transgressed. She was the wrong person in the wrong place. A wave of loneliness surged through her, perversely strengthened by the realisation that she had been invited to the farm not through pure altruism but because Kate and her father wanted to make her aware of their opinion of her.

But the old man had said scarcely anything. He had winked at her, and hinted at sympathy. She looked to him now for succour.

'Kafka's right,' he said. 'I read those books in my twenties, and made sure Kate read them, too, when she was old enough. Better than *1984* or *Brave New World* for telling you what you're up against.'

Twenty minutes earlier, Thea would have been delighted by this display of erudition in people she had been inclined to dismiss as peasants. Now it began to feel as if she'd blundered into something out of Kafka herself, or possibly Pinter.

'Why are you so angry with me?' she found the courage to ask, after a silence in which Kate cleared away the plates, and brought in a large apple crumble.

'You didn't know George,' came the oblique reply. 'Couldn't find a nicer man anywhere.'

'He could have told you all about Kafka,' added Granfer Jack, with a grunt that might have been born of rage or sadness or both. 'Out to get him, they were, from the first day he moved here.'

'And you let him live in your cottage,' Thea belatedly remembered.

'Least we could do,' said the old man. 'And much good did it bring him.' He shook his head, and this time there was no mistaking the sadness.

Chapter Twenty-Five

He took her back to the barn afterwards, the ice thicker underfoot, and his supporting arm even more necessary. She had demurred, conscious that he had been ill and would have to wrap himself up before venturing out. 'There's a moon,' she reminded him. 'I can see the way very well.'

'Best make sure you're safe,' he insisted. 'After all, there's a murderer about, so they say.'

At the door, he gave her a fatherly pat, and said, 'You mustn't mind Kate too much. She speaks as she finds, always did. Don't give her any more thought.'

The kindness was almost worse than the sniping had been. 'Thanks,' she choked. 'I'll try.' Then she hurried into the barn, where her faithful spaniel would greet her with uncomplicated love, that carried no hint of the character defects she was suddenly all too aware of.

It was still only quarter past nine. The empty house seemed to pulse all around her, too big for one woman, too far from any sociable human sounds. She turned on the television, desperate for distraction, but the programmes all seemed to be either crime thrillers, fatuous competitions or gardening. None did anything to divert her from the increasingly dark mood of self-dislike.

Because it was all true. Kate had seen through her mask to the mess that lay beneath. She had somehow discovered that she, Thea Osborne, was a useless mother, a selfish bitchy lover, a nosy interfering house-sitter. She was fit only for the company of animals, and was clearly destined to pass her days alone and unloved.

She remembered how rotten she had been to Phil Hollis when he hurt his back – an injury that had to some extent been her fault in the first place. She had barely even tried to show him sympathy, until it was too late. The two weeks she had spent in his flat, nursing him back to something like normality, had been grudging and impatient, at least some of the time. The truth was that Phil was too good for her – a decent, honest police detective, uncorrupted by his work, and ready to offer her companionship and security for the rest of their lives. Serves her right, then, that he had found a replacement that would do him a great deal more good, from the sound of it. His apparent dishonesty about what he wanted was easily explained: he hadn't wanted it with *her*. Once a more suitable woman appeared, who could blame him for changing his mind?

The few other men she had encountered since

finishing with Phil had all been treated with suspicion and criticism. She had turned into an untrusting shrew at some point since Carl had died, and failed to notice.

For half an hour she mortified herself with such thoughts. It sent her back to the dark days following Carl's death, but this time it was almost worse. This time she had to absorb the notion that other people didn't really like her as much as she'd thought they did. A notion that she found terrifying. Was she really to live another forty years like this? Was there really no partner out there, just waiting for the inevitable encounter?

And then, gradually, her psyche fought back. It reminded her that she had actually been a pretty good mother, a sincerely loving and attentive wife, and an averagely caring sister. She had been nice to people all her life, with a single shameful exception in the case of Phil Hollis. And when it came to that sort of relationship, with all the implications and hidden agendas, projections and unwise expectations – then most of the rules went missing.

She went to bed at the usual early hour, weary from a day full of high emotion and frustrating mysteries.

So much for Thursday being her favourite day.

Friday dawned late with another heavy covering of thick grey cloud that literally touched the tops of the hills to the west. Hepzie woke her with an unusual whining. 'What's the matter?' demanded Thea groggily. 'What time is it?'

The dog gave no reply, but the clock informed her that it was eight-forty – nearly an hour later than normal. 'Yikes!' she yelped, throwing back the duvet. *Yikes?* queried Hepzie, with a sceptical stare from her big black eyes. The long hair on the top of her head was tousled, her ears in serious need of a brushing. Cocker spaniels could easily look raffish, and Thea laughed. 'Who's a daft dog, then?' she murmured fondly.

Not me, said the dog silently, and led the way out of the bedroom.

Outside there was little trace of the deep snow of a week before, but Thea could still not evade memories of those fatal footprints and all the questions they had raised in so many minds. Why had George come this way, to begin with? He could have reached the same hollow field corner more directly from his own house. Had he been deliberately heading for Lucy's Barn? Had he wanted to see Lucy herself, forgetting or not knowing that she was away? Had he intended to reach Kate's farm, but veered off the track into the donkey paddock, losing himself because of the disorientating snow? Was he intent on suicide from the beginning, seeking a place in which to die?

Everyone said kind things about George. Decent, friendly, inoffensive. But there had to be a story to account for his impoverished state. Was it a breakdown, drug addiction, financial catastrophe? The first was the most likely, given the final outcome. Some people assumed that to commit suicide was by definition a sign of mental collapse. Thea herself was not so sure. She had glimpsed that starkly rational decision for herself, once or twice, after Carl had died. And Gladwin had seemed to be saying the same thing, when speaking of her sister. Was there anybody out there who knew the reasons behind George's action? Had they explained it to the police already, leaving Thea out in the cold of ignorance?

If she'd still been with Phil, she thought yet again, she would know some of the answers to these questions. She might even be of some use, instead of simply annoying everybody by her confused interference.

The ground underfoot was still frozen, but the air temperature was a lot higher than the previous evening. There would soon be a return to the familiar mild muddy winters of recent years. Granfer Jack had surely been wrong about the snow coming back – clinging to the weather patterns of the 1940s, forgetting that things were very different now.

The donkey was not in his shed, and at first she couldn't see him. Then she glimpsed his head, down at the bottom of the paddock, by the large gate into Kate's fatal field. His ears were pricked forward, and when she went down to see if he was all right, he clearly wanted to leave his own homestead and go next door. He seemed to think Thea would open the gate for him and let him through. 'No such luck,' she told him. 'And I can promise you the grass is quite a lot less green on that side, after those Herefords have been at it.'

He stayed where he was as she walked back to the barn, his gaze fixed steadfastly on the nirvana over the gate.

Jimmy was much as usual, walking stiffly into the garden, sniffing indifferently at one or two clumps of dry stalks left over from summer flowers. Hepzie trotted round him, plumy tail held high, goodwill coming off her like a halo.

The baby rabbits had scattered much of their cosy bedding as they grew and moved more each day. They wriggled and jerked as Thea watched them, the collective size of the six of them easily four times what it had been two weeks earlier. She gave them some generous handfuls of wood shavings to replace the dispersed mother-fur.

The cat had been outside when Thea first left the house, sitting on top of a wall, tail flicking. There was something other-worldly about that creature, Thea decided. 'Spirit' was the perfect name for it. She had already determined to keep her distance from the volatile beast.

The obvious well-being of all the livestock brought her a wry sense of satisfaction. 'At least I'm OK with animals,' she muttered. 'Even if I've been making a mess with people lately.'

There was more shopping to do, and Northleach beckoned. The chances of meeting anybody she knew seemed remote, even if she walked there with the spaniel. The groceries might weigh heavy by the time she got back, but the need for air and exercise convinced her, and she set off soon after eleven.

Walking generally served to keep her mind reasonably blank, especially with the dog to distract her. There were greasy puddles of melted snow still along the sides of the road, and the same poor visibility there had been for much of her stay. It all added up to a need to tread carefully, and this perhaps triggered the thoughts that pressed upon her. The mystery surrounding George and Bunny's deaths was no better defined than it had been five days ago. Instead of repeating the few known facts, she tried to construct theories from her impressions of the two people gleaned from things others had said about them. It was a habit she had acquired early in her career as a house-sitter, where there was seldom much evidence to support her assumptions about the people she met. When something happened that required an explanation, she would often begin from a vague 'What if…' and see where that led.

Now her question was: What if Janina had fallen for George – who sounded a nice man, and was another lonely individual in this small unsociable place, like her? What if he had rebuffed her, as he had perhaps rebuffed Tony, leaving her resentful and obstructive of George's friendship with the little boys? Would this have driven him to deeper depression and suicide? And where did Bunny come in? Could she have tried to argue George's case and enraged Janina to the point of murder?

It ran for a few minutes before she dropped it. There was a lack of conviction at the heart of it – the emotions didn't work. And she was unsatisfied with a scenario that did not include Simon in some way.

Everybody liked George and nobody liked Bunny – that was the single summarising thought that she was left with. It got her nowhere constructive, merely opening the way for more anguished worries on behalf of Nicky and Benjamin, floundering in a limbo of conflicting adults who showed little sign of knowing how to deal with them.

Northleach was as charming as ever. There were very few cars parked in the square, and only one man in the bakery when she went in. Hepzie waited irritably outside, unable to understand the reasons for her exclusion. Thea shared her feelings, and pulled sympathetic faces at her dog, through the glass. 'You the lady at Lucy's Barn?' asked the woman behind the counter, clearly recognising her from her visit on Tuesday. 'I heard you had a cocker with a long tail.' The aberration never ceased to elicit remarks, both positive and negative, although Thea had noticed a growing number of similarly unmutilated spaniels in recent months.

'That's right,' she said. 'I've walked here for a change, now there's no snow left.'

'Didn't bring that lurcher as well, then?'

'Jimmy? No, he wouldn't be able to cope.' How did the woman know about him, anyway? When did anybody ever see the reclusive animal?

'The van man knows him,' came the freely supplied

explanation. 'Lucy has a delivery from us, see. The dog comes out for a bun. We keep a bag of them for people's pets. Good for customer relations.' She laughed complacently. Thea found it hard to envisage Jimmy accepting such an offering, but then Jimmy was capable of quite a few surprises.

'How nice,' she said.

'Pity about all the trouble over there,' the woman continued. 'Those poor little boys. My grandson's in Ben's class. You have to explain it to all of them, you know. It's not easy at that age. They get in a panic about losing their own mums – shakes their confidence, especially the boys. These people, they don't realise the consequences of what they do. They don't think about how it affects the whole community, something like that. Twenty, thirty years from now, it'll still be talked about – the winter when poor Mrs Newby was killed. That and the snow, of course. Never seen snow like that in my life.'

Was this somebody who *had* liked Bunny, then? And surely she must have experienced similar snow before. She looked to be at least fifty – couldn't she remember 1963? Doing the sums, Thea concluded that maybe not. Thea herself had been born after that great adventure, which her parents described with almost euphoric merriment.

'I bumped into their father and uncle, last time I came here,' she said, hoping to keep the conversation going. 'They looked totally shell-shocked.'

'And so they might,' the woman nodded. 'Though I can't say I know the uncle. Can't honestly say I know the family at all, other than a few glimpses.'

'They don't get their bread from your van, then?'

A rueful expression answered that. 'Everything's from Waitrose for people like them,' she said. 'Must have been a real shock for that Polish girl, or whatever she is. Don't expect they have the like where she comes from.'

'Bulgaria, and I'm sure you're right,' said Thea, wondering briefly how it was that Janina's existence had filtered down to the shopkeeper. 'Have you seen her outside school?'

She shook her head. 'My daughter has, though. Said she was too pretty to be left so much alone with the boys' dad. Asking for trouble, as anyone can see.'

'Right,' said Thea heavily. It was all too obviously true, with all its painful implications. She went back to her tethered dog, who greeted her passionately, before being abandoned again while Thea went into the shop on the corner to buy further provisions.

The walk back, with a canvas bag slung over her shoulder, was a prospect she found even less appealing than before, thanks to an increasingly bitter east wind. The road out of Northleach was lined with small stone houses on both sides. Nobody was using the pavement, and little traffic passed by. The town was not on the way to anywhere, large new roads having been constructed to the north and east to obviate the need to drive through Northleach. The resulting quiet was a major factor in producing the out-of-time feeling. The little place was left in peace to potter along invisibly, not competing or displaying itself, but merely getting on with life on its own terms.

When a car drew up beside her, her instant reaction was wariness, an assumption of trouble. Somebody would want to know the way, or make a lewd suggestion. She braced herself, as the passenger door was pushed open clumsily by a driver leaning across the front seat. 'Dorothy said it was you,' came a woman's voice, and she leant down to see who it was. The small girl in the back was altogether familiar.

'Oh, hello,' she said, tentatively. 'Hi Dorothy. Are you still poorly?'

The woman nodded on behalf of the child, and Thea wondered whether she herself had ever looked so terrible, even in those first days after Carl was killed. This was a figure of desperate misery, a young woman, barely thirty, with greenish skin and sunken eyes. Not fit to be in charge of a child, or a car. When she spoke, her voice was strained: 'She said I should stop for you, because you were at Nicky's party. I'm Philippa – her mother.'

'Pleased to meet you,' said Thea, thinking she'd now got the full set, although little Wilf seldom seemed to put in an appearance, but also wondering how it was that she had taken back childcare from the capable Barbara. Dorothy looked anxious, and it occurred to

Thea that the child had wanted help in dealing with this distraught mother.

'Can we take you somewhere? It's cold out there.' The politeness suggested good upbringing, Thea noted, despite the undercurrent of something like hostility.

'Well...thanks. If you're passing the turn to Hampnett, that would be helpful. Is the dog all right? She can sit on my lap.'

The answering grimace ensured that Hepzie remained firmly off the upholstery, which was certainly spotlessly clean.

Thea had been a nervous passenger ever since Carl's fatal accident. She greatly preferred to be the driver, despite several minor collisions of her own. But it was not always possible to avoid riding with other people, and she made a point of concealing her feelings. Admitting to weakness only made everything worse, as far as she could see. Besides, her bag was uncomfortably heavy.

But Philippa was in no condition to drive competently. The car lurched in spasmodic surges, as she tormented the accelerator like a woman three times her age. 'Mother!' squealed Dorothy from her booster seat in the back. 'You're kangarooing.'

'Shut up, Dorothy,' snarled Philippa. 'You're making me worse.'

The drive should have taken three minutes at most, but there were traffic lights where the small road crossed the A429, and they had a long wait. Opposite them was a large building, and for something to say, Thea read out the lettering above one of its portals. 'The Old Police Station,' she murmured. 'Sounds interesting.' The building did seem incongruous, with no houses or other structures nearby. Thea tried to imagine how it would have been to be an inmate in one of the police cells. Without the busy road – which appeared to be a recent construction – it must have been quite isolated. 'I ought to go and have a look,' she said. 'I'm quite keen on local history.'

'You can't – it's closed in the winter, except for coffee.'

It was nowhere near enough time to gain a reliable impression of this ex-wife, friend of Bunny and young but neglectful mother. She must only have been in her early twenties when Dorothy had been born; Bernard past fifty. 'So...you're taking a turn with the invalid, then?' she ventured.

'What? Oh, you mean Barbara generally has them. Yeah. Well, it's complicated.'

She doesn't want to discuss it in front of Dorothy, thought Thea, understandingly, while at the same time intensely curious about her. This was a woman whose best friend had just been murdered, and who had taken it extremely badly, to judge by her appearance. The few reports Thea had gleaned about her suggested somebody selfish and of illiberal views. Bunny must have been at least ten years her senior, and therefore likely to have been a mentor. Had they enjoyed trenchant conversations over coffee, putting the world right while signing up for membership of the BNP? Or if not quite that, then UKIP?

She could not refrain from broaching the subject that could not fail to be on both their minds. 'You must be very shocked by what happened.' It seemed a safe enough thing to say, even in front of the child.

The response came readily enough. 'I'm devastated. Absolutely flattened. I can't even think straight. I'm scared stiff.'

'Oh?'

'Well, who wouldn't be?' Impatience with Thea's obtuseness made her handling of the foot pedals even more erratic, as they were released by the traffic light turning green.

'This is very kind,' said Thea. 'It's out of your way, I expect.'

'Only slightly, and there's no hurry. Besides, I didn't think you should be out on your own. Who knows what might happen?'

This ludicrously extreme version of Thea's own anxieties almost made her laugh.

They had both forgotten the child in the back. Now she spoke up. 'What happened to Ben's mummy?' she demanded. 'Babs says she's dead. *How* is she dead? Where did she go?'

Thea found herself approving greatly of the *how?* question. It made a pleasing change from the everlasting *why?* that she remembered from her sister's children.

Her own daughter had not been given to asking questions much at all.

'Shut up, Dorothy,' pleaded the child's mother, abruptly stemming any feelings of approval that might have come her way. 'Bunny was my *best friend*. And I just wish I could get my hands on the bastard that killed her.'

From being scared stiff to seeking physical vengeance in twenty seconds was not unusual, Thea told herself. Shock led to erratic emotions, after all. 'I'm sure the police will do a good job,' she said carefully.

'Are you? Seems to me it's a bit late for that, letting psychos go free to do whatever they like. This is what *happens*, don't you see? Not one of us is safe in our beds.'

A whimper from the back activated Thea's own anger. 'That's rubbish,' she snapped, turning to smile tightly at Dorothy. 'Absolute rubbish. A bed is the safest place in the world. So is a house, and a school. The world has never been as safe as it is now. You're not scared, are you, pet?'

Dorothy looked doubtful. 'I want Babs,' she said, undiplomatically.

'Well, bloody Babs can have you,' snarled Philippa, making Thea's blood run cold. The woman might be well brought up, with a nice car and good clothes, but she was every bit as monstrous as the rumours had implied.

'Drop me here,' said Thea, gripping the dog on her

lap. 'I can walk the rest of the way.'

The car jerked to a halt, and Thea scrambled out. It was only a hundred yards or so from the track down to the barn.

'Thanks very much,' she said, throwing a last supportive smile at Dorothy. The little girl returned an oddly complacent grin, and the car made a sudden leap forward almost before Thea had closed the door.

Rather to her disappointment, there was no visitor waiting for her at the barn. No Gladwin or Janina or sniffing Tony Newby. No lost children or stiffening corpses, either. The very absence unnerved her. Increasingly, she felt a tremor when she walked into an empty house, aware of potential attack on a burgeoning number of fronts. In the months after Carl had died, she had often entered her own house with a secret hope that he would somehow have come back, and be there waiting for her with his reliable smile and a mug of coffee. When that finally faded, she had progressed to a numb stoicism, which held no fear, only a dogged need to fill the rooms with light and music as substitutes for company. The house-sitting had seen her in charge of a number of empty rooms and strange dark corners, along with a few frightening incidents that she had coped with quite valiantly at the time. Fear had never been a problem – so why now? Why had she become this timid stereotype of a woman alone, scared of every sound, flinching at shadows, unable to escape the clutches of cold implacable fear?

Because, she answered herself, there was nobody on her side this time. Because it was wintry and frosty and everything was so unpredictable. And because the shock of seeing those footprints on a snowy morning a week ago had never really worn off.

She was quite aware that there was every chance that she had not encountered the person who had murdered Bunny. There were plenty of residents of Hampnett she had never even seen, not to mention people from further afield. And yet, the situation suggested that the murderer had not travelled far, the way the weather had been when Bunny died. Cars could hardly leave their driveways, buses and trains had been cancelled. All that was left was a person's own legs, or possibly horseback. And on the principle that most murders were committed by close relatives, she very probably *had* met the killer – however much she wanted to think otherwise.

She had nothing to congratulate herself for – Gladwin must have given her up as useless days ago. As a helpful amateur detective she had totally failed, unlike on previous occasions. Or had it perhaps been that she had never really made a difference? That it had been DS Phil Hollis all along, quietly pursuing his professional work and letting her think she was serving some purpose, when in fact she had just been a bit of decorative distraction? Looking back, it seemed all too persuasive a summary of all that had happened. Even when she had found herself in the thick of an investigation, in at the final revelations, she could hardly claim to have played a central role. And now, without Phil to guide and provoke, she was irrelevant.

Jimmy's next toilet outing was due. Although he was obviously able to wait for indefinite lengths of time, it seemed mean to expect it of him. Outside there was a glimmer of weak sunshine, and if she could keep him out of the east wind, he might actually enjoy the fresh air. That, after all, was what she was being paid to do: to make the impaired dog as happy and comfortable as possible. He seemed to take a faint sort of pleasure from the trips outside, especially if Hepzie was beside him. He walked delicately on his long, thin legs, head down, but ears erect. His unself-conscious emptying of bladder and bowel seemed to leave him satisfied.

'Come on, old boy,' Thea crooned at him, going into the conservatory. 'Come for a little walk, OK?'

She was used to having to lift him to his feet and wait as he got his bearings and his balance. Then she would hold his collar and direct him out into the garden. He never resisted, but stepped willingly after her. It was a melancholy task, in many ways, but from the dog's point of view, it wasn't so sad. He didn't know what he was missing, what his life might have been, running free over the paddock, chasing a ball or sniffing after wildlife. Hepzie apparently accepted his limitations without surprise or disappointment.

She could not explain afterwards why she did what she did. Something about giving Jimmy some extra time outside, or simply a whim of her own, born of nothing she could identify. Whatever the reason, she left the dogs in the wintry garden and went around the side of the house to the rabbit shed. Leaving the door half open, she went to the big cage, and unlatched it, and then bent down to extract two or three carrots from the bag on the floor. Sensing the treat to come, one of the rabbits began to nudge at the cage door, and finding it loose, lost her balance and fell out onto the floor of the shed.

Before Thea could grab her and put her back, the door of the shed was pushed further open and an unrecognisably energetic Jimmy came in like a bullet. The rabbit stood no chance, and with a muffled scream it died in the dog's jaws, after one swift neck-breaking shake.

'Jimmy!' Thea shrieked, and aimed a kick at him. Even as her foot connected with his shoulder, she regretted her action. He dropped the limp body and backed away, eyes staring. Thea picked up the victim and stupidly let it lie across her hands, willing it to revive. 'Don't let it be the mother of the babies,' she prayed aloud, all the time knowing that it was. Obviously she would be the most hungry, the one to come impatiently forward for the carrots. She knew from the colouration, the prominent nipples amidst the belly fur, and the cussed behaviour of Fate.

The disaster was as deep and terrible as that of the dead man in the field, in that moment. Was it remotely possible that she could rear the babies by hand, and if so, how? Would it mean being up all night with tiny bottles of special milk? Would she have to make a nest for them in the house, and ensure exactly the right temperature? Were they that important?

First, she dragged Jimmy back to the conservatory, clenching her teeth against an urge to thrash him for what he'd done. It was not for her to judge, she reminded herself – he was Lucy's first priority, and when it came to the point, a rabbit was almost certainly dispensable. Next, she switched on her laptop and searched the Internet for instructions on hand rearing baby rabbits.

There was plenty of it, and she began to hope she might save at least some of them. It appeared that the two primary requirements were infinite patience and warmth. They could manage baby formula, dropped extremely carefully into their mouths, and at their age it appeared that they might last through the night without a feed. They might even nibble at some solid food. Weaning could be achieved by seven weeks – which meant Lucy would be saddled with them for some time after her return.

The sense of loneliness increased, as she collected the babies in a cardboard box and took them into the house. With a teammate, the task would be fun, as well as much quicker. Carl would have revelled in the challenge, insisting on the immense care necessary if the milk was not to go down the wrong way and drown the poor little things. As it was, she would have to keep the dogs and cat firmly away from the improvised nest, sitting for hours in isolation. And for what? Was it possible that it was worth the trouble? Lucy hadn't even known the babies were expected. If only Thea hadn't said anything, she might have quietly let them die, and buried them out of sight, no harm done – apart from the slaughter of the poor, pretty doe.

But they were so very much alive that such a course would never have been an option.

Chapter Twenty-Six

She would have to go out and buy milk powder and a small feeding bottle, at the very least. Bourton-on-the-Water was the nearest place likely to sell such items, but she was not familiar with the shops there, and would hardly know where to start. Stow was better, but even then, she was unsure whether to try a normal chemist or a farm supplies place. Only after much dithering did she think she might walk down the track to the farm, and ask Old Kate. She would surely have everything necessary, readily to hand. But she would scoff at the idea of hand rearing rabbits. She would regard them as worthless rodents, something to be shot, not nurtured as beloved pets. And Kate's scorn was something Thea preferred to avoid if at all possible.

The websites had stressed the difficulties of the procedure; the need for experience and infinite care. Thea had never bottle-fed any creature, not even her own daughter. Kate would know how to do it – would give her instruction and perhaps active assistance, even while disapproving. It would be dark in an hour or two, the short day closing down far too early for comfort, making normal activity much more of a performance, with the need for a torch amid unseen hazards. Besides, people would not take kindly to unheralded knockings on their doors after nightfall. Where you might readily stroll down for a chat at nine on a summer evening, such a visit even at five in the winter would be seen as an intrusion.

But something had to be done, and the image of a large bag of specially formulated milk powder for baby animals, waiting only a quarter of a mile away, spurred her on, quelling the bubbling fear that threatened to prevent her from going outside at all, once it got dark.

She pulled on boots, gloves, hat and coat, shut both dogs in the conservatory and was just opening the front door when the phone rang.

She almost didn't answer it, thinking it was Lucy. If so, she would have to report the death of the mother rabbit. On the other hand, if it was Lucy, she could shoulder the decision as to what should be done with the babies. So she turned back and picked up the phone.

At first she couldn't make sense of what was being said. 'Could you come, do you think? There isn't anybody else at such short notice. They've all got their own families. Just for a couple of hours, until I get home.'

Eventually she worked out that it was Simon Newby, asking her to babysit his boys until he could get home to them. 'Or Tony,' he amended. 'I mean, it might be Tony who gets there first. I'm trying to get hold of him.'

Why me? Thea wanted to shout at him. *You hardly know me.* But she had been at Nicky's party, demonstrating her competence and goodwill. 'Where's Janina?' she asked.

'I *told* you,' he snapped. 'She's got to go back to Sofia tonight. Her stepmother's been in a car crash and there's nobody to take charge of the little brothers.'

He had not told her properly, burbling about an airport and sudden changes. 'Tonight?' she echoed incredulously. 'When exactly did the accident happen?'

'Yesterday, I think. Look…I realise this is a dreadful imposition. But the kids like you, and to be honest, I think they need a woman. I'd ask Kate, but she'll be too busy with her sheep and Granfer. He isn't at all well. We had all this before. There just aren't enough women around these days.'

She wanted to tell him about the rabbits and the dogs, and her disabling anxieties about going out. But she was, at heart, glad to have been asked. Just to be remembered as somebody who might come to the rescue was flattering. 'Where are you now?' she wanted to know.

He sighed deeply. 'At the hotel. I'm always at the

hotel. If you can't come, I'll have to have the boys here. It wouldn't be the first time, but it's far from ideal. They're not really old enough...' He tailed off, and Thea could imagine the difficulties all too clearly.

'Is somebody collecting Ben from school?'

'Oh yes. Janina's doing that. She's ordered a taxi to the airport for four o'clock. God knows how she got herself packed in time.'

By Thea's calculations, the au pair had had all day for that. A new thought struck her. 'The police,' she blurted. 'Have they said it's all right for her to go?'

After a short silence, Simon said, 'You mean they think she's a suspect for my wife's murder?' He gave a little snort. 'I think they abandoned that idea quite a little while ago.'

What have I missed? she wondered. Was the whole investigation over and done with, and she never even knew? Why would she find that so enormously startling?

'OK...well, it's ten past three now. I have a lot of things to do here. I *am* being paid to do them, after all,' she added defensively. 'It would be a stretch to get done by four.' It would be impossible if she were to attempt to feed the baby rabbits. Even acquiring the necessities would take longer than that. 'What time are you coming back?'

'Seven at the absolute latest. All you have to do is those three hours.'

'Can I bring the dog?' she asked daftly.

'Of course. Benjy loves your dog. Besides, we're convinced she's your daemon – how could you manage without her?'

Demon? She let it pass, suspecting she'd failed to grasp an allusion that anyone else would get instantly.

She persuaded herself that the rabbits would survive for a few more hours, nestled in their box in her bedroom, the door securely shut. Not only were they potential prey for the bizarrely murderous Jimmy, but Spirit the cat was undoubtedly at least as great a danger. She hurriedly fed the donkey and the remaining rabbits, and scrambled into her car at six minutes to four, the dog following her unenthusiastically. 'Your supper will have to wait until we get back,' Thea told her. 'It's too early to have it now.'

She arrived with a whole three minutes to spare, ahead of the taxi. Janina threw open the door, her eyes red and her hair in a mess. 'Oh, God, you are so good,' she exclaimed. 'Such a good woman. I feel so very terrible and guilty about all this. It is like knives in my heart, to leave the boys at this time. And it is all stupid Bunny's fault.'

Thea flinched at this fearless breaking of the taboo concerning speaking ill of the dead. Mightn't there be a thunderbolt any moment now, as a result?

'Are they all right?' she asked, only now really facing the implications of this drastic new loss. 'I suppose they can't be, really.'

'I told them I am coming back,' said Janina in a quiet voice. 'But it is not true. My stepmother's neck is broken. I guess she might never walk again.'

Or move her arms, thought Thea with an icy shiver. A paraplegic, with four small sons. 'That's dreadful,' she said.

'She was driving fast on an icy road. We have told her to be more careful, but she never listens.'

Which only made it worse, thought Thea.

'Listen,' said the girl urgently. 'I have things I must say. Things I ought to tell Simon, but he— Well, never mind. He is a child, in many ways, like a lot of men. Bunny did not talk to him like a grown man, and that was how it rested between them. Do you understand?'

'Not really,' frowned Thea. 'What are you trying to tell me?'

'Bunny – she had a lot of stupid ideas. About men abusing her sons, and the world being full of danger and risk. She was full of hate and fear. So stupid.' Janina shuddered. 'But she never said these things to Simon. He would not listen to them, just smiled and laughed if she was worried about anything. Always told her things would be fine, that everything was working well. And I...I was always on his side. Always thinking he was right. But now, she is dead. So she could have been the one who knew best, after all.'

An engine outside announced the taxi, and Janina wrung her hands. 'I do not know what is true any more,' she wailed. 'Perhaps the world is cruel and sick, as Bunny said. But listen, Thea Osborne...the important thing is that Simon knows nothing. We have protected him, in our different ways, even Ben. Even Tony. Everybody. So Simon is innocent, do you understand? More innocent than little Nicky even. More innocent than your fluffy spaniel.'

Thea's mind seized up under this urgent last-minute assault. 'OK,' she said. 'OK...now you'll have to go. You can phone me, if you like, tomorrow.' She grabbed paper from the hall table and rooted for a pen amongst the scatter of junk mail and newspapers. 'Here's my mobile number. I'll be able to tell you how everybody's doing.'

Janina finally departed with agonisingly minimal farewells. 'I will not see the boys again,' she said, with tears in her eyes, as she got into the back of the car.

The boys were in the playroom, watching television. Hepzie trotted in ahead of Thea, and permitted herself to be greeted violently by Benjamin. There was something disconcerting in the exaggerated hugs the dog was expected to endure, and Thea quickly interposed. 'Don't squeeze her so tight,' she said. 'You'll hurt her.'

Nicky was sucking his thumb, his gaze fixed on the TV. 'Hi, Nicky,' said Thea. 'Have you said bye-bye to Janina?'

The smaller boy shook his head, without shifting the thumb. 'It's sad, I know,' she pressed on, without yielding to the temptation to give empty reassurances.

'I'm going to stay with you until Daddy gets home... OK?'

The house was too hot, the radiators pumping out heat as if to compensate for the cold misery the family was living with. Nicky's cheeks were flushed, and Hepzie was panting from more than the vigorous affection she was receiving. Thea went in search of a thermostat – a search that took her upstairs, where she felt she really had no business to be.

She found the dial on the landing, between two bedroom doors. An irresistible curiosity made her peer through one open door into what was evidently the master bedroom. A large double bed took up a lot of the available space, the covers rumpled, and a pile of clothes dumped on one side. Had Simon started sorting through Bunny's things already? Or had the police left it like that after their searches? Never having met the dead woman, Thea had no sense of absence. The house she knew had only ever contained Simon and his children – and Janina. *There* was the absence, the loss of somebody crucially important. How fragile everything seemed, how truly terrifying. For a moment, Thea's nose and throat filled with sharp tears, her head constricted with the pain of what was happening.

It was a full ten minutes before she went downstairs again, to her poor little charges. She met Nicky in the main living room, apparently heading for the kitchen. 'All right?' she asked him.

'Need a drink,' he said.

'Come on, then,' she said. 'I'll get it for you. Maybe it's time for a biscuit or some cake as well, do you think?'

He looked at her, his head held sideways as if listening acutely for something. 'We had cake,' he said. 'Janina gave us cake.'

He climbed onto a chair, and sat tidily at the kitchen table, waiting for the drink. Thea found pineapple juice in the fridge and gave it to him in a glass. 'No,' he said. 'That's my cup,' indicating a blue beaker on the table.

'Sorry. Do you think Ben would like some as well?'

There was no response to that.

'I'll go and see, then.'

She went back to the playroom, but was arrested at the door by a high voice, apparently addressing the spaniel. 'No, Benjamin, you can't come. Go *home*, Benjamin. Mummy has to talk to George by herself.'

Thea froze, dimly aware of some kind of acting out going on. Something that might well be therapeutic if allowed to continue.

'You *pervert*, you *bloody pervert*,' shrilled the child. 'You just leave my kids alone, do you hear me? I'll make you sorry, I'll make you a…' The little voice sank and faltered. Whatever the word had been was lost, and then he recovered, 'You have to leave. Do you hear me? You have to leave this place and never come back.'

Hepzie suddenly became aware of her mistress standing just outside the door, and began to wriggle from the child's clutches. She whined when Ben held her tighter. Thea had little choice but to make her presence known.

'It's OK, Heps,' she said, approaching the huddled pair. 'Just let her breathe, Ben, OK?'

The look on the boy's little face was stony. What exactly had he witnessed? Would it ever release its grip on him, or were nightmares and flashbacks his lifelong fate? What was the current thinking on debriefing a six-year-old, anyway? Encourage him to relive it, or change the subject and hope to bury it deep?

Benjamin made the decision for her. 'I was bad,' he said. 'I followed them, when Mummy told me not to. She said I had to go home. I was shivering in the snow, and it was nearly dark, and she said *Go home, Benjamin. Do as you're told for once.*'

'Where did *she* go?'

'To George's house. We were going to find his sledge, and go out with it the next day. I was excited. But she said we couldn't. Then she shouted a lot at him.' He bowed his head, weighed down by what he had witnessed. 'He hit her and she fell over.'

'George hit Mummy?'

Ben nodded.

Thea tried to make sense of the story. When had it happened? Thursday – it had to have been the Thursday, when the schools were closed, and the world was in snowy chaos. 'Where was Daddy?' she wondered.

'In the house. Mummy came back, and I saw her in the lane, out of my window. I ran out and told her about the sledge, and she said, *I'll see about that*, and she went to shout at George.'

'So Daddy didn't know she'd come home?'

Blankness greeted that question. How did he know what adults knew?

'Why didn't you tell him? Or Janina?'

'George said I shouldn't. He said we could go sledging if I never said what had happened. But if I told them, he would have to go away and never come back. He was crying,' added the child, and his own tears began.

'But he's gone anyway,' said Thea, without thinking.

'It was *me*. I was bad. I told Uncle Tony. George never said I couldn't. So George had to die, and it was because of *me*. And now Janina has gone as well, because she doesn't like me.' Quiet tears slid down his cheeks, and Thea knelt down and wrapped her arms around him, some commiserating teardrops falling onto the top of his head.

'No, you weren't bad, Ben. It wasn't anything to do with you. Janina has to go because her mother had an accident. Not your fault in any way at all. You are *not* bad, Ben – you have to believe me about that. It was all the grown-ups who were bad.' Most of all, she realised, bloody Bunny, and her paranoid sidekick, Philippa.

Carefully, Thea reviewed what she had learnt. Her first instinct was to phone Gladwin and pass it all on, just as she'd heard it. But already she knew what the response would be: *It's not evidence, only hearsay.* If you repeated what someone else had told you, it didn't count in a court of law. The police would have to question Ben directly, and make him say it all again. Perhaps he wouldn't mind that, perhaps it would even be helpful for him. But perhaps not. For Thea, recalling the tormented little face, it seemed too great a risk. After all, George had killed himself after murdering Bunny. There was no retribution possible, no loose ends to be tied.

Except, of course, for Simon and Bunny's other relatives. Didn't they deserve to know the whole truth of what had happened?

Already, too, unexpected loose ends were dangling before her eyes. Had George really been a paedophile? If so, who else might have suspected, or even known for sure? She remembered Janina's parting words, insisting on Simon's innocence – or had it been ignorance? Blinkered wilful refusal to face facts about damage to his own children? If Bunny had confronted George, didn't that imply that she had some hard evidence against him? And if there was no truth in the accusation, why had he hit out at her, hard enough to kill her? Why such a powerful need to silence her, if it was all fantasy in her own twisted mind?

The need to tread delicately was obvious, as was the lack of urgency. She could give herself time to think it all through, and perhaps consult someone other than

Gladwin. Quite who this might be remained obscure, for the moment.

Simon arrived home an hour later, harassed and resentful. 'This is too much,' he protested, 'Janina going off like that. It makes things impossible for me.'

Thea could quite see. Any one of his troubles alone would be enough to justify panic and self-pity, but he had three or four big challenges: the death of his wife; the needs of his children; the demands of his job – and the overwhelming implications of a murder inquiry. She ached to rescue him, to reassure him that everything would work itself out. She forgot, for the moment, the distress of Simon's elder son.

'You should probably contact social services,' she suggested. 'They might have some help to offer.'

'What? You mean they'd take the boys into care, because I'm not a fit father?'

'Of course not.' She looked at him intently. Janina had been right – he was hopelessly immature, with no idea how to manage the situation. 'But if there's nobody else, they'll give you some support.'

'There's Barbara,' he said. 'She's good with children.'

At least he hadn't suggested Philippa, she thought ruefully.

'Simon…Ben needs *you*. At least for the next few days, I think you have to forget the hotel and concentrate on rebuilding Ben's security. He's very shaken. He knows something about what happened to his mother. Try to encourage him to tell you about it. You're the central person in his life, now.' She ought to tell him everything Ben had said, to pass the burden onto the shoulders where it properly belonged. But she couldn't rely on him to handle it responsibly. He might argue with the boy, or laugh the story away as make-believe. There had to be a reason why Bunny never shared her fears with him, and until this was apparent, Thea was afraid she might only make things worse.

'Oh, God,' moaned Simon. 'I suppose you're right.' He gripped his head in both hands for a moment, as if fearing it might explode. Then he looked up. 'Tony! I'll see if Tony can come and help. Why didn't I think of that before? He's brilliant with the boys – understands them a lot better than I do.' He gave her a look full of pathos. 'And thank you very much for coming to the rescue today. I should have said that sooner. I'm really very grateful.'

'That's OK. Anybody would have done the same. But—'

'I know. You won't be able to keep doing it. I understand. We'll manage now. Tony's self-employed – he can come here for a week or so, until we get sorted. I can't believe I never asked him before. I suppose I was only thinking about women.' He smacked himself lightly on the brow. 'Ought to know better.'

The sudden brightening was almost more disconcerting than his despair had been. 'Well, I hope it works out,' she said, doubtfully, feeling a burgeoning sense of guilt at leaving the wretched Ben with the two boyish brothers that were his father and uncle.

Chapter Twenty-Seven

It was Friday evening, the weather looking ominous again, the thought of further snow a dread out of all proportion to the probable results. It was like a rollercoaster, where you survived the first appalling drop, only to find the prospect of a second one almost impossible to bear. She needed to talk to somebody, but had no idea who might fill that need.

In the end it was resolved for her, not entirely satisfactorily, at least to start with. Gladwin phoned at nine. 'Where were we?' she asked, disarmingly.

'I have no idea,' Thea laughed. 'It's been a very busy day...again.'

'Oh?'

'Janina's flown back to Bulgaria, leaving Simon not coping with his kids.' The urge to reveal Ben's testimony was massive, but still she kept her counsel. Once uttered, the story would be impossible to withdraw again.

'Yes, I know. And we don't have any good news for him, sad to say.'

'That's a shame. Is he still under suspicion?'

'He's in the frame, although we've got almost nothing on him.'

'I saw the Philippa woman this morning. Bunny's best friend. Have you met her?'

'No, but I've read her statement.' Something in Gladwin's tone made Thea sit up. A picture was coming inexorably into focus, thanks to Ben's story. Much of what Philippa had said was making more and more sense. From one moment to the next, it all seemed crystal clear, as if it had been sitting there all along, for anyone to see. And yet...

'She thinks George killed Bunny,' she said. 'Doesn't she?'

'She's got more sense than to say it outright, but yes, I think that's what she believes.'

'That would be very convenient, wouldn't it,' said Thea. 'Neat and tidy.'

Gladwin didn't reply directly. 'You know...it's odd, in a way, the amount of time and effort we put into understanding a straightforward suicide. Do you remember that bloke in South Wales who killed his wife and kids and then himself, some years back?'

'Not really,' said Thea.

'Well, the police spent *months* investigating his finances, love life, past history, just to find a reason.

They already knew who'd killed them. It wasn't necessary to get the whole story – but they felt they owed it, somehow, to the family. Well, it's a bit like that here. We know George Jewell killed himself, but we've still been going through his house inch by inch.'

'And have you found anything?'

'Masses. Too much, if anything.'

'Somebody moved his body,' Thea reminded the detective. 'Was that a crime?'

'Technically, yes. Not reporting the discovery of a dead body is a crime. It usually implies something more serious, of course.'

It all felt too sad and serious to continue. People were dead and nothing was going to change that. 'Sonia…I think I have to ring off now. I've got some orphan rabbits to feed.'

'Good God. What happened?'

Thea told her.

'Bottle feeding might work, I suppose. Have you got the gubbins?'

'Sort of. I found an eye dropper thing in Lucy's bathroom cupboard. I suppose I'll have to use diluted cow's milk. I never had a chance to get proper baby milk.'

'You need a bottle and a teat. I've got one, and some milk powder. We had a litter of puppies a few years ago, and I got a kit for feeding newborns, just in case. We never had to use it, but I have some experience. Shall I bring it round to you?'

'What...now?'

'Absolutely. They won't last all night, will they?'

The detective superintendent arrived twenty-five minutes later, swinging a bulky carrier bag. 'I brought everything I could think of,' she laughed. 'Cotton wool for their bottoms, a bit of natural fleece to lie on and all the feeding equipment.'

It was not much of a partnership: Gladwin did all the work. With infinite care, she introduced a tiny rubber teat into the little creature's mouth, and waited for it to get the idea. 'They must have been hungry,' she murmured, as the third one took to the artificial food with alacrity.

'They're so *sweet*,' said Thea. 'I couldn't just let them die, could I?'

'Of course not. A life is a life, as my father always said. Did I mention that I grew up on a hillside in Cumbria? We were always having to rescue dying lambs. Not that the farmer ever thanked us. He said a cade lamb was more trouble than it was worth.'

'Cade?'

'Orphan. Or rejected, more likely. Sheep don't have a very long attention span. They forget they're supposed to be taking care of their offspring.'

'What did your father do?'

'He was a baker. But we didn't live over the shop. My mother said she needed a view. You could see about ten mountains and three lakes from our house.'

As each little rabbit was finished, Thea was given the task of massaging its stomach, to aid digestion. 'Actually, I think they're old enough for it to work by itself, but it can't do any harm, as long as you don't press too hard.'

'Will they survive, do you think?'

'Most of them probably will. Mind you, they'll be psychologically damaged.'

Thea laughed at that. 'It'll make them better pets if they're fixated on people.' She had a thought. 'Maybe we could give one to Benjamin. He likes animals.'

Inevitably, this took them onto the subject of the murder. 'Poor little mite,' sighed Gladwin. 'Makes you wonder whether people ever stop to think of the consequences of their actions.'

'People? Murderers, do you mean?'

'Among others.'

'They don't, of course. No more than Jimmy spared a thought for Jemima's babies when he killed her.'

Gladwin gave her a long severe look. 'Animals are different, and you know it,' she said.

'Yes, they are...but I doubt if a person in the act of killing somebody has the slightest notion of the implications.'

'Unless those implications are part of the motive for doing the killing.'

'Phew...that's a bit deep,' Thea protested.

'Think about it,' Gladwin persisted.

Thea thought, knowing she was being pushed into a corner, that she had very little choice left to her. 'Um...' she began. 'I do have something I should tell you, but I'm worried about where it might lead. Something somebody told me.'

'Hearsay,' nodded Gladwin. 'Where would we be without it?'

'What?'

'Come on. Half the crimes we solve are only brought to book because of something someone's told us he overheard in the slammer. We have to wangle it so as to get the perpetrator to incriminate himself somehow. It's a game, and if you're holding a joker, or even a six of diamonds, I'd appreciate knowing about it.'

'You already think George killed Bunny, don't you? You know it fits. Well...apparently somebody actually saw him doing it.'

Gladwin's eyes narrowed, and her head tilted to one side. 'Really?'

'Somebody who wouldn't make a very good witness in court.'

The detective's shoulders slumped. 'Like a child, you mean?'

'Precisely like a child.' And Thea told her everything Ben had said that afternoon. The two women forgot their roles for a few minutes, as they considered the consequences for little Ben and his family.

Then Gladwin straightened, and said, 'It doesn't fit, though, does it? Who moved his body? Who texted Simon after Bunny was dead?'

'Kate?' whispered Thea. 'She could have seen George in the field, and moved him.'

'That's possible. It would be in character. But *why*?'

'Oh, there are too many questions,' Thea burst out. 'They just go on and on until my head hurts. I don't know how you can bear it, following all these futile clues, trying to work out who's telling the truth – and never really completing the whole picture.'

'It's my job,' said Gladwin simply. 'And just for the record, I'm still not convinced it was George who killed Bunny. Maybe he just *thought* he had. I told you before – there are anomalies.'

'Like what?'

'Like timings and head injuries and the position of the body. It's all there, somewhere, but we've still got to assemble the pieces.'

'Well, it's past eleven,' Thea pointed out. 'We'll both have to sleep on it.'

'I doubt you'll get much sleep. You'll have to do all this feeding again at about...' she glanced at the clock on Lucy's wall '...three a.m., or thereabouts.'

'No! It'll take me *ages*. Here, let me do the next one, while you supervise. I'm not at all sure I can manage it.'

'Well, I'm not noble enough to come and do it again. I only saw my boys for ten minutes this evening as it is.'

'Twins,' nodded Thea. 'I remember.' What she could not remember was whether the father was still on the scene. It was hard to see how Sonia could hold down such a senior job without substantial back-up from a second parent, but she could make no assumptions. Why not ask? 'Is their dad at home?'

'Paolo? Oh yes. He thinks the rabbit story is hilarious.'

'Is he Italian, with a name like that?'

'His mother is. We were at school together – childhood sweethearts. Married for fourteen years. I realise it sounds dull.'

'Not at all. It was much the same for me.' She stopped herself from going any further. It would be presuming far too much on Gladwin's good nature to dump all the persistent grief and fear on her now. Besides, she already knew the basics, from their previous encounter in Temple Guiting.

She fed the last rabbit with embarrassing clumsiness, but at least she didn't choke the poor thing. Finally they were all settled into their new nest, apparently satisfied. 'I'm *enormously* grateful,' she gushed. 'Do you want something to drink before you go?'

'Better not. It's getting cold out there, and these

little roads get very icy. Plus I have to be up at seven tomorrow.' She gave Thea a very direct look. 'I'll phone you in the morning. We're not finished with all this – you do understand that, don't you?'

All this did not mean the baby rabbits.

Chapter Twenty-Eight

Hepzibah could not understand why her mistress switched on the light at three in the morning, went downstairs to warm some milk, and then spent over an hour with the little things in the box by the bed. She knew she was banned from going near them, and was quite happy to obey. They smelt of people, now, and a hint of sheep from the stuff they were lying on, and besides, she had never quite got the taste for killing things. Huffily, she turned her back on the proceedings, and curled up tightly on top of the bed.

Thea dreamt of dogs with great sharp fangs, and a great herd of huge Hereford bullocks crowding around her as she tried to prevent them from trampling on an unruly collection of kittens. A child was being crushed amongst them, too, but Thea had no way of reaching him. She woke with a powerful sense of helpless panic.

The rabbits had an early breakfast, at seven, the

process taking a mere fifty minutes this time. All six were alive, but two seemed worryingly limp. The inexorable routine of feeds every four hours or so was already beginning to feel like an impossible burden. One website had suggested that solid food could be introduced at just over two weeks, which was a hopeful idea. There was nothing to be gathered outside in January, but lettuce, cabbage and carrot could be bought easily enough.

But her thoughts were mainly on the Newby family. Simon had taken over the parental reins, at last, but nothing else was resolved. Benjamin had been emphatic that he could not reveal his secret to his father, but had seemed relieved when Thea told him that she might be able to make things all right, at least as far as weighty secrets were concerned. She had repeatedly assured him that nothing was his fault, that things would sort themselves out without him having to do anything. He had smiled bravely and returned his attention to the telly as if the exchange between them had never happened.

Donkey, rabbits, Jimmy – they all had to be seen to. With no time for coffee, Thea was outside attending to her duties, trying not to feel resentful. Lucy had paid her well to act as substitute, and she had no grounds for failing. True, it had been Lucy's carelessness that led to the birth of the baby rabbits; Lucy's dog that had killed Lucy's doe. But it had been Thea who let the dog see the rabbit – something everybody knew was liable to lead to tragedy.

She was halfway across the donkey's paddock before she saw him. A man was standing in the shadowy opening of the shed, his arm around the animal's neck. A cold hand fingered Thea's heart, her guts did their familiar spasmodic dance, and her throat went dry. There should not be anyone there. Childishly, she repeated this fact to herself, and remained on track to confront him. 'Hey!' she called, her voice much less strident than intended. 'You shouldn't be here.'

He faced her with a slow melancholy smile. 'Oh, hello. Sorry. I came with some carrots for him. We're old friends. Lucy knows I visit sometimes.' He indicated the camera hanging round his neck. 'He's very photogenic.'

She let it go, reassured by his smile and the friendly attention he was giving the animal. 'Did Simon ask you to help out with the boys?' she asked him.

'Oh, yes,' he said carelessly. 'But I won't be needed until lunchtime, when I'm to collect Nicky from nursery. I felt like a bit of fresh air, while it's dry. They say it'll rain later on.' There was a flatness to him that reminded Thea of the woman, Philippa. The shock of a sudden death and its aftermath, that only seemed to escalate in the first few weeks.

Her mind was mainly on the baby rabbits, and Jessica's promised visit the next day, with a few spare thoughts for Janina, Gladwin and little Ben. Tony

Newby wasn't even on the list. 'Well, let me give him some hay and get on with my other jobs,' she said. Should she be offering him a mug of coffee? Somehow she thought not.

'OK. I'll be off in a minute.'

She went back to the house, preparing herself for another bout of bunny feeding. Bunny – for the first time she made the meaningless link with the dead woman's name. One of life's small, silly coincidences that made you smile and wonder whether there might, after all, be some vast cosmic pattern to it all.

With no prompting, Gladwin turned up at eleven, bouncing down the track too fast and slewing the car to a stop. 'I absolutely should not be here,' she panted, 'but I couldn't resist. After all, this is the centre of the investigation – I can swing it with my conscience, just.'

'You're the second visitor of the day,' said Thea, and recounted the odd discovery of Tony Newby in the donkey shed.

'What time was it?'

'Just before nine, I suppose. I was a bit slow getting going, after being up in the night with these little scamps.'

Gladwin went strangely still and thoughtful. 'Seems peculiar,' she said. 'Do you mind if we go over there for a look?'

'Of course not...but why?'

'We need to find Mrs Newby's mobile. It's a key

factor in the whole story. Of course, it'll be in a skip or a river by now, but I suddenly got a bit of a hunch.'

'You've been fixated on that donkey all along,' Thea accused.

'It's not the donkey I'm thinking about,' said the detective.

In the shed, Gladwin began running her hands along the top beam of the walls, where there was a cobwebby ledge. Thea watched her with growing scepticism. In the corner of the area where the hay was kept, where the donkey was barred from going, a plastic bag slumped innocuously. What was in there? she found herself wondering. It looked empty, crumpled and abandoned. A blue and white sack, made of the sturdy plastic designed to keep rodents out. When full, it had apparently contained sheep nuts. She could just read the word 'Ewe' in black letters. 'That wasn't there before,' she said.

'What?' Gladwin looked over her shoulder, her hand still reaching up to the ledge.

'That feed bag. It wasn't there before.'

In one fluid leap, Gladwin pounced, dragging the bag from its corner, and shaking out the crumpled sides. Then she reached inside.

She brought out a metal cylinder, which turned out to be a biscuit tin – one that had contained a stack of round cookies: the kind sold at Christmas by fancy food shops in Stow or Cirencester. She prised off the lid, and peered into the interior. With two fingers, she withdrew a rolled piece of paper.

'It's like a treasure hunt,' said Thea daftly.

'Listen to this,' said Gladwin, in a small voice: *'Dear Tony...by the time you read this I'll be dead. You might guess the reason for it. That dreadful woman has been at me again, worse than ever, and I simply can't take any more. I'm afraid I actually hit her earlier today – quite hard, as it happens. She'll recover. People like her always do. But I've burnt my bridges now. She'll raise hell when she comes round. So, Tony, I'm taking advantage of the snow. I'll walk over to you, and pop this through your door. Then I'll take some Scotch and finish myself off with hypothermia. It won't take long. I'm rather looking forward to it. But I'm not too keen on the damage the crows might do to me, so would you be a sport and shift me home again, after the event? Leave it till nine or ten in the morning. Don't try to save me, Tony. That would be cruel. I'll give you a clue – start from Donk's shed. Lucy's dear Donk can be my last living contact. Romantic fool that I am.*

'Thank you, Tony, for your understanding and affection. I regret that I never responded. Damaged goods, me. Very damaged. But not in the way that vile woman said. They might believe her, though...

'Goodbye, my friend. Have a good life.

'George.'

Thea said nothing, repeating the lines to herself, seeing the final scenes and her own part in them. How narrowly she had missed everything, how close she had come to saving George, and catching Tony as he moved the body.

Gladwin looked at her, and then said, 'There's another line at the bottom, in a different pen. Different writing. It says, "I love you, George".'

'So that's it then, is it? Tony found the letter on Friday morning, went to George's house, found Bunny's body, chucked her in the ditch and then went for George. But why dispose of Bunny like that? And take her phone – I assume that must have been him?'

'Well, it's not here, but yes, I think we can make that assumption. But Thea… George didn't kill Bunny.'

'What?'

'She had a blow to the head which didn't kill her. The pathologist had his doubts, but had to do tests first. Now he says she was alive nearly twenty-four hours, and was then choked to death. Possibly smothered.'

Thea's eyes widened. 'Bloody hell,' she said.

'Indeed.'

'It's so unfair, though, don't you think? Two men who seem altogether decent, both driven to the end of their tether by a thoroughly nasty woman.'

'Since when was anything fair?' said Gladwin.

2017
58
1969
59
28

19
2017
1960
57

2017
1958
59
59

Chapter Twenty-Nine

Saturday afternoon was spent with the animals, as usual, everything imbued with a sense of sadness and futility. Gladwin had gone off with her Exhibit A to arrest Tony Newby, in the process further compounding poor Simon's problems. Outside it was drizzling, in that maddening English fashion which was neither one thing nor another.

Then Lucy's phone rang, and Thea braced herself to explain yet again that no, there was nobody here who could fix their computer.

'Thea?' came a familiar voice, crystal clear. 'It's me, Janina.'

'Hey! Hello. Did you get home all right?'

'Oh yes. In spite of twenty centimetres of snow. In Bulgaria, snow is not a problem.'

'Right. And how's your mother?'

'She is not well, but quite cheerful. Of course, her treatment will cost us all our money – everything I earned in England will be gone in a week. My father has been trying to borrow from his friends, but nobody has much.'

'That's awful.'

'Yes. Many things are awful. How are Simon and the boys?'

'A lot's happened since yesterday,' she began tentatively. 'They know who killed Bunny now. They arrested him a little while ago.'

'Not Simon?' The voice was hollow with dread. 'Please not Simon.'

'No, not Simon. It was Tony. Because Bunny was being so rotten to George. I expect you knew about that?'

'Poor George. She was afraid of him, you see. The way he looked at her. He could not hide what he thought.'

'What *did* he think?'

'That she was a fool. That she did not deserve those sweet boys. That she could do nothing but harm in everything she touched.'

'And you thought the same, didn't you? You said so, the first time I met you.'

'We all did. Tony, too. And even Ben was beginning to see that she was not worth very much.'

'How ghastly for *her*,' said Thea. 'Don't you see that? You all pushed her into a corner, and made her worse. She had to find a scapegoat, to make her feel better.'

'Yes, I understand it now. I understand why George

might take the force of her feelings. But I don't see why Tony—'

'Because he loved George, and hated what she was doing to him. And it got a bit more complicated than that, at the end. She made very specific accusations.'

'Oh, I understand. That came from the Philippa woman, her friend who left her children, and then blamed everyone else for her own behaviour. She is the one who first talked about paedophiles. She made Bunny see everything even more darkly.'

'It's all so *sad*,' said Thea.

'Yes,' agreed Janina, speaking from snowy impoverished Bulgaria. 'Yes, everything is sad.'

Sad, but no longer frightening, Thea realised, at the end of the day. The sensations of fear had subsided so gradually that she did not notice they'd gone until bedtime. When she got up on Sunday, the baby rabbits were all still alive, and had begun to nibble tentatively at the shreds of cabbage she gave them. Outside, the sun was shining, and the temperature had risen to a heady five degrees. Around the edges of Jimmy's toilet patch there were daffodil spikes poking a full four inches above the ground. Under an apple tree at the end of the garden a semicircle of snowdrops had produced fat buds as if by magic. Tony Newby would be receiving fair treatment at the hands of the police, encouraged to disclose the full truth of what had happened over that snowy night. Simon's children would be given as much cherishing as was humanly possible, women emerging from amongst family and friends – and perhaps a new nanny as loving as Janina had been. Like the little rabbits, they would survive and grow, which was at least a start.

All of which left her with her own life to consider. Where would she go next? Would she find the courage to embark on a fresh house-sitting commission, or had this wintry experience deterred her from ever doing it again? She thought back over the places she had been – Blockley, with its tilted streets and ancient field systems; Frampton Mansell, with its historic canal and mysterious woods – places she would never have got to know without the house-sitting work. But there were no fresh jobs in her diary – she had advertised during November, but nothing had come of it. People were cutting back on holidays, and the cost of a sitter on top of the other expenses was less affordable now that money was tight. Perhaps, after all, she would find herself a proper job, become self-reliant and in the process acquire something closer to normality in the eyes of people like Old Kate.

Jessica and her mysterious 'friend' were due to arrive soon. The prospect of this diversion was entirely welcome. She could lose her worries in the maternal role for a while, taking them to lunch and encouraging them to talk about their own concerns.

The car came warily down the track, as if unsure

whether it had taken the right turning. Hepzie gave her single *someone's coming* bark, and went to the door. Thea let her out, following slowly, and watched as her daughter drew in beside her own car. From the passenger side, a man emerged, standing uncertainly, looking over the car roof at Thea.

He was tall, with broad shoulders. And he was black. When he smiled, his teeth shone bright against the dark skin. 'Hi,' he said.

'Mum, this is Paul. He's a detective sergeant.'

'Pleased to meet you,' said Thea, with a smile. 'Come in and have some coffee.'